THE SURVIVORS BOOK TWO

THE SEARCH

NATHAN HYSTAD

Cover art: Tom Edwards Design
Edited by: Christen Hystad
Edited by: Scarlett R Algee
Proofed and Formatted by: BZ Hercules

ISBN: 9798342680370

Also By Nathan Hystad

PROLOGUE

*T*here was nothing enjoyable about this experience. The entire planet was covered by clouds, saturated with moisture. The dampness sneaked up on him. Everywhere he went, water dripped on his head. It crept into his boots. He didn't think he could take much more of it, but tonight might give him the out he'd been waiting for.

Sarlun treaded from under the awning, peering at the blinking light across the street. He hid his face, lifting the cowl higher.

When he thought the rain might be slowing, it began again in earnest. The locals were stalky creatures, their skin impervious to the constant humidity. One of them walked by, growling under his breath.

Sarlun nodded to him, getting no reaction in return. What had drawn him to the Belash Bazaar was that no one cared what kind of being you were. To them, Sarlun was the least appealing species to visit their world in ages.

As far as he could tell, none of them had ever met someone from Shimmal before, and that suited him just fine. Sarlun had spent the last couple of years running and hiding, but it was time to stop the charade.

He navigated the ceaseless puddles, trying to avoid the deepest, but failed miserably. Water surrounded his pants to the knees, and he stepped out.

This was the final stop on the trail he followed, and he couldn't fail.

Sarlun checked his tablet, comparing the sigil on the building's doorframe to the one on his screen. They were identical. The Bazaar had its share of miscreants, as did any location of this nature. It made the old Udoon Station look like a daycare.

He heard a commotion and jumped aside, predicting what was about to occur. A man flew through the exit, landing in a heap.

"If we ever see your pox-ridden hide in here again, it'll be the Backyard for you," the bouncer said.

The Backyard was a mass grave the people of the Bazaar used to dispose of the downtrodden. It was said that no one could survive there for longer than twelve hours. Sarlun wasn't certain he wanted to test the theory, but he was committed now.

The man in the street staggered to his feet before tipping over again. He reeked of Artificial, a common drug sold in nearly every back alley on the planet, from what Sarlun could surmise. He was tired of this hellish place.

But he deserved to carry out his penance. He'd given the orders to kill Dean and Mary Parker, and for that, he would never recover. But he could seek a moment of redemption before his demise.

Tixa was supposed to be here tonight. After weeks of determined hunting, Sarlun had found out who oversaw this gutter of a world, and where he'd be on this particular uninviting night.

"Hold on, stranger," the bouncer said when he attempted to enter. The man put a hand on his chest, and Sarlun bowed his head in deference.

"I apologize for my poor judgment. Perhaps you could let me in, so I can buy a drink from this fine establishment," he said.

The guy shoved him. "Not tonight. This is for the

Belash only." The door slammed in his face.

Sarlun paused, letting his heart rate settle. He needed to act today, since finding Tixa in public had proved so difficult. He wasn't willing to spend weeks more in the Bazaar for his chance.

Someone screamed in the distance, and Sarlun hurried toward the sound. Two men were cornering a Belash woman, a child clenched to her chest. "Leave me alone!"

"Give him over," one of the men said.

"I will not! He's my son. I have his papers."

Sarlun cringed but reached into his robes, touching the gun. It was forbidden for an outsider to carry a weapon, but he wasn't walking these streets without protection.

"Pass him to me!" The bigger of the men grabbed for the woman, and she kicked him in the shin. Sarlun grinned, but flinched when the guard struck her across the cheek. The other guy snatched the kid, tugging on his legs.

"Let them go," Sarlun said, stepping from the shadows.

"And who are you?" He was big, his skin wet and glistening. His eyes were narrow and black, his nose deformed from too much Artificial use.

"I'm someone you don't want to anger," he answered.

The pair began to laugh, their voices clogged. "How about we settle this the old-fashioned way?"

"I don't think so." Sarlun shot him in the neck, the homemade gun sending a sharp projectile through his thick hide. The bigger guy lunged, but Sarlun was faster. He used his opponent's momentum, slamming his head into a garbage pile. He shot him too, not wanting loose ends. The woman gawked at him, clutching her child tight.

"Don't hurt me."

"I wouldn't dare," he whispered, ear cocked to listen for more trouble.

She came closer, her eyes wide. "It's you…"

He'd already saved five others from ambushes by Tixa's people, and obviously, word was beginning to spread. He'd tried to be as careful as he could so he wouldn't attract attention.

Sarlun threw his cowl back on, concealing his snout with a beige scarf. "Don't tell anyone. Get out of here before anyone else sees you. And stay off the streets until Tixa is dealt with."

"Dealt with? He's the Nishtak. There is no better life for us," the woman said.

"Perhaps it's time for someone else to take over." Sarlun rushed off, scaling the side of the building adjacent to the bar. He retrieved a rusted scope, touching the auto-focus to stare through the window. The place was packed with locals, purple and white drinks sloshing over the edges of their cups.

It took forever, and Sarlun's body ached from his crouching position. Then he sighted the man. Tixa was smaller than most of the Belash people, his hair long and abundant; a contrast to most of the hideous bald men he employed. Sarlun wondered if he preferred to be accompanied by these freaks to make himself appear better, and wouldn't put it past him.

Sarlun reached under the ventilation ducting, preparing the long rifle. He methodically clipped it together, and when he snapped the scope to it, Tixa wasn't in view. The bar doors were open, and half of the drunk patrons had spilled into the alley, boisterously singing a dreadful song about swindling tourists for their offspring.

"Where are you?" he whispered, searching for Tixa.

"Who? Me?"

Sarlun swung the gun around, but the Belash man knocked it aside, kicking Sarlun in the throat. He grabbed for it, but found his hand pinned to the rooftop. Tixa's boot crunched his knuckles.

"Why are you so determined to kill me?" Tixa asked.

"This world will be better off when you're gone," Sarlun said.

"Perhaps. Unfortunately for you, that won't be today." Tixa motioned to his guards to detain Sarlun, and he shouted as they wrenched his arms behind him. "You realize that I only do what the Shareholders ask of me."

Sarlun blinked, staring blankly.

"I see you haven't heard of the Shareholders. Let me fill you in." Tixa laughed, standing inches from Sarlun. "Once I supply them with my quota, they're going to promote me off this dump. Then the people can have their new leader."

"Why are you telling me this?" Sarlun thought about his daughter, Suma, and how he'd never be able to hug her again. He wouldn't see her children, or bounce them on his knee during the holidays.

"Because no one comes out of the Backyard." Tixa punched him in the gut, and Sarlun keeled over, puffing out a lungful of air.

Sarlun was hauled off the roof, carried down the steps, and dragged into a waiting cart.

He was blindfolded, stripped of his personal belongings, and they were off to the Backyard. Its location was supposed to be as big a secret as any on Belash Bazaar, but Sarlun already knew where the prison sat. He'd attempted to break in, but it was impossible. As far as Sarlun was aware, none had survived, but that couldn't be true. It was probably a rumor, used to scare people straight and keep them from revolting against Tixa.

The trip took hours, the hovering cart ride bumping with the wind. When it finally stopped, the pair of nasty guards rolled him off, booting him in the ribs before removing his blindfold. "Welcome to your new home," one of them said.

The other unlocked a thirty-foot-tall gate, the hinges groaning as it opened. Sarlun had made a mistake. He shouldn't have come here. It was as foul as the whispers in the streets suggested. The sky was black, a constant plume of exhaust rising from somewhere close by. It smelled like rotting meat, but at least it wasn't raining. He chuckled at the thought, and realized he must have sounded off his rocker. The guards glanced at one another and shrugged, motioning him through.

He stepped inside and listened to the gate close and latch, then the lock clicking in place.

Sarlun stalked forward and peered up, feeling a raindrop on his brow.

He stared at the structure with disgust. "I'm coming… sister."

ONE

"Don't touch…" I was too late. Hugo was tossed by the force, the energy blast sending him skidding onto his back.

"Whoa, that was pretty cool," he said, obviously having the time of his life. I helped him up, and he grinned.

I wanted to reprimand Hugo for disobeying me, but these were his last years as a kid. I needed to stop being so hard on him, as long as he wasn't doing anything that put his life in danger.

"Why are these still powered on?" he asked.

I stared across the empty alien city, shaking my head. "How can we know? For every world that's inhabited, there are a thousand with nothing but rocks and sand. But occasionally, there's a place like Pestria," I said. "A planet that was once thriving, but has since turned into a wasteland."

Pieces of the city littered the area, reclaimed by nature over millions of years. Suma had sent core diggers with us, and I reached for one, handing it to Hugo. "You want to do the honors?"

He didn't respond as he grabbed the device. He probably hadn't been expecting the weight, and I laughed when it tugged his arm lower. "Forgot that gravity is slightly stronger here," he said.

Hugo knelt on the hard-packed dirt and activated the digger, then set it down. Lasers shot from the base, cutting into the ground, and he glanced up at me. "How far?"

"Let's start with five hundred kilometers and go from there," I said, patting him on the shoulder.

I patiently waited as he worked, programming the unit, and gazed at the pieces of the city remaining visible. Who were these people, and what had happened to them? The universe was constantly expanding for the Alliance, our network growing with rapid efficiency, but part of me was concerned about it. I thought we might be stretching ourselves too thin, but Mary and the board disagreed. So I went along with them, choosing to side with the Alliance president, even if I didn't completely agree with my wife. I wouldn't let my opinion become a point of contention. I knew that no matter what we encountered, we'd always be fine.

We'd proven that time and time again.

"Dad, can you double check this?" Hugo asked, presenting the details. I did a quick scan and offered a thumbs-up. I didn't usually attend this kind of mission for the Gate-keepers these days, but when Hugo had asked, I had to say yes. He'd been busy over the past year, and we only saw each other every couple of weekends for a few hours, at best.

"That'll do it." I noticed a light blinking on one of the spires.

"Okay. It's starting." Hugo hopped up, dusting his knees off, and we watched as the core digger silently lowered into the ground. "How long does it take?"

"We have a while. How about you tell me what's been going on in your life?" I said.

Hugo tapped his helmet's facemask and scrunched up his nose like he had an itch he couldn't scratch. "Not much. It's been busy, and I want to do a good job when I'm on mission."

"I've heard from the team. You're doing better than good," I proudly told him.

Hugo's eyes grew bigger. "Seriously? They said that?"

"You're in the forefront to be the youngest lead ever," I said.

"Second youngest," he reminded me.

"Well, it's hard to compete with Jules, isn't it?" I laughed.

"You have no idea," he sighed.

A year or two ago, Hugo would have resented the comment, but after spending a few weeks on an adventure involving a planetary hunt and the First World, Hugo had gained some perspective. I thought that witnessing what she was capable of firsthand had grounded him.

The light blinked again. "Hugo, I think this entire network is still powered up."

"Really? We did the preliminary scans," he said.

"Those energy defenses are on, as you proved… twice. But there's more. Look." I pointed at the spire's peak.

Hugo squinted in its direction. "Could it be linked to the defenses?"

"Maybe." Something about this city was beginning to bother me. Half of it was covered by water, the top layer frozen. The other half had weedy grass with shrubs, but nothing resembling trees. Part of me yearned for wisdom, or connection to the universe still, but I'd passed on the torch to Regnig. He was now the Recaster, operating from the Void, though none of us had seen him since. I'd often wake up, forgetting I was only a man now, and relief would flood my body when I remembered.

I could take a back seat to the cosmos, watch my kids grow and start their own lives. Jules was engaged to Dean, and the idea of my daughter being old enough to make a decision of that magnitude seemed more alien than this planet. Hadn't I just been enjoying the Yankee game on TV, eating a bachelor's meal in my house?

But when I thought about all the things we'd experienced since the Kraski arrived, I felt every year of my age, despite having the physical appearance of a man under forty, thanks to the extenders we'd taken.

"Dad?"

"Huh?"

"You're doing it again."

I smiled at him. "When you're my age, you'll over-analyze everything too. Come on, let's check the results."

Hugo pulled out his tablet and brought the application up. "That's strange."

"Where are the readings?" I took the device, restarting the program. "There's no link. It's gone."

I heard a whistle, and tackled Hugo aside when an object flew out of the digger's hole.

We sat, observing helplessly as the digger clanked in front of us. It sparked and hissed, then gave up the ghost.

"What happened?" Hugo jumped up and kicked at it, rolling it over.

I peered into the hole, wondering the same thing. The soil below my boots rumbled, the light on the spire blinking more rapidly.

"We have to go," I whispered.

Hugo stared at me blankly. "What?"

"Move!" I pushed him forward, and he ran, me trailing behind. I risked a glance past my shoulder and creatures shot from the recently opened cavity, taking flight into the sky.

They were all bunched up, a cluster of dark gray bats, rising to the clouds before they began diving for our position.

Hugo was faster than me, racing across the frozen turf.

Pieces of the archaic structures stuck out from the ice, and Hugo bypassed one as the animals fluttered near my head.

I fell to the surface, sliding on the slick ground. I banged into the building and stared up at the flock. They were each the size of a cat, with large front talons and tiny red beaks. From what I could tell, they had no eyes, so they were likely used to being underground, until we'd disturbed their sanctuary with the core digger.

"Dad, this way!" Hugo called, and I scrambled to my feet, slipping to the far side of the structure. He had a hole carved into the wall, and offered me his hand, tugging me within as the horde caught up to us. We found a piece of furniture in the room and turned it on end, shoving it against the hole. They seemed to retaliate, but only momentarily.

"I think they're gone," I huffed.

"What is this place?" Hugo flicked his suit's lights on, and I did the same, getting a better sense of our surroundings.

"Probably an office." There was a desk along the near wall, a strange chair under an obviously alien keypad. It had five buttons. I tried one, and the display lit up, shining onto the wall with an unseen projector.

A video played, and voices spoke through speakers tucked somewhere in the corners. I hit the record button on my wrist, not wanting to miss out. It might be possible for someone to translate later.

"It's showing the city," Hugo whispered as the drone footage lowered, slowing as it passed the spire still jutting from the middle of the urban region.

People walked in the streets, some waving as the drone approached. "Who are they?" I muttered. They seemed familiar: bipeds with muted green and brown clothing, narrow faces, and elongated heads. Their eyes were large, their smiles genuine. And now they were gone, all dead. I wondered how long ago this video had been taken.

"The power's still on, though," Hugo said. "That's impressive. Rivo's going to want a gander at this."

Hugo was doing his job, yet it felt slightly detached. I was worried about what had transpired with the local population, but Hugo was concentrating on the technology we could obtain from visiting the planet. That was what the Gatekeepers were trained to do, so I couldn't fault him. But maybe I could use this as a teaching moment, to remind my son there was more than furthering our Alliance's status by utilizing these lost innovations.

"What do you say we keep investigating?" I asked him.

"We're supposed to observe, record, report," he said without pause.

"But you're with me, Hugo. And I have a better idea."

"Is that so?" Hugo grinned, and I could see his wheels spinning. He was ready for another adventure with his father. Most of the Gatekeepers' work was simple. Traveling to barren worlds with nothing but gases and ice grew tiresome, especially for a seventeen-year-old.

"Let's explore below the ice," I said.

"Dad, if anything goes wrong, you'll take the blame?" Hugo lifted an eyebrow.

"With the Gatekeepers? Of course," I assured him.

"And with Mom. I'm more bothered by upsetting her."

"You and me both." I waved him forward. "Let's see what Pestria has to offer." I walked to the exit, choosing to descend deeper into the structure instead of returning outside. We could check it out, and I expected we'd be heading home within a day, hopefully with answers rather than questions.

"*A*nd what do you have to say to that, Ambassador Parker?" Jarlo asked. He steepled his long fingers and waited for her response.

Jules cleared her throat, wishing she'd paid closer attention to the conversation. She'd been to three of these meetings in the past four months, and this was the first time anyone had asked her opinion. "I think that the Nulach will be the perfect fit for the Alliance. We can help one another in so many aspects. We're astounded by your soldiers' discipline, and your government's forward thinking," Jules told him, flipping the switch in her mind. She'd been sitting patiently for hours, daydreaming her primary mission: finding Sarlun.

But that was on the back burner because of the influx of aliens contacting Mary's office about joining the Alliance. Word had spread since the contest, and they were somewhat famous since liberating the people of Zecos Three from Planetary Provider Inc. And because of their involvement in the events at the First World, particularly with the part about the Cosmos, and the Recaster, they'd all requested Jules be present at the meetings, which irked her to no end.

"Very well spoken, Jules Parker, but there's more to a partnership than shared resources. And the Nulach are not looking to join an Alliance that is focused solely on war," Jarlo said. He was a wrinkled man, with deep recesses throughout his face, but she couldn't pinpoint his age, since all of the Nulach were the same in that regard. She'd seen a baby with heavy folds in its chubby cheeks.

Her mother shifted in her seat, setting her palms on the table. "I assure you, we're not seeking war. There are—"

"I'd like to hear this from the Ambassador," Jarlo cut

her off, and Mary pursed her lips, glancing at Jules.

"As my mother, the president of the Alliance of Worlds, was trying to say, we're actually more interested in expanding our community. Filling our colony worlds Haven and Ebos with like-minded individuals. We want to create intellectual teams of varying races, which we think will bring all our people to the next level, whether we're talking about energy technology, food growth optimization, health care, or the arts. Knowledge is an asset, and we'd be remiss not to share it with one another. That is how the Alliance will truly grow and prosper," she said.

Jules stared at the group of Alliance delegates, and then at the Nulach dignitaries. Was this what she'd become? She didn't want to be sitting here discussing the benefits of the Alliance with these people. If they couldn't see that from the start, maybe they weren't a good fit.

"That is a lot to consider. Please allow us to deliberate. We'll reconvene at a later date." Jarlo stood, indicating the meeting was over.

Jules bowed her head gently, as per their custom, and waited until her mom exited before following.

"That was uneventful," she muttered.

"On the contrary. I sensed Jarlo was about to send us on our way. You salvaged the relationship," Mary said.

"Me?" Jules pointed at her own chest. "I barely spoke."

"But the words were powerful. Maybe you should think about a career in politics," her mom said with a grin.

"Don't you dare." Jules smiled, letting the rest of the Alliance members past her. "I'd rather stick a fork in my eye."

"Jules, your future isn't decided yet." Mary motioned at her counterparts. "I'll see you in a few. I'd like a word with Jules."

The elevator door closed, and Jules was alone with her

mom in the foyer. "What's up?"

"I know you're annoyed at these trips, but you've become a figurehead for the Alliance."

"I thought Dad had that role locked up," Jules said.

"He did… and does, but he'd prefer to stay behind the lines these days. He's having fun, and he deserves it."

"But, Mom…"

"Let me finish," Mary said.

Jules nodded and peered at the sprawling city below. The Nulach were an advanced society, with hovering transports and portals located all around the streets, providing faster travel from school or work to home. Jules had initially wondered if it was all a ploy to get their population to increase their hours, since their commute was limited. But after some investigation, they were all treated quite well, with low crime and high intelligence scores.

"I've already spoken with the next group and explained that you're unable to attend, but I thought you could record a message, relaying the same information you just gave Jarlo."

Jules' dour mood brightened. "You're letting me off the hook?"

"In a sense. Suma's not doing well."

"What do you mean? I just saw her—"

"I spoke with Elex, and he's uneasy. Slate's also expressed concern. We have to help her find Sarlun," Mary said.

"That's what I've been saying for the last year!" Jules put a hand over her mouth, realizing she'd shouted the last bit. "What changed?"

"Suma's… we're all worried about her. And the baby."

"*Baby?*" Jules was surprised. "Why didn't I know?"

"It's too soon, and in the Shimmal culture, this isn't shared until they're confident both the child and mother will be healthy," Mary said. "So don't say anything to her. Wait for Suma to tell you on her own terms."

"How did you find out?" Jules asked.

"Elex thought it was important I know." Mary didn't expand on the reasoning. "You'll be heading to Ebos from here, so pack your things."

"What about Dean?" Jules had barely seen her fiancé in the last few months.

"He can't leave New Spero. With all the influx of recruits from our new partnerships, Magnus is more in demand than ever. And since I've been taking all your attention, it's just Malir and Dean on the front lines. Slate's been trying to assist, but he's busy with his own family."

Loweck and her Uncle Zeke had finished their adoption, providing an orphan from Zecos Three a loving home. Their little girl was beautiful… and a handful at eleven months old.

"Okay. I'll do it." Jules hated the idea of leaving Dean for another run, but soon they'd be married. It had been almost a year since their engagement, but neither of them was in a hurry. Jules was still young, but she was confident in her decision. Dean was the love of her life.

"Good. Thank you for understanding. It's time we brought Sarlun back, so we can find a way to usurp the power from Hulope. The Alliance needs Shimmal, and their people require us. She's a tyrant, making deals with the likes of Nix Benah. Who knows what other unions she's forming? Thank goodness Lom of Pleva is gone, because I wouldn't be surprised if she attempted to team up with him. Or Ovalax."

Jules shivered, recalling the monster that had inhabited her father. "I'll do everything I can to bring Sarlun back safely."

"I know you will." Mary hugged her.

The doors to the boardroom slid open, and Jarlo stood in the entrance, a smile on his sagging face. "You're still here. We have come to a decision."

"Welcome to the Alliance," Jules told him, knowing that they'd agreed to enter the coalition.

"Thank you, Jules Parker." Jarlo walked them to the elevator. "Perhaps you'd dine with me to celebrate."

"We'd love to," Mary said, joining him in the lift.

Jules smiled, but all she could think about was traveling to Ebos to retrieve their missing ally.

TWO

*S*arlun had heard countless rumors of the horrors of the Backyard, and none of them were remotely accurate. In person, it was far worse.

Black smoke rose from a giant stack, the concrete monolith coated in dark soot. The air was filled with the gunky smog, making his breathing difficult. He'd only been here for one day, but he could hardly tell a difference between dusk and dawn.

The area was massive, and he wondered how big the Backyard was. Sarlun stuck close to the exit for the first hour, realizing he'd made a terrible mistake. But after the initial panic subsided, he'd focused on the task. No one escaped the Backyard, but he doubted that could be true.

Sarlun had yet to see another soul, which motivated him. Where had they all gone? He'd been on the planet for a few weeks, and had witnessed ten criminals being escorted from the city by Tixa's guards. They had to be in here somewhere. The ground was slimy, a layer of soot on everything. He wiped his heel forward, finding cobblestones beneath the grime. This had once been a city of its own.

The buildings were half-rubble, their old bricks lying in piles. Had someone dismantled them, or was this a testament of the passage of time? There was no way to tell.

Sarlun was grateful they hadn't taken his cloak, and he

18

raised the cowl to shield his head. It was cold today, and his breath misted out of his mouth. He scrunched up his snout and sneezed. The Backyard was even more inhospitable than he'd expected.

The massive smokestack continued to dispense pollution, and he froze while staring at it. If there was smoke, that meant someone had to be fueling it. With a purpose in mind, he started toward the huge destination.

It looked like it was a mile away, but by the time he reached it, the sun had shifted across the sky. It was nearly impossible to see through the haze, but occasionally, the wind would blow the clouds apart enough to notice the ball of light. He figured he'd traveled three times his estimation, which spoke to the vastness of the region.

Sarlun climbed the hill surrounding the stack and placed his hand on the stone. It was hot: not scalding, but warm. He stayed near it for a few moments, letting the heat penetrate his cloak to his skin.

"There has to be a way below," he whispered to himself. His own voice sounded strained, like he'd been inhaling too much of the polluted air. It wasn't as if he had a choice.

Sarlun circled the tower, which had a diameter of around twenty feet, and spotted metal rungs rising high on the far side. He tested the lowest one, and it held. Maybe if he could climb them, he'd have a better vantage point of the Backyard. He'd make a mental map, noting any landmarks of interest. And if there was a population, they'd be easier to spot.

This confirmed his decision, and Sarlun tied his cloak tighter, taking the rungs upward on the smokestack. The benefit was the heat, and after the first twenty yards up or so, he was sweating. Drips of black soot rolled down his skin, but he ignored them, climbing higher.

A few of the rungs were loose, and he was careful to test each of them as he ascended, skipping any that seemed dangerous. It took a while, and his muscles started to protest, but he made it to the top. Sarlun slung his arm through the top crossbar.

He couldn't see the edges of the Backyard, only the gates he'd arrived at. The city beyond wasn't in view, meaning it was some distance from here. He'd expected to have a panorama of Belash Bazaar, but it was nowhere in sight. This did little to dishearten Sarlun. It just suggested that the soldiers were farther from the Backyard than he'd anticipated. That was a good thing. Near the gate, the walls rose forty feet high. There was no way of scaling them, not without preparation. Perhaps someone could carve foot and handholds in the stone, but it would take years of work, and in these conditions, he doubted they'd be able to live long enough to see it through.

He concentrated on what he saw: a mound of garbage to the east, maybe four miles from his position. A town, with their buildings mostly intact, to the west, and it was even farther. To the north was emptiness, fields of nothing, all covered in the same soot and ash. The gate was to the south.

The smokestack vibrated, and he clung harder as a thick bellow of fumes belched from the top. The air grew more putrid, and he began hurrying his descent. His legs and arms were turning rubbery, and his fatigue caught up to him. Sarlun stepped on a broken rung and fell, his cloak billowing in the wind as he plummeted. Something caught him, and he was lowered down.

Two men stared at him, their eyes white against their soot-stained faces. "Who are you, stranger?"

"I'm new here," Sarlun said, dusting himself off. They spoke the Belash tongue, which Sarlun could translate with his previous surgical modifications.

The guys were a foot taller than him, and from what he could tell, they were almost identical. "What did you do to get exiled?" They stood apart, and he noticed the long rods on their belts. They were armed.

Sarlun considered his answer and decided to go with the truth, guessing that other exiles would have no respect for the ruler who'd sent them here. "I tried to kill Tixa."

The guy on the left threw his head back, laughing a deep growl, while the other did the same, slapping his own knee as he bent over. "That's a new one, stranger."

"How close were you?" his partner asked.

"I thought I was going to be successful, until I turned around and found Tixa behind me." Sarlun grinned like it was a funny story, not the reason for his death sentence.

"We're honored to have you, stranger. Welcome to the Backyard. I am Erem. This is my brother Oran."

"I have a name," he said. "But I prefer Stranger, if it suits you."

"As you wish, Stranger. Are you hungry?"

He was, but had given up hope of finding sustenance in this desolate wasteland. "I couldn't ask you to share…"

"It would be our pleasure. Come, Stranger. We will show you our home—and yours as well," Oran said, stepping away from the stack. He handed Sarlun something from one of his many pockets, and Sarlun unfolded the cloth, finding a chunk of bread within. He took a bite, and once he broke past the crunchy exterior, he salivated at the taste of the rich food.

"This is delicious," he said.

"You will have to let Chef know. She appreciates the feedback, despite her gruff exterior," Oran replied.

Sarlun made a note to do that. "How did you know I was here?"

Erem pulled an old scope, the lens aged. "We watch the gate."

"Many do not survive the first night. We have a rule. If you make it a day, we will seek you out. If not…" Oran glanced at the ground.

"How many make it a day?" Judging by their expressions, the number wasn't high.

"Very few. Most find a means to end their pain."

Sarlun swallowed another bite of the bread. "How dreadful."

"Don't get us wrong. Many people that come to the Backyard are bad. Some deserve their exile," Erem said.

"And you?" Sarlun asked.

"We like to think we have atoned for our wrongdoings," his brother answered for them. "Let us leave it at that."

Sarlun finished the loaf, returning the cloth to Oran. "I can appreciate your frankness. I'm doing some atoning of my own."

"Then perhaps we are more alike than our outward appearances suggest," Erem told him.

"How far to your home?" Sarlun's body was tired, and he needed something to drink.

"It is not far," Oran said, grinning.

The landscape was still bleak, the buildings even more forlorn in this direction. Erem slowed his pace after an hour and walked past a pile of bricks, stopping at an entrance. A light shimmered, and he disappeared.

Sarlun's heart raced in his chest. "What just happened?"

"We have a few tricks in the Backyard. Come. The others will be eager to meet you." Oran vanished behind his brother.

Sarlun glanced over his shoulder at the smoke still

billowing into the sky and sighed. He stepped into the glistening light.

THREE

*J*ules hadn't been on Ebos for a while, and she was astounded by how much progress they'd made. It had only been a few years since they'd first set foot on the planet, but with the cooperation of so many worlds, their new colony had expanded beyond anyone's initial dreams.

"This makes Haven look like a town," she whispered.

"It basically is," someone said from beyond the portal entrance.

"Sergo!" Jules smiled at the Padlog. "What are you doing here?"

"Slate warned me you'd be coming, so I wanted to greet you, since your dad is away." Sergo buzzed for a second, rubbing his palms together like only an insect could.

Jules eyed him dubiously. "This has nothing to do with me, does it? Maybe it has something to do with your three little bees flying around at home."

Sergo sighed and slumped against the wall. "They're a handful. It was actually Walo's idea, if you can believe that. She said I needed to see the universe again, and I had to agree."

The portal stone was perched in the middle of the city, and Jules gawked at the remains of *Outpost*, the fallen warship that had crashed to the surface when they'd faced off against Ranul and her cronies. They'd left the massive vessel, utilizing her hundreds of quarters in the early days of

24

construction. Now they used it as a reminder of the hard-ships and sacrifices the Alliance had made in order to begin this colony—which had since been aptly named *Outpost* it-self.

It had also been the last time she'd seen Sarlun.

"You okay, Jules?" Sergo asked as they traversed the promenade. It was quiet, despite being the middle of the day, and Jules wondered why.

"I am. Do you know what's going on?"

"They're unveiling the new Gatekeepers' Academy. You didn't hear about it?"

Jules grabbed Sergo's wrist. "What? The Gatekeepers' Academy?" She swallowed, struggling to believe she hadn't been informed. "This is crazy. How can they have built an academy, and no one told me? This is impossible."

"I thought you knew! It's been all over the forums lately. Haven't you followed along?" Sergo asked. A couple of transports flew through the air, navigating right. Jules' gaze tracked them.

"It's near the lake?" she asked.

"That's right. Fresh water." Sergo had a hoverbike waiting, and he motioned to one beside it. "Wanna ride?"

Jules grinned. Papa never let her use these. He said they were too dangerous, even though she knew for a fact he'd operated them on many occasions in his younger days. It was like he forgot she could fly, and had a protective shield ready at all times.

Sergo powered his on with the push of a button, and Jules did the same. The bike leveled off, and she tucked her feet in, gripping the handles. "Race you." And Sergo was gone.

Jules frowned and gunned it, shooting away from the portal's grounds. *Outpost* lingered in the backdrop, and slowly shrank as she headed away from it. She concentrated on the bike, but still noticed the population as they moved throughout their city. It was filled with such diversity. From the corner of her eye, she spied Molariuns, Keppe, Padlog, Humans, and even a couple of hybrids, as well as Inlorian, Motrill, and Bhlat. It was amazing to see them all together, but Jules felt a moment of sadness that there were no Shimmal people among them. Only Elex and Suma were here to represent their race.

Jules trailed after Sergo, who went dangerously fast through the streets. A series of hovering vehicles sat gridlocked as they neared the edge of town, and Sergo rose over them. Jules did the same, giving an apologetic wave to a family of Toquil. The little ones were so cute, and the smallest lifted a wing, her beak opening wide. It made her miss Regnig fiercely.

She almost clipped a sign overhanging a building's entrance and swerved to the side, avoiding it. Sergo slowed, lowering to the street past the traffic jam, and Jules saw the new academy. There were two statues on either edge of the courtyard, each covered with cloth to keep them hidden.

"This is incredible." Jules parked the hoverbike and strode toward the building. There were hundreds of people gathered, with countless more coming from the city. "Sergo, level with me. Why wasn't I informed about this?"

"Because you're the guest of honor," Dean said, appearing from behind a crowd of familiar faces. Rumi and Patty were with him, Natalia smiling with Magnus next to her.

She kissed Dean in relief. They were supposed to be planning a wedding, but neither of them had time for the minutiae surrounding such an event. He looked doubly handsome in his formal wear, and she noticed they were all dressed to the nines for the occasion.

"I'm the guest of honor?" She glanced around, finding

so many familiar faces.

"That's right, Jules Parker. We've named an entire wing after you," Suma said.

"Suma!" She hugged the Shimmal woman, and then her husband, Elex. "I was coming to work with you."

"Your mother called earlier, but this takes priority," Suma told her, despite the obvious longing in her voice to return her father home.

Rivo wore a black uniform, the Alnod Industries logo on the shoulder. "You look well. This engaged life suits you."

Slate and Loweck came from inside the building. A floating stroller moved in step with them, and it stopped when they did. "Jules! You made it."

Uncle Zeke hugged her and stared adoringly at his girl. The child smiled, trying to grab hold of Slate's finger. "Brae likes you, Jules."

"Well, I like her too." Jules leaned in, rubbing the girl's cheek.

"It's almost time," Magnus said.

They hurried for the end of the courtyard, and Jules held Magnus and Dean back. "You knew about this, didn't you?"

"Of course we did. We helped design the weapons training lot, as well as arranging the simulators," Dean said.

"I could strangle you," she muttered. But in reality, it was quite a privilege to be held in such esteem by her friends and family. Jules had only wanted to help people, ever since she was a young girl, not that much older than Brae. She hoped to be an inspiration to this next generation, as Zeke, Mary, Natalia, Magnus, and her Papa had been for all of them.

Dean kissed her again. "Take that back."

"Okay, fine." She smirked and began to walk.

Countless people filled the area, and Jules guessed there were a couple thousand witnesses by the time they settled. Dozens of recording drones were in the air, capturing and relaying the event to every Alliance partner. This was a big moment. A second Gatekeepers' Academy was desperately needed, even more so given the recent influx in membership. No wonder her mother had been ignoring her requests for something like this to be built. It had already been done.

"Where's Papa? And my mom?" she asked Dean.

Dean gaped at Magnus, then at Slate.

"What is it?" Jules growled.

"Your dad and Hugo haven't checked in yet," Slate said.

"What do you mean? Where are they?"

"They went to Pestria, a world along the outer rim planets in the Galetrom System," Slate informed her.

"And why hasn't someone gone to investigate?"

"It hasn't been long enough. Plus, your dad said he wanted a bonding trip with Hugo. I think they're probably sleeping under the stars and swapping stories." Slate crouched when Brae began fussing in her stroller. Loweck picked the child up, soothing her with the effortless skills of a mother.

"And you know where Mary is. You were supposed to be on that trip with her, but we heard you had enough fake pleasantries with potential Alliance partners," Suma added.

"It should be an easy decision," Jules muttered. "But they act like we're trying to take their tax money."

"Aren't we?" Magnus shrugged, and Nat slapped his arm.

"Indirectly. We're also aiming to… never mind." Jules glanced at her own clothing, realizing it wasn't practical for something this important.

Dean leaned in. "Right this way, Ms. Parker."

"See you later, Ju," Rivo said.

"I still can't believe you surprised me," Jules told Dean as they entered the foyer. It was grander than the one on Haven, the ceilings rising up fifty feet, the glass designed to send refractions against the far wall in intricate patterns, displaying the shape of a globe.

"I wanted to so many times, but everyone pressured me to keep it a secret."

"Why?"

"You'll see." Dean led her down a hallway. Their footsteps echoed through the vast space, and they passed countless offices. Most of them were unlabeled, but one at the end stood out.

JULES PARKER – PRESIDING AMBASSADOR

She touched the letters etched into the frosted glass. "They gave me my own office?"

"Don't worry, no one expects you to sit and work every day." Dean punched a code in, and it opened.

Jules was relieved at the comment—not that she couldn't see herself doing such a role at a different point in her life. Just not yet. She had too much to accomplish. She couldn't settle down…

Jules realized what she was thinking, and glanced at Dean. Could she marry him? Buy a house? Start a family? She suddenly felt far too young for any of those things.

She almost stepped away, leaving the office, but forced herself to stay. She was being ridiculous. Of course she loved Dean, and wanted the whole package. Then why was she so hesitant?

"Ju, are you okay?" Dean asked.

"I…" She swallowed. Her powers increased, pulsing through her core and into her extremities. Their latent abilities coursed in her veins, and she struggled to keep them there. Images flashed in her mind. Sarlun running from a gigantic worm, humanoid beings lumbering toward him. A Shimmal woman in a cowl, her face obstructed by shadows. Heat. So much heat. Jules wiped beads of sweat off her forehead as if she was being cooked alive.

"Jules!" Dean snapped his finger, and her gaze focused. The pictures vanished, and she noticed the cool breeze circulating from the vents.

"I have to help Sarlun," she whispered.

"Jeez, can't you wait until this is over? What's gotten into you?" Dean picked up a neatly pressed uniform, handing it to her. "I'll give you a minute."

He closed the door, and Jules sighed a heavy breath, wondering what the heck had just happened to her. She'd experienced countless strange occurrences over the years, but this was so fresh, so invasive, she knew Sarlun was in danger. It was imperative that she help him; otherwise, she wouldn't have witnessed those scenes. Had they happened already, or were they signs of things to come? And who was the woman in the daydreams? She was from Shimmal, but she was too tall to be Suma, and older. Was it Hulope, the lady that had usurped all power from Sarlun and sealed their planet off from the Alliance?

Jules didn't think so. There was something about her…

Dean knocked on the door. "You done yet?"

"One minute!" Jules hadn't even started changing. She did it in a hurry, using a mirror along the wall to add the finishing touches. Her curly hair was a bit unruly, like usual, and she tried to temper it with a ribbon. When that didn't work, she removed the bind and let it go. It was wild, and so was she. Jules grinned at the notion and went to the hall, taking a final glance at her office. "I like this."

"I thought you would." Dean smiled widely and offered his arm. "Shall we?"

The Search

When they went outside to the courtyard, the mood had shifted. The gathered crowd stayed on the grounds, just off the circular concrete pad, and a young Padlog choir stood in three rows, their voices angelic and haunting as they sang. Jules heard words speaking of courage and bravery emitting from the insectoid children, and it warmed her heart.

Dean broke off, standing with his mother and Magnus. Jules realized something she hadn't really considered. Now that Magnus had married her Auntie Natalia, he'd become her father-in-law, and the woman she'd thought of as an auntie would become her mother-in-law. She glanced at Patty, who waved. That was her sister. She'd been so busy with work that these important details had slipped her mind. To her, they were just family, and always had been. Now they'd be connected by an even tighter bond. The revelation flooded her emotions. Mix in the strange visions of Sarlun, and the surprise of today's Academy unveiling, and she felt the tears forming. They blurred her sight as Karo exited the building, wearing his Gatekeeper's garb. Ableen stuck beside him, her green eyes bright and inviting as she smiled at Jules.

The chorus ended, and the entire area went silent.

"People of Outpost and beyond, welcome to the newest of what we hope will be many more Gatekeepers' Academies," Karo said. His long white hair hung over his shoulders, and he raised his arms, making the crowd erupt with applause. "The Gatekeepers are an old tradition, previously led by Sarlun, and we hope to continue his passion with our vision of the future."

The word *vision* sparked something within Jules, and she pictured Sarlun racing from the worm, garbage on the ground. She shook it off and concentrated. Jules was beside Karo, standing aimlessly, since no one had given her direction.

"I will continue to run things on Haven for the time being, and I'm pleased to announce that Zeke Campbell and his lovely wife Loweck will be taking the reins on Outpost," Karo said, and Slate waved at the people while they cheered.

He joined them, standing beside Jules. "You're coming here?" she asked.

Slate spoke from the corner of his mouth. "It's time to give our ship a new legacy. *Light* needs someone younger. We have a kid to think about."

Jules didn't like how time was going by so fast. The previous generation was slowing down, but that gave her and her friends opportunities. Still, she preferred a universe where Papa and Slate fought for their ideals in the field, not from behind a desk.

Karo waited until the clapping ceased before continuing. "The Gatekeepers are about more than exploration. They bring a sense of stability to the Alliance. We're an organization that allows any member to apply, and because of that, we're pleased to announce that we have students from all twenty-three Alliance races enrolled at this very academy for the coming semester."

Jules applauded with everyone else. This had been the dream since the start, even before she had been born. She noticed the Bhlat Empress there, huddled in conversation with the Supreme. They seemed delighted as well.

"Gatekeepers have a mantra."

"Observe. Record. Report!" the crowd echoed, bringing a laugh to Karo's lips.

"That's right." He pointed to those three very words carved into the building above the massive doorway arch. "But we'll be beyond that. We teach your children rules and compassion. Strength and honor. Discipline and courageousness. Together we will shape a better future for the Alliance, and it all begins now."

Two humans walked to either side of the courtyard, each grabbing hold of the ropes on the pair of statues covers.

"Without further ado, I give you Regnig's Academy, a place for learning as much as interplanetary exploration training!" The first cover dropped, revealing a ten-foot statue of Regnig. It was the perfect depiction of Jules' elderly friend. They'd removed the red lines from his single eye, and his beak was slightly ajar, his tongue visible between it. She studied the talons and smiled at the familiar robe on his back. A tear fell from her eye, remembering the hours of conversation they'd shared.

She used to flap her wings when she'd visit him, dancing through his library. Jules filled with sadness at those moments, and how Regnig had always been kind to her, even when she was in those uncomfortable early teen years. He'd been a grandfather figure, a best friend, and a mentor. "I miss you, Regnig," she whispered to herself. Slate held her hand, not even glancing at her, and she appreciated the gesture.

The group of Toquil near the front embraced each other, and Jules felt a surge of pain that they hadn't gotten the chance to meet Sager earlier. That had been his real name at one point, long before he'd met any of them.

"And none of this would have been possible if not for the heroics of a special person. Without them, the Alliance wouldn't have persevered, and we'd have lost so many more lives to our enemies."

Jules smiled, knowing full well this had to be a statue of Papa. Dean Parker was a fixture among the Gatekeepers and the Alliance.

When the person tugged the cover off, she almost

choked.

It was her.

The statue showed a curly-haired woman in a Gate-keeper's uniform, her arm outstretched to the stars, with a confident expression.

"Jules Parker, we want to thank you for everything you've accomplished, and know that you have a permanent place here at Regnig's Academy. The training wing is hereby forever known as: The Jules Parker Institute," Karo said, smirking at her.

Jules had never heard such applause. The cameras floated closer, and she wiped the dampness from her cheeks. Karo motioned to the spot in front of them, as if she was expected to give a speech, and she closed her eyes, doing a trick her mother had taught her for such occasions.

When Jules opened them, the calmness returned. "I'm at a loss for words, but I've always preferred action to them anyway."

The people laughed, and Magnus nodded to Nat, likely agreeing with the sentiment.

"I was the youngest student in history, but I think that record will be broken soon. Because we're advancing, and you are all seeing the value to raising bright and effective children. We visualize the opportunity, because look around: Outpost is the future. This is what we're meant to do, not hide on our worlds while others are suffering. While some of you are losing your star or dealing with food supply issues. No. We won't stand by and ignore these atrocities. We're in this together." Jules paused, not wanting to overdo it. After spending the better part of the last year with Mary on her dignitary meetings, Jules saw herself in a new light.

"Regnig was the brightest star I've ever met. Please remember him as you walk the halls of his Academy. Honor him by reading his biography, by studying his notes and manuscripts. Become a better student because of Regnig's desire to learn and share his wisdom. That's your purpose. And most of all…" She smiled and waved at a young student wearing her first-year garb near the courtyard. The Keppe girl beamed, giving a gap-toothed grin. "Have fun!"

Jules stepped back, stealing another peek at the pair of statues. It didn't feel right that none of her family members were around for this moment, but she knew they'd watch it on the feeds at a later date. Jules returned her gaze to the crowd, finding her friends, and decided that her family was there after all.

FOUR

"*D*ad, check this out!" Hugo knocked on the sheet of ice above us. "I can see the light through it now."

"Given the depth, the ice is quite pure. I think it's midday on Pestria." I squinted, catching the glow of the star past the thick layer.

I used my tablet, viewing our path behind us. We'd exited the building almost a full day ago, and had managed to tour most of the city since then. It was a marvelous sight.

"What could have made these?" Hugo asked.

The city was filled with tunnels, all nearly perfectly shaped. The corridors were round, like someone had drilled sideways with a large machine, but whoever did it was long gone. We'd seen no sign of a living being anywhere on what was previously ground level.

"Where are the people?" Hugo asked.

"Did you ever read about Pompeii?"

Hugo kept walking, his lights reflecting off the tunnels shiny surface. "Yep. Mount Vesuvius erupted, covering the city in ash."

"It was frozen in time, forgotten until an excavation revealed it years later."

"But the people were still in it," Hugo said.

"That's right. They must have evacuated Pestria," I suggested, trying to see if Hugo would pick up on my train of thought.

"But they didn't have space travel."

"And how do you know?" I asked.

"Well, I don't, but we haven't seen any evidence." He pointed to the right. "They have these vehicles. Three wheels. They have axles, which means there's likely a motor under the hood."

The cars were bigger than a minivan, but without roofs, making for an extremely clunky convertible. "Earth had space shuttles before we had flying cars."

"But, Dad, not really. We just kind of flew into orbit. Does that even count?" Hugo asked.

I cringed, thinking about the astronauts I'd grown up admiring. "It does, but that's not the point."

"Yeah, the point is, if there was a world-ending catastrophe, Earth would have been screwed."

I considered the comment. "What would we have done if a life-destroying asteroid or massive flood occurred? Or, as we were always concerned with, a nuclear devastation?"

Hugo was deep in thought, his feet planting on the slippery surface below him. Our boots had spikes, which made traversing this ice tunnel much easier. "If we couldn't leave, we'd have to hole up somewhere. Maybe an underwater bunker, or something buried far below ground. Wait for the fallout to become manageable. It would be a huge undertaking. We'd need a power source, have a means to grow food and filter air."

"And this city. What have we determined?" I grinned when he grasped my clues.

"There's power. Those shields were operational." Hugo looked at the path. "And we've even noticed a few lights in use."

"That's my boy." I clapped him on the back.

"You think they're still here?" Hugo asked.

"Could be, but I doubt anyone would have survived

this long. The best guess is they've been trapped in ice for five thousand years. They could have emerged," I said.

"But it's frozen. Why bother if they built a viable home?"

I hadn't considered that. "I guess you're teaching me."

"Speaking of, I think we missed the Academy's unveiling."

I went rigid and made a fist. "I can't believe it. This was a big day for Jules, and we should have been there for her."

"She'll forgive us, Dad. We're on a mission. Jules, of all people, can appreciate that."

He was right, but that didn't make the guilt vanish from my gut. "I wanted to see the look on her face when she saw Regnig's statue."

"Yeah, Regnig's Academy is epic. And Jules got her own statue," he said.

"What?" I didn't follow.

"They built a statue of Jules. It's on the opposite side of the courtyard," Hugo told me. "Wait, you didn't know about it?"

I shook my head. "I guess I was supposed to be surprised with her." I felt even worse.

"Nothing we can do now. Not like we can turn back time." Hugo took a step forward and stopped. "We can't do that, can we, Dad?"

I laughed, shoving his shoulder. "Keep moving."

I was having fun with my son, and hoped we could solve the mystery of this vacant city. But if we were going to do it, we had to pick up the pace. We could only stay on Pestria for another day, maximum, before they sent reinforcements.

"Can I see the map?" Hugo reached for the tablet, and I conceded it to him. He zoomed and changed the focal point, muttering under his breath. He was as tall as me now, his shoulders just as broad. I still pictured him as a young boy, obsessed with playing video games, but he'd quietly become a man faster than I anticipated. "That's it!"

"What did you discover?"

"The tunnels only criss-cross in one location. See this." He tapped the screen about a mile from our position. The yellow light indicating our suits blinked on the left side of the display. "This has to be a hub."

"A hub? Like a train station?"

"We have this on New Spero. The hovertrains all connect in the center of the Terran sites and branch out from there."

"Meaning…"

"We found a major clue to their disappearance. I think we'll see where they are if we check it," he said.

"Then what are we waiting for?" I lifted an eyebrow. "Let's move."

He offered the tablet back, but I declined. "You keep it. I'm following your lead."

———

*A*t first, Sarlun had expected to be transported elsewhere, but that wasn't the case. He was still in the Backyard, only behind an invisible curtain. Oran and Erem took him through their village. They were obviously well-liked, since everyone they encountered sought their attention. A few people asked after Sarlun, but most didn't offer a glance, and he was okay with that.

He did notice a few stares, as if seeing a Shimmal man was something to note. He couldn't tell if it was because they'd never met one, or because his sister had indeed been in the Backyard and they recognized his race. Sarlun wanted to ask them, but decided on lying low for the moment. She'd been there many years earlier, by his estimation, and Sarlun doubted any could still be living in this squalor after so much time.

Citizens were in the streets, mopping the cobblestones with filthy rags on the end of thick wooden stakes. He was astounded to see how much cleaner it was in this village, hidden behind some technological forcefield.

Even the air was less pungent. He could still see the smokestack in the distance, but it was blurred, like a mirage. The buildings had been recreated, the bricks mismatched, and the mortar was discolored, but it did the job. These people had homes, and despite their outward appearances, they seemed content. Everyone's clothing was soiled, their faces covered with soot. Sarlun guessed water was a rarity.

"Why do you waste water on the streets?" he finally asked Erem as they passed another man scrubbing the stones.

"The rain here is undrinkable. We use it to wash our clothing and the town," Erem said.

"How inspiring," he commented.

Erem poked a finger at Sarlun's chest. "Are you criticizing our methods?"

"No. Nothing like that. I meant it, wholeheartedly."

Erem's frown shifted into a smile. "You are different, Stranger. We don't meet many prisoners like you."

Sarlun wiggled his small snout and tapped it. "One's that look like me?"

Erem cleared his throat. "Out with it."

"Have you met another person from Shimmal?"

"I don't know."

"She would have had my features."

Erem ignored him, waving a woman over. "Tessa, this

is Stranger. We found him at the Stack."

"Planning to jump off, were you? It's a common way to end the pain," Tessa said.

"Are you human?" Sarlun asked, astounded to see one this far out.

Tessa seemed equally shocked. "You know what a human is?"

"I'm from the Alliance." Sarlun blinked repeatedly. "Or I was."

Tessa's eyes filled with tears. "Tell me... how are things?"

"Good, I suppose. How did you get here?"

"I was on *Vast*, sent to explore the Ishio System. There were rumors of a crystal, something the Parkers wanted," she said.

Sarlun thought about the portal spheres, and kept his mouth closed. *Vast* had been reported missing about a decade ago. It had been a tough few months, with *Mettle* vanishing around the same time.

For some reason, her mention of the crystals reminded him of the sphere he'd tried to conceal. He hoped that no one had accessed it under his collection room floor. He'd done his best to hide it there, mostly because he trusted nowhere else. Sarlun had visited the world several times, learning of the ten-headed Amendors, but didn't want them unleashed on the universe, so he'd kept it secret. "What happened?" he prompted her.

"We didn't find anything of the sort, but managed to encounter a rift in space. We tried everything to avoid it, but got caught in the gravitational pull. We shot our escape pods out, but even those didn't break free. I was on the bridge when we were torn apart. The captain ordered us into spacesuits, but I was the only one sealed in when the hull was breached."

"I'm sorry," Sarlun mustered.

"A trader found me a day before my life support would have expired," Tessa whispered, touching her cheek. "They were good to me, until we came to the Belash Bazaar. The trader sold me to the highest bidder. I was with them for five years, working in their storage compartment, running inventory systems and cataloging their items."

Sarlun sensed where the story was leading, given that she was in the Backyard with the rest of them. "And you fought?"

Tessa looked abashed. "Not at first. I worked for Tixa's staff for one year. A human. He thought it was the most marvelous thing. I was exotic. He showed me off to his visitors, making me serve them meals and drinks. I learned of a trader ship coming to town, someone that helped free people like me, and I ran. When I reached the docks, Tixa was buying more staff from the 'liberator.' I was sent to the Backyard for my attempted escape."

"How long?" Sarlun asked.

"I've been here for four years."

Sarlun struggled to imagine living in this place for that kind of duration, and shivered. "And you two?"

Erem and Oran glanced at one another. "We've lived in the Backyard for seven years."

"Seven?" Sarlun grimaced, and noticed more people flooding the streets.

"Eleven," a gnarled woman said, her hair gray and tied in a rag.

"Twelve… give or take a few months," another local man said.

He thought about his sister, Shula, and how many years ago she'd vanished. Last seen at the Belash Bazaar. "And none of you have seen someone like me?" he asked.

Tessa shook her head. "Not directly."

"What does that mean?" Sarlun asked.

"There's a record keeper of all the Backyard residents," Oran told him.

Sarlun's hopes climbed. "Can I meet them?"

"She's dead, but the records remain. Someone watches over it. It's not close, and the journey can be perilous," Erem said.

Sarlun cracked his neck, rolling his shoulders. "I'm prepared."

"Good for you. I'm not." Oran chuckled. "We rest. There's no sense in rushing into things. Time doesn't exist as it does elsewhere in the Backyard. Come, I'll show you to your quarters."

"What of home?" Tessa asked.

Erem stood in her way, shooing her off. "Speak with him later. I think Stranger needs to understand this isn't a temporary stop."

Tessa nodded somberly and returned to her work.

Sarlun kept his cowl off to display his prominent features. If anyone had met his sister, he wanted them to be reminded of her.

He was led to a clean building; the entrance was marred with soot-streaked footprints, but was otherwise pristine.

"In here." Erem pointed. "Water is in the kitchen."

They left him alone in the house, and Sarlun sighed, taking his cloak off. The cot was small and patched together, but it was better than sleeping on the floor. He used a latrine, impressed with the series of tubes exiting the wall and heading to the street, then below ground.

Sarlun went to the kitchen and saw a machine. A glass sat beside a metal nozzle, and Sarlun flipped a large red switch. The device rattled and coughed before funneling water from an outside source.

"It must be on the roof," he muttered, glancing up.

The water was black near the top of the bending tubes, and it flowed, changing to brown, then yellow, until finally a clear liquid poured into the glass. "Impressive." He tested it, finding it sour but palatable. These people were the definition of resilient. He'd expected to encounter angry, mutated thieves, but instead had found a real community.

"Assemble! They've come again!" Erem's voice bellowed from the street.

Sarlun dashed to the exit and saw clunky robots stalking to their village, kicking up soot and dirt. "What's going on?"

"Tixa has sent his cleanup crew!" Oran hefted a giant club. "Arm yourself, Stranger."

FIVE

The day had been tiring, but now that everyone had vacated the area, Jules enjoyed walking the Academy with Dean, despite her exhaustion. It had been an emotional rollercoaster, seeing her own statue, and remembering Regnig with a vivid clarity.

"We probably won't see everyone together until our big day," Dean told her, their fingers intertwined as they strolled through the empty halls.

"I guess not."

"Are you sure you have to leave?" Dean stopped, facing her in front of the training yard. Jules peered at the field, smiling at its pristine condition. That wouldn't last, not when some freshman blasted a hole in the middle of it because he forgot the safety on his pulse cannon. Jules could be blamed for a similar incident. She'd had a lot on her mind back then.

"Suma wants to find Sarlun, and Papa agrees it's time to bring him home," she said.

"You don't have much of a lead," Dean reminded her.

"Someone sent Suma and Hulope the same footage, which suggests she might be on his trail already." Jules wouldn't let Hulope get to Sarlun first, but months had gone by since the night of her engagement.

"If Suma can't find the location, why would Hulope be able to?"

"Whoever sent the files knows where he is," Jules said. So far, they'd been unable to track the sender down, but that was the key. "Dean, that's it."

"What is?"

"Suma's been so focused on discovering where the clip took place, when she should have traced the sender." Jules grinned and kissed him. "I have to go."

"What do you mean? This is our last night…"

"Sorry. I'll make it up to you," she promised.

"I can come to *Outpost* with you," he said.

"You're leaving in the morning with Magnus and your mom. Just stay here and get some sleep." She kissed him again, lingering for a moment longer. "Trust me. I'll bring Sarlun home."

"Then will you relax for a while? Maybe we can chill on Bazarn for a week or something?"

"Sure. Deal." Jules rushed off, pausing near the exit to wave goodbye. She hated doing this to him, but Suma had been looking at the problem from the wrong angle. Jules jumped, shooting her sphere around her, and launched to the crashed warship near the fringes of Outpost.

She was sure people could see her, but she didn't care. It was late and the massive moon glowed brightly, making it feel like daytime over the city. It truly was a beautiful place. She'd spent years growing up on Haven, Earth, and New Spero, but thought this might take the prize.

Jules imagined raising a family here, and letting the kids experience many remarkable cultures. They could fish at the lake on weekends, and dine at a famous Bhlat chef's restaurant in the evenings. Learn to make pottery from a Molariun artist. The options were endless. But that was for the future, and she wasn't ready to give up her youth so quickly.

The trip was fast, traveling as the crow flies to the

repurposed warship, and Jules settled to the entrance, glancing at the cameras pointed at her. The doors were huge, and they slid open at the hangar, allowing her access.

Two Keppe guards were there to greet her. "How are you guys doing tonight?"

"Very well, Ms. Parker," the left one said. "Congratulations on your honor today."

"Thank you." She smiled at them and kept walking. "Would you tell me where I can find Suma?"

"She's on deck four, room zero."

That was the captain's quarters. She'd occupied them for a brief moment a couple of years ago, before she felt qualified for such a position. Jules slowed her steps, appreciating the warship. It had been the first of its kind to be in the field, and she was grateful it was still being utilized. When she arrived at Suma's, she felt guilty, given the late hour, but she rapped her knuckles regardless.

Suma answered a minute later, her robes pulled tight. "We have to stop meeting like this."

"Is there an emergency?" Elex asked from inside the dark room.

"It's just me… Jules." She lifted a hand when the lights turned on.

Elex exited the bedroom and sat at the table. "Make yourself at home."

Suma stifled a yawn. "Couldn't this have waited until tomorrow?"

"The message. Who did it come from?"

"My source at Udoon routed it," Suma said. "You know that."

"But how did he get it, and why… did it go to Hulope?" Jules gritted her teeth, recalling the woman as she tried Suma, attempting to find her guilty of treason. Suma would be dead if it wasn't for Jules and Papa rescuing her.

47

"He said it was in the instructions. The directions sent it to me and to Sarlun's old address. He claimed he had no idea what was transpiring within the Shimmal ranks."

"Likely story," Jules said. "We're visiting Udoon."

"Seriously?" Elex asked. "We already did that."

"I'll find out where the message came from. Then we'll have a real trail. I understand that you trusted this guy, but I don't. For all we know, he was paid off to do this, and hide the message's origin from anyone."

"And how will you learn if that's true?" Elex asked.

Suma laughed and started to brew some coffee. "Don't worry, it's decaf. And, Elex, you obviously haven't gone on missions with this young woman. She's almost as infuriatingly good at getting her way as her father. Speaking of, where is Dean?"

"With Hugo. They're investigating some world." Jules struggled to remember the name. "Pest something."

"Pestria?" Elex perked up.

"That's it."

"Interesting," he whispered.

"Why?" Jules grabbed cream from the fridge as the wonderful aroma filled the space.

"I spoke to Dean about it a while ago. I'd been researching vacant worlds… by that, I mean the ones that had previously been occupied, but now the populations are missing. It's not as uncommon as you might expect. The Gatekeepers have explored hundreds of the portal map locations. 91.2% are unoccupied, and of those, 84% have no life or the capacity for life as we know it. 3.9% have an intelligent population, capable of technology and community. But there are also 1.7% of the investigated planets that have all the infrastructure of a thriving people, only they're empty."

"Sterona was one," Jules said.

"Yes, but we've learned what happened to those people, and helped colonize the remaining refugees. Weren't you born there?" Elex asked.

"Yep. That's where Suma met Papa," Jules said. Sometimes it was hard to recall how much older Suma was than her, especially considering that Uncle Zeke and her parents treated Suma like she was a niece.

"Pestria was another of those. Half the city coated in ice. The rest of the continent was bereft of civilization, but I have a hypothesis." Elex took the offered cup from his wife.

"What's that?" Jules accepted a coffee too and stirred in a dollop of cream.

"Have you heard of the Galbaria Theory?" he asked, blowing on the steaming beverage before testing it.

"Don't think so," Jules admitted.

Elex rolled his eyes and his snout twitched. "No wonder we have more explorers than scientists. It's a good thing I'm subbing in at Regnig's Academy. We need to teach our youth more of this, and less about weapons."

Jules didn't argue, because he was probably right. "What's the theory?"

Elex's face grew animated, and Suma plunked to the chair beside him, wrapping her short hands around the cup. "Galbaria was Shimmal's most renowned expert on planetary cores. He was the first person in the known universe to drill all the way into one. 2300 kilometres on a small planet near our home. He believed that there was enough energy within our cores to power the entire world, if applied correctly."

"Okay, I'm following," Jules said.

"Here's where it takes a turn. Galbaria grew restless with the speed of his research and became obsessed. He was denied access to Shimmal's core, with the leaders deciding that it was too dangerous to reach it without knowing just what might happen should the atmosphere come in contact with the interior. The heat comes from decaying radioactive elements, and they were correct to err on the side of caution."

"So what happened?" Jules asked.

"He tested the theory on another world, one of comparable sizes to Shimmal, and we later found out through his studies that he was doing so on an occupied planet. The journals were discovered much later. I've discussed this in detail with Regnig. He'd stumbled upon an original copy of Galbaria's files, and his notes were extraordinary. For a Toquil, he had a vast knowledge of complex equations," Elex said.

"You sound surprised," Jules quipped.

"I meant no offense. I just didn't expect it from Regnig. He was one of a kind," Elex recovered.

"Agreed. What happened to Galbaria, if his research was left behind? Did he die?" Jules took a drink, warming with the coffee.

"That remains a mystery. The journals grew increasingly erratic, with talk of linear core links between solar systems. It was tough to follow, but the countless scholars who've spent their lives working on deciphering Galbaria's work can agree on two things. First, that Galbaria was mad. Second, that he believed in Reflective Worlds."

"Reflective Worlds." Jules repeated it. "We saw another Earth! They do exist."

"It could have been a fluke," Elex suggested. "Given all the planetoids out there, and the immensity of space, the idea that two might be identical isn't out of the realm of possibilities."

"Do you believe that?" Suma asked him.

"Perhaps. I don't have enough data to draw a

conclusion."

Jules kept on it. "What about the Reflective Worlds?"

"Galbaria thought that if you reached the core, some would have a gateway within, linking them to their partner planet."

"And what does this have to do with Pestria?" Jules asked him.

"There are some interesting results from the Gatekeepers' report that suggest the planet's atmosphere has been exposed to the core," he said.

"It's radioactive?"

"No, it's perfectly safe, and there's no reason the people couldn't live within the environment." Elex finished his coffee. "Other than the fact the world is covered in ice."

"Are you suggesting that Pestria might be connected to another planet within its core? And that's where the population might have gone?" Jules wished she could contact Papa and ask him why he chose that place to visit with Hugo, when there were so many other unexplored destinations at their fingertips.

"Again, it's just a theory, and an ancient one. I believe in science, and despite Galbaria's supposed mental health issues, he was a brilliant intellect. It's possible. But… I highly doubt that Reflective Worlds exist, and there should be no danger on Pestria," he said.

"Good. Can we focus on our task, since this has nothing to do with bringing Sarlun home?" Jules stared into her cup, wondering what they'd find within Earth's core. Would it transport them to the other place she'd seen on her journey to the First World?

"Yes." Suma brought out a tablet. "We'll head to Udoon in the morning and meet my source. I don't care how you do it, but we need to bring my father home. I've heard stories regarding Shimmal, and it's bad. Hulope already tried to screw us over by partnering with Nix Benah, and there are reports she's offering any Kraski or former PlevaCorp employees amnesty on my home. We've stood by in the shadows for too long. It's time to liberate Shimmal and return her to her former glory."

Jules couldn't agree more, and went to the quarters next door, where she closed her eyes, finally drifting into a fitful sleep. Images of Sarlun battling a robot appeared for a breath, and then there was darkness.

———

Sarlun wished he had a gun, but the heavy iron rod would have to suffice. He swung it with all his strength, clanging it against the metal man's temple. His head caved in, electrical wires shorting and flickering before his eyes darkened and he collapsed to the ground.

"Behind you!" Sarlun shouted at Tessa. She ducked and avoided the robot's weapon. They clutched objects like energized chainsaws. The flickering power spun in an oval, slicing the stone as the enemy missed her.

Tessa whirled around, jabbing her spear into the robot's neck. The weapon kept lifting, and Erem was there to knock it aside. He clubbed the opponent in the back of the neck, and it was no longer operational.

The robot clanked to the alleyway, and Sarlun searched for another target. But they were all dealt with. Two people were clearly dead, and another five injured. Tessa rushed to an old woman, tearing a piece of her own shirt to bandage a bleeding cut. Sarlun joined her, ushering the wounded into a hospice, complete with makeshift gurneys.

"What were those things?" Sarlun asked through gasping breaths.

"Tixa sends the Cleaners every now and then. Usually only twice a year, but that's the third time in six months," Oran said, his left eye swelling up. It was already bruised.

"And they try to kill you?" Sarlun hefted a heavy man up with Erem's help, and they began to cleanse his wounds with clear water.

"Either he wants us dead, or just to remind everyone that it's hopeless. I think he gets off on torturing his people," Erem said. "Last time, they killed four of us. You're a warrior, Stranger."

"I'm no warrior," Sarlun whispered.

"But you fight like one, and for that, we are grateful." Oran patted his back.

"They'll make it." Tessa navigated the room as if she'd done this a thousand times. Others arrived to assist, and soon all of the patients had been seen to.

"How can you live like this?" Sarlun asked them.

Oran cracked his knuckles. "It's all we have."

"You were supposed to be hidden. We entered the invisible barrier."

"It only works for so long. We will move it again. But they will find us," he said.

"I'll get you out of here," Sarlun promised.

Oran clenched his jaw, and his brother looked at the floor. "Don't speak like that."

"Like what? With hope?" Sarlun coughed, finding black soot on his hand when he covered his mouth.

"Those are dangerous ideas, Stranger. We've been here for years, and if there's one thing we know, it's not to be optimistic. It only hurts more when nothing changes."

"You've attempted to escape? These are mere walls surrounding the Backyard."

"And drones with lasers, and more of the Cleaners, and soldiers, and…" Oran leaned on a table. "It's fruitless."

"We'll see about that. You said you'd bring me to see the Record Keeper. Does that still stand?"

"You saved my life," Tessa told him. "I'll personally escort you."

"Us too." Erem spoke for himself and his brother, who nodded solemnly, like he had no choice but to oblige.

They went outside, and people were dragging the robots to the largest building on site. "What are they doing?"

"We dismantle them. Make water purification filters, and any other contraptions we can think of," Oran said. "Why waste good electrical components?"

"And their weapons?" Sarlun glanced at one of the energy saws.

"They don't work without their power source." Tessa pressed the button, but it did nothing. "And we require them for our machinery."

"Then hardwire one in," Sarlun said. "Make the sacrifice. It'll be much easier next time the Cleaners come."

The brothers glanced at one another. "We could do that."

"Will more Cleaners be sent?"

"Not for a while. Unless Tixa has found a reason," Erem told him.

Sarlun was beat, and he needed rest. The city was darkening, and he assumed the sun was finally set. It was tough to know beneath the blanket of smog.

He went back to the home, climbed into bed, and instantly fell asleep.

Sarlun woke hours later, his body feeling rejuvenated, his mind clear of cobwebs. Today was going to be a good day.

"You're up," Tessa said from the kitchen. She offered him a glass of water when he joined her, and he accepted it with a nod of his chin.

"Thank you."

"Are you ready?" She wore different clothes, these clean and patched with various colors.

Sarlun slipped his cloak on, feeling the warmth. Mornings in the Backyard were abnormally chilly. "I am prepared."

When they exited the building, Erem and Oran were waiting for them, long staffs in their clutches. "We have something you may enjoy." Oran pulled his cloak open to reveal the robot's weapon. It powered on with the flip of a chrome switch, the energy chain spinning noiselessly.

"You did it," Sarlun said appreciatively. "That was fast."

"We didn't get much sleep. But this was more important," Oran informed him.

The sky was still dark, the smog feeling lessened today, and Sarlun caught a glimpse of the glowing sun beyond. The villagers were all emerging from the various structures, their eyes wide, their expressions grim.

"Tessa, I don't understand why you're leaving for this man," someone said. "Is he worth the danger of crossing the Backyard?"

"Time will tell," Tessa whispered. "But I believe so."

Sarlun smiled at her. "If you point me in the proper direction, I can venture…"

Tessa lifted her hand. "No. I made a promise, and I intend to stick to it. Plus, it's been a while since any of us have neared the Mountain of Refuse."

Sarlun thought about his view from the smokestack, and knew where they were going.

Erem said goodbye to a woman near the edge of the crowd, and they touched foreheads before he broke away.

"Is that your wife?" Sarlun asked.

"We do not make such commitments in the Backyard.

For time is fleeting, and our spirits cannot endure any more pain." Erem stalked past him into the lead. His staff clipped on the cobblestone, and they were off.

Their group walked in silence for ten minutes, passing by the invisible barrier once again and re-entering the middle of the Backyard. "Are others out here?"

"Yes," Tessa said. "But they are not as they once were. They've changed."

"Changed how?" Sarlun asked, peering around.

"When you're fending for your own life, you do things… eat whatever you can. It's about survival. That's why we opted to work as a team, and to protect each other. But these… they're feral. If you encounter one, ignore them if possible. Some are more violent than others. It's the Artificial. We also think Tixa is experimenting on them with his drugs."

"And if ignoring isn't possible?" Sarlun inquired.

"Kill them," Oran said firmly.

Sarlun nodded. "Very well."

"Tell me of home, Stranger," Tessa prompted him an hour later. They moved east, the smokestack still billowing blackness into the air from a distance.

"You know of the Shimmal, right?" he asked.

"Yes. That ostentatious man leads them. The one from the Gatekeepers," she said.

He grimaced. "Sarlun."

"That's him."

"You don't respect Sarlun?" There was a bit of humor to this conversation, but he also felt guilty for his deceit.

"I suppose he's fine. My father wasn't much in the way of alien relations. He complained about everything. Thought Dean Parker was giving too much credibility to his alien alliances, and not enough focus on our own people," Tessa said.

Sarlun considered this, and could appreciate the perspective. "And you?"

"Look, I was ten years old when the Event transpired. I was torn from my home like everyone else, separated from my family, and I saw two of my classmates die from dehydration on those Kraski ships. I know not everyone is sympathetic to what we've gone through, but I still see their faces when I close my eyes."

Sarlun blinked, trying to imagine the horrors this woman had witnessed in her life. From a near-death experience at ten, to her crew dying, to captivity by Tixa at the Belash Bazaar. And now… this desolate wasteland to contend with. "You might be the strongest person I've ever met," he admitted.

She stopped and stared at him. "I don't think that's true, but thanks for saying so. There have been many moments I've thought about giving in, but something pushes me on."

"Good." Sarlun noticed that neither Oran nor Erem was within earshot, and assumed they were giving Tessa some privacy. "You asked to hear about home. Where was that for you?"

"New Spero. It was the only way to join the crews. They weren't hiring out of Earth, and my family stayed in New Columbus. Spent two years at Terran Three before I was brought on board."

"New Spero is thriving. We've… they've built an Institute there, in the desert. They train soldiers from around the Alliance, which has expanded dramatically."

Tessa let out a low whistle. "How remarkable. And the Parkers?"

Everyone wanted to hear what Dean was up to, even though they didn't really know him. He was royalty. "Mary leads the Alliance as their president, and Dean…" He paused, not wishing to give himself away. "I think he's still roaming the galaxies, saving the day."

"Sounds about right. I met him once," Tessa said.

"You did?"

"Twice, actually. He was there when they landed the Kraski ship, returning us to Earth after they failed to throw us into the sun. He came over to me, took my hand, and asked me what my name was." Tessa stared at the smog-covered sky. "Dean Parker found my family in the logs and ordered someone to bring me to them, even though we were two states apart."

"But Dean had no authority," Sarlun said.

"They listened to him. I knew he was special then."

"And the second time?"

"Before *Vast* took off from orbit. He gave a rousing speech, and his daughter came wearing that Gatekeepers uniform. Cute girl. She still in school?" Tessa asked, and Sarlun actually laughed.

"Sorry. No. Jules Parker is working with Magnus at the Institute."

"That's good. Magnus seemed like a good man."

Sarlun didn't have the energy to elaborate. She didn't need to know that their real Magnus had died on *Horizon*, or that Jules had traveled to another dimension to kill Lom of Pleva and managed to bring another Magnus back with her. How many occasions had he not been present for in the last couple of years? Suma…

"Did you say something?" she asked, and Sarlun caught himself.

"It was nothing."

"So the Alliance is thriving. Good to hear." There was a little sarcasm in her tone, but he could tell she missed home too.

"I'll bring us out of here," he promised again.

"You need to stop doing that. We just met, Stranger. Why would you be loyal to us?"

Because I failed my daughter. I let Ranul brand me with my father's curse, and almost killed my best friends… Because I am a shell of a man… "I have penance to pay. And this seems like a good start."

Tessa smiled at him. "Now that, I understand."

Erem and his brother halted up ahead, and they clinked the ends of their staffs together. "The Feral are nearby."

Sarlun listened, catching howls on the wind. The noises grew louder.

SIX

I didn't want to admit it to myself, but I was having a blast beneath the ice on Pestria. Hugo was in his element, stalking through the corridors like he belonged. The trek was perilous within the city, the tunnels growing slicker as the air warmed.

"I can't figure out why it's melting," Hugo said, dipping a gloved finger into the puddles near our feet.

"It must be the sensors. The city is watching. We came inside and activated some ancient trigger," I told him. That had to be the reason.

Hugo showed me the map. "We're nearly at the hub."

"Then let's keep moving." I went first, but stopped when I heard a noise echo through the cavity.

"What the heck was that?" Hugo whispered. His gun was out before mine, and I had to give him credit for his quick reaction.

"Could be nothing." But I didn't think so. I checked the outside air temperature, finding it was five centigrade. Above melting. We'd kept on our suits, even though the air was hospitable within the ice city.

"Dad, it's the ice… it's cracking!" Hugo gestured above his head, and I saw the first hairline fracture expanding on the surface.

My chest grew tight. "We have to get to safety!" I pictured the entire network of tunnels collapsing and sending us into an early grave. It would take weeks to extract our bodies once the Gatekeepers sent reinforcements.

Hugo ran, his ice picks sending shaved bits of snow behind him. I sped after him, eying the growing crack. The blocks were shifting, the sound like a lonely whale in the ocean. The hub was only a hundred meters from our current position, and the corridor slanted down. Hugo tripped on his own feet and slid on his belly. I dove while the tunnel broke apart, giant blocks raining from above. I jumped over one and fell, slipping the rest of the way.

I bashed into something, and saw it was Hugo. "It's okay, Dad."

We were in a building, the corners supported by giant metal girders, the walls solid. "The hub."

Our escape route was fully blocked with chunks of ice. I ran to the far end of the space and found the exit to be covered as well. There were more corridor entries in the hub, and they were all clogged.

"There's no way out," I whispered.

Hugo smirked. "Sure there is. Down."

Our lights illuminated the building's interior, and I saw circular doorways. I went to one, pressing a bright green button, and it slid to the side, blocking the ice barricade. I did the same with the others, sealing the exits.

There was one more, and it was beneath our feet in the center of the wide room. "If this doesn't have a tunnel, we're stuck here, son."

Hugo knelt, touching the green indicator button. "Here goes nothing."

We stood clear of the disc-shaped door as it swung wide, revealing a hole. "Nice work, Hugo."

I crouched, shining my light as far as it would go. The tunnel dropped for ten feet, and angled like a slide after that. "Maybe we should take a break." I was tired, but could tell Hugo wanted to dive headfirst into the next phase of our mission.

"You knew what was under here, didn't you?" Hugo took his helmet off, the air valve hissing momentarily.

I did the same, removing the pack clipped to my back. "Maybe."

"Why are we really on Pestria, Dad?" Hugo sat down cross-legged and rummaged through his own bag. We each carried provisions, should we be separated.

"I may as well come clean."

"I knew it!" Hugo broke a piece of his energy bar off. "You had ulterior motives."

"Nothing so conspiratorial. I wanted to spend time with you."

"But…"

"It's Regnig. I can't stop thinking about him, and…"

"And what?" Hugo took a bite.

"I've been seeing things," I admitted.

Hugo looked worried. "Tell me it's…"

"No, not like before, and definitely not because of Ovalax. No, this is different. I think Regnig's trying to tell me something."

"He's with the Cosmos. Is that even possible?" Hugo asked with his mouth half-full.

"Regnig is the Recaster, so I think so."

"What's he showing you?"

"Remember when I told you about the spilled wine in his home?"

"Yeah, it gave you a clue."

I drank from my bottle and tore open a package of dried fruit. "It's almost like that. I've seen maps in my coffee. Planets in my bathwater."

"Of what?"

"Pestria."

"What's so special about this place?"

"That's what I wanted to find out. I figured you'd be game for an exploration," I said.

"Why didn't you just tell me before?"

"I didn't know what to make of it until I got here. Then it felt right, like we were on the proper track. I'm certain Regnig is guiding me, Hugo."

Hugo smiled and folded his garbage, shoving it away. "That's pretty cool. You miss him, don't you?"

"It's Jules I worry about." I could handle myself, but Jules was more attached than anyone to the ancient Toquil man.

"She's tougher than you think," Hugo said.

"I think she's plenty tough."

"Not like that. I mean up here." Hugo tapped his temple. "Why would he lead you to Pestria?"

"It's a mystery. Where did the people go? That's our mission. We solve that, and maybe Regnig will leave me alone," I told him, not sure if I really wanted him to or not.

"Well, only one way to solve it, Dad."

"We go into the hole," I muttered, finishing my snack. "I'm glad you came with me, kiddo."

"Someone has to protect you, old man." Hugo offered his hand, helping me to my feet.

"Old man… I'm only… okay, I just did the math." I'd taken the life extenders and felt young, but the years were still adding up. "I'll go first."

"Have it your way." Hugo stood at the tunnel's mouth.

I grabbed hold of the ledge to hop into it, and let go.

––––––––

*T*hey docked on Udoon Station, grateful to have the

wormhole generator to make the trip. *Light* was a bit of overkill, but since Slate wasn't in need of it, Jules figured no one would mind. Suma and Elex peered around nervously, but Jules had been here on countless occasions. She'd even saved it from being destroyed at least once. Even though they had a tenuous relationship with the Alliance, they still allowed gambling, drugs, and illegal trading.

Jules didn't really care, as long as they didn't break their agreement. If she heard of any people trading transpiring, there would be dire consequences. The group running the station knew her stance, and she was constantly assured it was prohibited.

"Miss Parker, we didn't know you were visiting," Amsea said. The woman was a fixture here, the second-in-command of their hierarchy. She had three eyes and gray skin, her mouth pulled tight into a smile. Jules wasn't sure if that was cosmetic or natural. Either way, it was off-putting.

"I didn't think I needed to give notice," Jules told her.

"You don't, but… we could have seen to your usual suite."

"We're not staying." Jules strode into the promenade, wearing her white Institute Ambassador uniform, gathering more attention than she might have wanted if this was a covert mission. It wasn't. She wanted their snitch to know she was there. "Have you met Suma and her husband, Elex?"

"I don't believe so." Amsea's eyes glittered, and she bowed respectfully. "What can we…"

Jules leaned in and whispered her instructions. "Close the docks. Do not let a single soul leave. If you see anyone scrambling, tell me." She passed the woman an earpiece, feigning it off like she was giving her a bribe, should anyone be watching. "And secure unit 73." Jules glanced at Suma, who nodded her confirmation that was her contact's suite.

"Consider it done." Amsea hurried off, setting the piece in her ear.

"What do we do now?" Elex asked. He was out of place here. Elex was at home in the laboratory, not on a dangerous mission.

"Wait," Jules said. "I have an idea."

They walked through the promenade and into the Station's primary halls. She searched for the time, but recalled there were no clocks on board Udoon. People of all kinds lingered in the facility, many scurrying away at the sight of an Alliance uniform, especially one denoting her as an ambassador for the area's strongest military presence.

Elex stayed close to his wife while they traversed half the station, heading into a bar. Her dad had told her stories about his first time on Udoon, when they came to meet Kinca and Lom of Pleva.

The bouncer was a massive alien with three arms and an angry scowl. He didn't lower to her stature as he stood there.

"We'd like a drink," Jules said.

"*Lesshesh bareds visha*," he croaked.

"Allow me," Elex told them. "*Bechee sovlish daar elian.*"

The big man shrugged his giant shoulders. "*Doolosh?*"

Elex went still. "*Ghosil… ghosil eeruptus.*"

They stared at each other, and both hollered out laughter. The alien bouncer stepped aside, still snickering as they entered.

"What was that all about?" Suma asked Elex.

"I told him a joke. It's impossible to resist that one," he told her with a grin.

"Nice work," Jules admitted. The place was packed,

but a table cleared out when they saw Jules Parker striding through the bar. A robot quickly wiped the surface, and a thin Padlog woman buzzed over with a tablet.

"What'll it be?" she asked.

Jules ordered a coffee, and Suma started to when Elex raised a finger, asking for three Padlog nectars.

"Those are potent," Jules warned him after the server had left.

"Sergo made me promise to try one if I had the opportunity. When in Italy… isn't that a human saying?" Elex asked.

"Close but no cigar," Jules told him, and his brow furrowed.

Elex was proving to be quite the interesting character. Jules rarely saw this carefree side. She could understand why Suma was so smitten with the guy.

Jules' coffee arrived with the three nectars, and she lifted her glass, clinking them with her friends. She'd taken one sip when the earpiece beeped. *"Miss Parker, we've apprehended the suspect. They were found trying to jettison from escape pod C-14."*

"We got him," Jules told Suma, and then said into the mic, "We'll be right there."

She stood up, but Elex stayed. "He's in custody. Let's stay and enjoy the drink."

Suma pushed her glass away, and Jules remembered she was carrying a child, but no one was supposed to know.

Jules wanted to tell him that every minute counted on Suma's father's trail, but the truth was, he'd been absent for years and obviously didn't want to be found. So she sat down and sipped the drink. It was sweet, but not in an overwhelming way. Jules drank half and switched to her coffee as she glanced around the bar. Creatures of all shapes and sizes occupied the establishment, and she thought she saw a familiar face.

"I'll be right back." Jules couldn't believe it. How was Regnig here? Her heart hammered in her chest as she stared at her old friend. It was him. The glossy eye, the slightly opened beak. His graying feathers were ruffled, his head tilted like he was listening to a conversation, even though he was alone at the bar. She tapped him on the shoulder, and he turned.

Can I help you? The voice wasn't his, the face no longer his either. The beak was shorter, the eye glossy from drink, not age.

"Sorry, I thought you were someone else," Jules told the Toquil.

I wish I was. He picked up his drink and slurped it through a straw, burping.

Jules hurried to the table and dragged them away. "Let's get out of here."

"Who was it?" Suma asked, craning her neck to see.

"Nobody." Jules stole another glance, wondering why she'd seen Regnig yet again.

When they arrived, Amsea stood near her office, motioning them in. "We'll bring the detainee."

"Thank you," Jules told the woman, and the door closed. "How did you even make this contact?"

Suma's snout twitched. "Sergo hooked me up."

"Of course. So we can't trust a word he said, not if Sergo used to operate with them," Jules said.

"We trust Sergo now," Suma added.

"True, but that doesn't mean the people he associated with wouldn't sell you out in a second. It's obvious this one did."

The door opened, and a young woman entered, her hair long and purple, her eyes marked black like a raccoon's. Jules didn't know what race she was, but her nails resembled sloth claws, sharp and long.

"Why were you running?" Suma asked.

The guards stayed, but Jules waved them away. "She's tied up. We'll take it from here."

Jules had no doubt she could stop this woman from escaping even without bound wrists. They left their captive in the room with Jules and her companions.

"Answer the question," Jules said forcefully.

She plunked to the empty chair, her hair falling over her face. "They'll kill me."

"Who will?"

"I was told to send you the file. And I lied before. Obviously, you see that now, or you wouldn't have brought the wonder girl." She glanced at Jules, smirking. It took all Jules' strength not to wipe the expression from her face. Jules had no empathy for spies and snitches, even if Suma had hired her.

"What's your name?" Jules asked.

She stared at the floor. "Zarin."

"Tell us what happened." Jules softened her tone, leaning on Amsea's desk to stay higher than their captive.

Zarin blew at the strands and slumped back into the seat. "Why bother? Are you going to kill me? Because I'd rather take my chances with you than the organization."

Jules glanced at Suma and Elex. They seemed as surprised by this revelation as Jules was. "What organization?"

Zarin laughed. "You guys think you know everything. The Alliance is this big happy family, but there's more happening behind the curtains than anyone can even imagine."

"Then fill us in," Jules whispered.

"Just send me to Traro or wherever. They won't be able to find me there."

Jules could sense this wasn't going in her direction, and didn't want to lose the opportunity for information.

"Suma, can you take Elex and check in with Amsea about our ship's provisions?"

"But we…" Suma stopped herself. "Right away." They left Jules alone with the young woman.

"You can't intimidate me," Zarin sneered.

Jules shrugged and lifted Zarin with a tendril of invisible energy. She wrapped it around her throat, tugging it ever so slightly, and Zarin's eyes grew wider. "Now, what were you saying about this organization?"

"You're not so tough," Zarin managed to say while her throat was being constricted.

Jules used another lash, cutting through the woman's binds, and she set her down. Zarin rubbed her neck with her free hands. "Come on, then. If you have something to say, go for it." Jules stood with her arms at her sides.

Zarin didn't move. She obviously knew who Jules was, and anyone would be foolish to try to strike her, even if they were desperate. "You're in over your head."

"Why?" Jules asked, and exhaled, making a show of relaxing to convince the woman to do the same. It worked. Zarin returned to her seat, her swagger diminished.

"Look, I only know what I've seen on the Black Hole," she said.

"What's the Black Hole?"

Zarin laughed, the noise uncomfortable. "What do you guys even do? The Black Hole is the forum we use to communicate with one another. We share jobs, information, people's data…"

"You steal things. Identities? Money?"

"I don't. Some do. I'm legit," she argued.

"Right. Where did you obtain the footage of Sarlun?"

"I already told Suma, I found it for her while running a facial recognition pattern in the regular feeds."

Jules frowned, noticing Zarin's cheek twitch. "You're

lying. This will go a lot smoother if you just tell me the truth."

Zarin flexed her sharp talons, the long nails clicking together. She glanced up with those big raccoon eyes, her demeanor shifting from brave to scared. "Promise you'll protect me." Her voice changed too; it was lighter, softer.

"From whom?"

"Have you not been listening at all?" Zarin shouted. "The organization that wants to create chaos in the Alliance. They put Hulope in charge of Shimmal."

Now they were getting somewhere. "Go on."

"Promise me," she repeated.

Jules sighed and nodded twice. "We'll bring you to New Spero. To the Institute. Magnus could use someone who understands this stuff. Let us hire you."

"Work for a human? I'd never—"

Jules raised a hand, a beam of energy flicking from her fingertip. "If you mess with me, the organization will be the least of your concerns."

"New Spero. Sounds nice. I've lived on Udoon for years, more recently the station when the heat got too much," Zarin said. "The local law enforcement claimed I was doing something illegal."

"Were you?"

"In a traditional sense, sure, but compared to these others on the Black Hole, I'm a Deity," she said, laughing at the comment.

Jules didn't crack a smile. She wondered if the comment was meant for her. *You're no longer a Deity, Jules,* she told herself. But she still had the powers of one.

"Okay, I'll spill."

Jules sat on the desk again and waited.

"There's an entire thread about the organization on the feeds; you just have to know where to look. They cover their tracks well, but one of my friends did some digging and traced the posts down. They pay… extremely well, but the organization must contact you. There's a spot where you can offer your services, but it's almost funny. They claim to be a stonework company, seeking miners to work on their teams. You fill out an application form and hope to get a response."

"And you did?"

"Eventually. A year out. They asked if I had any connections within the Alliance. I knew Sergo had gone clean, and contacted him. Suma messaged me a few days later, and this made the organization very happy. They sent the file, and I was given implicit instructions. The recipients were Suma and Hulope," Zarin said.

Jules was getting somewhere. "Show me everything. You'll be safe at New Spero."

Zarin grinned, her big eyes relaying amusement. "Miss Parker, you're never safe from the organization. That's what I'm trying to tell you."

SEVEN

Sarlun sought to catch his breath, but it was growing increasingly difficult. His legs ached, his snout dripped sweat, and they weren't even halfway to their destination.

"Will they stop tracking us?" he asked Erem. The bigger man glanced at him, as if he'd forgotten Sarlun was with their group. It took him a moment to respond, and Sarlun saw resignation mixed with his counterpart's fear.

"The Feral don't care for their own health. They will hunt us to the ends of the Yard and back," Erem said.

"Which is why we must kill them," Tessa told them.

"We should circumvent the Feral instead," Oran countered. "They're not bright."

Tessa closed her eyes and took a deep breath. "We've tried to lose them for the last three hours, and no matter where we go, more come."

Sarlun peered at the giant pile of trash a short distance away. "What about there?"

"No one enters the Mountain of Refuse. Not even the Feral," Erem muttered.

"Why not?" Sarlun wiped his forehead, smearing soot on his sleeve.

"It's too dangerous," Tessa whispered.

"That can't be true. If the Feral won't follow us, then that's our path."

"Stranger, you don't know the Backyard like we do. It's

filled with perils at every turn. There's a reason we don't venture from our sanctuary." Oran hefted his club higher when one of the Feral howled. They scanned the horizon, not seeing the beasts that had once been men and women, just like them.

"Some sanctuary. The Cleaner robots attacked you," Sarlun said. "Nowhere is safe, not even your precious home. You can mop the streets all you want, but you're never going to survive if you stay put."

The brothers shared a glance. "You have enough optimism for all four of us. Show us the way, Stranger."

Tessa grabbed Oran's arm, speaking in hushed tones so Sarlun couldn't overhear their conversation. She looked upset, but when they broke apart, it shifted to determination. "Fine. We'll gamble for our friends' futures."

Sarlun took in his surroundings. The sky was dreary, a haze of black and gray smoke drifting on the breeze, coming from the smokestack miles away. He could still see the monolith there, constantly belching poisonous darkness over the region. It was beyond bleak, and Sarlun could feel his own energy being sapped.

It took all his strength to put one foot in front of the other as he approached the heaps of garbage. The ground was no longer stone-covered. Nothing grew from the layer of dirt, and it was so hard-packed, not even the brothers' boots left a mark in it as they went.

Sarlun licked his lips, wishing he could down a full canteen of water, but their supplies were limited, so he settled for a sip. It only made him want more.

The mountain was a half-hour from their position, and it grew in size as they traversed the dirty land. Every now and then, Erem would halt, tilt his ear into the wind, and wave them on.

Sarlun was getting colder as he resisted the wind with

each step, but he had nothing to warm himself with. It cut through his cloak, and he cinched the garment tighter, leaving the cowl down so he could see his path.

The Feral were silent, but he sensed their presence despite this fact. Sarlun had ventured on enough alien worlds to know when a local predator was stalking him, and he had the same sensation right then.

He removed the Cleaner's weapon and powered it on, standing firmly. "They're coming."

The ground sloped from the edges of the garbage heap, and Sarlun noted where the mountain border was. The Feral lingered near the perimeter as if they were too afraid to enter, as Tessa had suggested. It wasn't until they'd reached a dead end that the Feral emerged from their hiding spot, charging for Sarlun and his new companions.

"There's too many!" Erem shouted, wielding his iron rod.

Tessa took a weapon from her pack and cranked a rope tight, loading a sharp projectile into a crossbow. Sarlun positioned his energy chainsaw defensively, telling himself these Feral were just flesh and blood people who'd turned to monsters as a result of their time in the Backyard. They were hungry, their minds afflicted with months of gradual poisoning.

They would die.

Ten or so arrived, their limbs flailing, their jaws wide. In that moment of attack, Sarlun experienced profound pity. The Feral had pockmarks saturating their skin; their eyes were pure red, their teeth falling out.

He hated to say it, but their dreadful appearance made it easier to end their lives.

Oran was right. They weren't intelligent, just wild. But they were abnormally strong.

A woman with thick, greasy hair bashed into him, dirty

nails clawing at his face. Sarlun struck her in the nose with his elbow, hearing a crack, and she fell, Oran ending her misery.

Tessa felled a short, wide man with her crossbow bolt and reloaded in a flash. Erem was a powerhouse, taking on a pair of vicious Feral while Sarlun joined Oran to encounter another two.

"Behind you!" Tessa shouted, and Sarlun ducked. Teeth gnashed the air where his neck had been, and Sarlun lashed out, slicing the opponent's neck.

It all ended as soon as it had begun, and Sarlun gawked at the filthy dead people, wondering how long it would take him to end up Feral if he couldn't escape the Backyard. He suddenly felt stupid for ever coming here. If his sister had entered, maybe she'd never left. What if Shula had turned into one of these monsters?

"You okay?" he asked Oran, who was bleeding from a cut on his cheek.

"Just a scratch," he said.

"You know what can happen. Hurry. There might be more." Tessa rushed into the Mountain of Refuse's border, passing stakes in the ground. Sarlun sensed a shift in the air when he traversed over, but nothing had physically changed.

More Feral arrived, dozens of them. They paused at their deceased, sniffing the air, and bellowed in fury.

"They won't follow us," Oran said.

And he was right. These Feral were even further gone, their skin sallow and deteriorating, like zombies from the comic books Sarlun had seen Leonard reading years ago. They stopped at the invisible boundary, pacing a line in the dirt.

"Let's keep going." Sarlun struggled to turn his back to the enemy, so he jogged away.

They rested a few minutes later when they were out of view from the Feral, and Tessa dropped her pack, sifting through the contents. She cleaned Oran's wound, and he gritted his teeth. Sarlun noted how kind Tessa seemed while doing the work, her hands nimble and practiced. The cut was soon patched and secured with a bandage.

"Thank you," he told her.

"The last thing we want is for you to become Feral." She stowed the supplies and slung the pack on her shoulders. Sarlun noticed that the crossbow didn't leave her sight, and she carried it at her side as they went deeper into the pile.

He couldn't tell what kind of trash it was, since everything was rotting and coated in black grime. "Who put this here?"

"Tixa. He's been dumping heaps for years. The rumor is, he's feeding something." Erem slid his iron club into his belt.

Sarlun peered around the area, trying to see what might be hiding within the loaded garbage. "What kind of creature would live amongst this trash?"

"We don't know. Several say it's a slithering monster with a forked tongue. Others say it's *Darethel*, the tortured soul," Oran said.

"Who is Darethel?" Sarlun asked with a shiver.

Tessa kept walking but glanced at Sarlun. "He's the demon of the afterlife," she said in English. "I don't recall what you have on Shimmal, but it's like our Devil."

"Why would the devil resort to such an inhospitable venue?" Sarlun asked.

"As Oran suggested, it's just a rumor." She spoke the local tongue again.

Something rustled from a ten-foot-tall mess, and Sarlun jumped. A four-winged carrion bird lifted, taking a wet piece of cardboard in its dirty beak.

"Apparently, not everything is scared of this place," Sarlun whispered.

"Let's stay quiet. The sooner we leave, the better." Erem took the lead, trudging through the chaos at a faster pace.

Sarlun's body protested, but he forced himself to keep going.

From a distance, it had been impossible to judge the sheer magnitude of this mountain, but being among the sopping stinky heaps, Sarlun guessed they might never escape. None of them spoke as they struggled on.

Sarlun passed his time by thinking about Suma. His precious daughter. She deserved so much, and Sarlun had been preoccupied for most of her life. He'd been entrenched in Shimmal politics, as well as the Gatekeepers, his undying fascination with other cultures, and their history. Then when the Alliance was formed, he'd had an entirely new vision to attend to.

And the curse he'd been forced into had always lingered in his mind. It wasn't fair, but nothing in life often was. Every blessing comes with a curse. That was an old Shimmal adage, and he believed it to be true.

Sarlun picked out markers on the top of the mountain to estimate distances, and he realized they were making better progress than he'd initially thought. Oran walked with utter determination, his brother only slightly slower. Tessa kept her eyes on the environments, her crossbow always prepared for an attack.

But none came.

Eventually, Erem slowed and crouched, placing a palm on the ground. "Did you feel that?"

Sarlun had, but it might have been his imagination. His legs felt lifeless.

The area vibrated again.

"He's here," Oran mumbled.

"Who?"

"Darethel," Erem finished.

The center of the mountain erupted, garbage flying everywhere for a square mile or so. It rained down on their group, pieces of trash splatting to the surface.

"Run!" Tessa bellowed, and Sarlun didn't have to be told twice.

He peered over his shoulder as he sprinted, and saw the creature emerge from the gaping hole blown into the peaks of trash. It was straight from a nightmare: a soot-stained worm, its mouth twenty feet across, teeth sharp and as black as the rest of the acrid Backyard. It slid down the slopes, wriggling and creating a bigger mess as it neared them. Sarlun guessed it was roughly a hundred meters in length, and the smell…

"The border's ahead!" Erem shouted, pointing to his right.

A group of Feral people stood as if anticipating their arrival, and Sarlun didn't know where to go. Either direction was certain death.

Erem must have been thinking the same thing, because he hesitated.

Tessa didn't. She surged past the markers, shooting a Feral man in the head, and kept running. Sarlun joined her, cutting an arm off with his weapon, and they burst through the horde just in time to see the worm reach the group of Feral.

Darethel no longer cared about them. It had plenty of food. The Feral attempted to fight the worm, as if sensing they might get a meal out of it. But the worm was faster, stronger, and evidently smarter. It devoured them with impunity.

Sarlun ran like never before, outpacing his counterparts, and only stopped when his legs gave out. He fell to his knees, keeling over and coughing in shallow breaths. He spat on the ground, and it came out black. This place was a nightmare.

"Come, Stranger. There's a safehouse nearby." Erem helped him up and kept his arm around Sarlun's shoulder for support.

As promised, they encountered a building, the stone walls strong and seemingly impervious to the elements. They were clean, a shiny white beacon in the desolate wastelands around them. Tessa went to the door, punched a code into a pad, and it opened.

Sarlun passed out.

"*T*his is more fun than I expected," Hugo said.

"Fun?" I strolled down the tunnels, knowing we were heading deeper into Pestria with every minute. The corridors were an endless thread of switchbacks leading us into the planet. So far, we'd seen nothing but the perfectly hollowed-out passageways, and I was beginning to wonder if we'd made a mistake coming here.

"We have food and water, and we're together. It feels like we're on the cusp of discovery," Hugo told me.

The pressure was different, and my ears popped. I thought we'd be fine going lower, especially since we were traveling so slowly, but I started to wonder if we shouldn't have been returning to the surface.

"We could always come back," I said.

Hugo stopped and put his hands on his hips. "Dad, you know as well as I do that the moment we go home, you'll be pulled into something else and I'll be sent to another world on a Gatekeeper mission. This is our chance to hang out before that happens."

"You're right, son."

Hugo was filling out, and I was confident he'd outsize me within a year or two. He got that from Mary's side. Her father had been of hearty stock, she'd told me. It looked like those genetics were living on in Hugo.

"Do you think that we'll find anyone down here?" Hugo asked.

"I really don't know. I hope there's a clue to what happened."

"Dad, did you ever read about the Reflective Worlds?"

"Nope. Maybe I'd heard them mentioned? Mirror planets of some kind?"

"In a sense." Hugo kept walking, his suit's lights aiding our direction. I'd turned mine off to conserve power several hours earlier. "We saw another Earth on our mission to find the First World. It was insane."

I was curious why he brought this up now, but didn't press him. He was clearly on a train of thought.

"We researched the term when we went home. Well, I did. Casidy helped for a while."

"What happened with you two? I thought that was going well," I said casually.

Hugo shrugged ahead of me. "She started seeing this other guy. Older. More missions under his belt. It's all good. I wasn't that into her."

I knew for a fact he was, because he'd confided in Mary a month earlier that his heart was broken. "You'll find another girl," I promised him.

"I know."

"So what about these Reflective Worlds?" I directed him back on track.

"They might be attached to one another through a link within their cores."

I paused to consider this. "Like a portal?"

"I guess. But different. They're natural, not placed by Theos or Deities or whatever. I think the planets join at the same time, but they can change due to conditions, and other circumstances."

"Explain how," I said.

"That's a whole can of worms, Dad. The star is probably number one, then the beings on the planet. It's suggested that the stars would have to be similar for the Reflective Worlds to even begin their growth… and that two identical species of animals might emerge."

"I've heard about this," I said. "Regnig spoke of it once, but only in passing."

"Yeah, that's where we got the details."

"Why did you bring this up now?"

"Because we're far below the planet's surface. Maybe they left through the core."

Goosebumps tingled on my arms. "Won't that be quite the story if we encounter a link."

"Sure would. We'd be the first in the Alliance to do so."

"If they exist, it might be a new dimension for the Gatekeepers. I bet someone can design a tool to determine if there's a core link within a planet or not. We'll need to study Pestria, and the secondary world it's connected to," I said.

"Dad, you always make it sound so simple." Hugo turned at the bend in the corridor, and we began in the opposite direction, only lower as the tube descended at about a twenty-degree angle.

I checked the odometer on my wrist and tapped Hugo on the shoulder. "We should stop. We've walked for twenty miles."

Hugo smirked. "Feels like half that. We have to speed up."

I laughed, seeing how much he reminded me of… well, me. "Now we're talking."

The corridors were no longer carved in dense ice. It was just stone, likely meaning they were still within the mantle.

Hugo sat cross-legged, and I joined him on the ground. "What do we have that can assist our travels?"

Hugo opened his pack and dumped the contents. I did the same, taking stock of our gear.

"We have to get there sooner," he said.

"If we're going all the way to the core, it'll be a long process." We didn't have enough food to last more than a few days.

Hugo lifted a foldable crate, snapping it open. The box had two lengths of metal, with three two-inch-diameter wheels on it. He slid the first free, and then the second, handing it to me.

"Roller blades?" I asked.

"Something like that. But we're going to need propulsion," he said.

"Good thing the suits have built-in jet-packs these days," I reminded him. They weren't as powerful as the real things, but they worked for short periods when you were in a bind.

"How can we get them onto our…" Hugo stopped when I pulled the welding kit loose.

"We can't attach them to our suits, because that goes against protocol."

"*You must never modify their spacesuit, not for any reason. Doing so may affect one or more functions, resulting in injury or death.* Safety Guidelines Section Two, Subsection AZ."

"Very good. Someone studied the book," I said with pride. I didn't know any of these details, just the overall standards.

Hugo had a drill-core, and he grinned. "Let's use these panels. Our feet would slip right into the brackets."

No one would be upset if we disassembled the technology if it offered an opportunity to discover something important far below Pestria's surface. "Go for it."

He dismantled the device, handing me the first brace. I used the welding tool to connect the wheeled bar to the bottom of it and tested the durability. Hugo stood on his with one foot, and rolled down the decline a few meters before stopping with his other boot. "Cool. It works."

I did the same to mine, and we both had operational skates—for one foot. "If we go too fast, it'll be hard to decelerate."

"Then don't." Hugo flipped his propulsion stream on.

"Leave it on the first level," I warned him, but he shot forward, nearly toppling over. "Hugo, what did I say?" I muttered, grabbing my pack and shoving in my spilled gear. I sped after him, wondering how deep these tunnels would take us.

EIGHT

"Where am I?" Sarlun croaked in his own tongue, the squawks going unanswered. The room was pitch black, and he rolled to his side in a panic. Was he at home in his bed? It was far more uncomfortable than his pillowy mattress. The smell was what struck him: a mixture of soiled clothing and blood. "Hello?"

The door opened, sending a beam of light from outdoors, and a man filled the entrance, his visage blurred with the intense brightness. "Stranger, you've awakened," he said.

It flooded back, the entire story. His betrayal, Suma, Dean Parker…

"How long have I been out?" he asked. The ground vibrated gently, making him think about the giant worm from the dump.

"A few hours. We've scoured the path ahead and found it clear. Can I help you up?" Erem asked.

Sarlun shook his head, his snout wiggling with the movements. "I'll be fine."

Erem handed him a canteen. "Drink. We have a source in this refuge." He gestured at the counter, where another of the water filtration units sat. This one looked manufactured, not a pieced-together conglomerate of broken robots.

Sarlun didn't need to be told twice. He drank until his

thirst was quenched, and pulled the canteen away, water spilling from his lips. They were cracked, and stung at the touch of the liquid, but he didn't care.

"The others?" Sarlun asked.

"Tessa is praying," he said.

"Praying?" Sarlun hadn't expected that.

"To the Deities. She picked up on a distant religion while living among the traders. I don't know what the gods are, but she reveres them. Ever heard of the Deities?" Erem asked.

"No," he lied. He couldn't very well tell this man that his closest friends, Mary and Dean, were parents to one. Sarlun hadn't spent a lot of quality time with Jules, but his daughter had, and she loved her as if they were sisters. Sarlun liked being a role model to the girl… No, she was a woman now. It all made him feel extremely old. "What about you? What do you believe?"

Erem flipped on a switch, and a faint glow emitted from a clunky lamp. "Me? Nothing. From my experience, there is no higher power. Or they'd have prevented me from deserving this fate."

"And do you? Deserve this?" Sarlun went to his feet, feeling slightly better for the brief resting period.

Erem nodded. "I suppose I do. I won't deny it. Many proclaim their innocence until the day the Sickness takes hold, or they turn Feral, but I'm not so obtuse. I hurt people. I pay the price."

"And your brother?"

"Wrong place, wrong time."

Sarlun understood. They were close, and Oran wouldn't let his sibling go down for his crimes without tagging along. It was almost admirable, but Sarlun speculated Oran would have been more helpful by staying free. Not that being free on Belash Bazaar was ever a reality, because

Tixa owned them all, one way or another.

"Ready?" Tessa poked her head in and smiled when she saw Sarlun. He grinned back, realizing she reminded him of home and his friends.

"How's Oran?" Sarlun prodded, recalling the cut he'd endured.

"He's well with no ill effects. The Record Keeper's place is only five hours' walk from here. We should be going," Erem said.

They exited the building, but not before Tessa grabbed something from the cupboards. The cans were sealed with screw-top lids, and she undid one, sniffing the contents. "Smells like dogfood." She dipped a spoon into it anyway and took a bite, handing it to Sarlun. He swallowed a mouthful, being careful not to insult her gift. The brothers ate without comment, and he got a second round before the can was empty. She set it on the ground near the door and whispered a thanks to the purveyor of the waystation.

"Who tends to this place?" he asked her.

"No one knows, Stranger, but they keep it stocked. I'd say that's a miracle, wouldn't you?" Tessa asked.

The trip was easier now that they'd left the Feral people behind, along with the massive trash worm. He did worry what other mysterious obstacles they might encounter within the Backyard, but didn't mention it.

Erem and Oran kept silent, and he sensed their discomfort. Their movements were jittery, their clubs too tightly gripped. Once or twice, he noticed Oran watching him when he didn't think Sarlun was paying attention, and it irked him.

"What's known of the Record Keeper?"

"Nothing more than details lost on the wind. No one lives long enough to remember their name, but I've seen their home. Witnessed the pictures. I suppose the Backyard was once more of a community, before the rot took hold. They say that the smokestack was installed after Tixa obtained his position of power. Since then, the experience has become drastically worse," Erem said.

Sarlun hadn't seen his sister in so long, he wondered if she'd found the Record Keeper, in the years before the smokestack. He guessed she was part of the early survivors, but where had she gone from here? He still pictured her as a young woman, her eyes bright, her tongue sharp. She hated their father with a passion, and rightly so, given his deal with Ranul. Shula had left them when Sarlun wasn't of age, and she'd never even said goodbye.

He'd spent years trying to locate her, but this was where the trail ended. Belash Bazaar. The records indicated she'd been discarded past the tall stone walls about forty years earlier, and in Shimmal years, that wasn't long. But for Backyard years, it was countless lifetimes ago.

What if she'd become Feral too, and was wandering the region, searching for flesh to consume?

"You're quiet," Tessa told him.

"I was remembering someone."

"We all have those, don't we, boys?" She gave the brothers a thin smile.

"Wouldn't have a beating heart without lost love," Erem said.

The soot stains had lessened here, with more miles between them and the smokestack. It made sense why fewer of the Feral would be this far out. "Why don't you move to this corner? It seems much safer."

"Because the gates are on the opposite side." Tessa peered in that direction.

"And you want to help the ones that make it," Sarlun whispered, appreciating their selflessness. They'd probably saved his life.

"What is it you truly seek?" Oran asked him. Something screeched in the distance, and Sarlun noticed a gigantic creature perched on the stone fence a mile to their left. The others didn't seem to care, so he ignored it.

"I'm searching for someone."

"You actually expect to free yourself from here?" Erem removed his club, rotating it between his hands.

"Yes."

"And you'll get us out too?"

"Yes," he repeated.

"Okay." Erem slowed and surveyed the valley below. The ground dipped a hundred feet, revealing another large section of useless land. Sarlun smiled at a single growing green plant and he rushed to it, crouching near the cracked dirt.

"There is life," he said.

"What does it matter?" Erem didn't seem impressed, but Sarlun took a couple of drops from his canteen, offering them to the pitiful vegetation.

Tessa grinned as he did so, but the brothers were less fascinated. "We're close now."

They marched on for another half hour, but time was difficult to interpret beneath the blanket of smog. Sarlun's heart sped up when he sighted the rounded structure, the walls and domed ceiling made of clay and muck, the roof thatched with dead tree limbs. It was much larger than the previous waystation, though not as pristinely maintained.

The three of them stood at the entrance, the doors tall and narrow.

"Are you not coming in?" he asked.

"No. It's bad luck," Erem said.

Sarlun stared at the dented slabs. "I thought you'd been here before, Tessa."

"I have, but never inside."

"Then you don't know what you're missing." Sarlun almost knocked, but realized it would be foolish. Instead, he reached for the iron handle, and pulled. The door hinges groaned, but conceded to his strength.

"Farewell, Stranger," Erem said.

"Yes. This is the end of our journey. We should be getting back."

"Will you not wait for me?"

Tessa leaned in, kissing his cheek. "Don't forget us, Stranger."

"What if there's nothing to find? You'd abandon me out here?" he asked.

"I prayed on it, and the Deities spoke. You will escape." Tessa lifted four fingers, making the sign of her gods.

"Goodbye, Stranger." Oran offered his arm, and they clasped wrists.

"It's Sarlun," he whispered. "Not Stranger." If felt wrong to separate without this bit of information.

"Sarlun?" Tessa's eyes filled with tears. "It can't be."

"It is," he said.

"We've met. On New Spero… you were so… different."

"I have a feeling you were too," he surmised.

"Spoken like a wise man." Tessa bowed her chin. "I wish we could come along."

"Then do."

"It is not to be." She turned around, and the trio began their journey home.

Sarlun focused on the door, wondering how much credence he could give to her beliefs. "Hello?"

He entered the room and came face to face with one of the Cleaner robots.

"This is bad, Jules," Magnus said.

"How bad? On a scale of one to ten." Jules crossed her arms and stared at the leader of the Institute.

"About a hundred." Magnus scratched his stubble. "The organization isn't known by any individual name, but there's mention of them if you dig deep enough. Ever since you brought Zarin here, she's shown me countless references to the Black Hole."

"The Black Hole. I can't believe this," Sergo huffed. "I thought I could trust Zarin, and I handed her details to Suma."

"You were acquaintances when you were a thief. Did you think everyone else would straighten out because you did?" Magnus asked his Padlog friend.

"Not exactly, but…"

"It's actually a good thing," Suma said.

"It is?" Sergo sat in his chair.

The meeting room was mostly empty, with the four of them in conversation about their next steps.

"We have a lead. Someone within this organization knows where that footage of my father was taken," she reminded them. "Now all we need to do is locate them."

Sergo buzzed and let out a laugh. "You don't find these people. They've spent decades ensuring it. I tried to contact them when a job went sideways years ago, and…" He dropped his smirk and drummed his fingers on the table. "I shouldn't get into it."

"Don't worry, Sergo, we won't make you return to a life of crime," Jules said. "Papa already did that a few years ago with the Sect of Memories."

"Good, because I have kids now. Walo would be

devastated." Sergo sighed with relief.

"We'll have to bring Zarin with us," Suma suggested.

"I promised I'd keep her safe on New Spero." Jules didn't want to break her word, even to a criminal like Zarin.

"Nowhere is safer than being with Jules Parker," Magnus added. "There has to be a way to discover where the communication was sent from."

"Let's see." Suma tapped the display screen. "Send her in."

Jules had been waiting for this.

Zarin wasn't handcuffed, but Malir accompanied her. He grinned at Jules and stayed outside in the hall while the door closed.

"I thought I was done," Zarin said. Her raccoon eyes were darker, the marking on her face a shadow in the dim room. "You told me I'd be working with the Institute nerds to heighten security and stuff."

"Consider this your first job." Jules pointed to an empty chair. "Take a seat."

"What if I don't want to?" Zarin barked.

"Sit." Magnus' tone seemed to startle her, and she obeyed. He was imposing when he wanted to be. Jules had witnessed that on numerous occasions.

"We've seen your communications with the organization. Where did it originate?" Suma asked.

Zarin sneered. "If I dig any farther, I'll be killed. Simple as that."

"We're looking for Sarlun, as you know. Thanks to you, so is Hulope. I won't let him slip away, or end up in her clutches, because she'll string him up and make an example of my father." Suma's voice softened. "Please do this for me. Jules will protect you."

Zarin glanced at Sergo, who nodded. "They're good people, kid. It's better on this side, trust me."

The young woman peered at everyone in the room and sighed. "It came from a place called Ghorson."

"Ghorson. Never heard of it," Magnus said.

"No reason you would have. It's a mining colony a million light years from anything."

"So the mining front is real?" Jules asked.

"They might have a base, or they're rerouting messages through its network. I can't know for certain without visiting."

"Gather your things," Jules muttered.

"How are we getting there?" Suma brought up the Crystal Map. "This doesn't have anything labeled by that title."

Jules took the tablet and handed it to Zarin. "Where is Ghorson?"

Zarin flinched but grabbed it, shuffling the images to zoom on the edge. "Here." She left the screen open, and Jules searched for a nearby portal.

"There's one in that system," Jules said. "The Gatekeepers haven't explored this Shandra yet."

"That's probably for the best. I assume you'd be killed upon entry," Zarin muttered.

"Then we better be careful." Jules remembered the Shandra number, along with the symbol associated with it. There was something oddly familiar about it. Five circles, all slightly overlapping, with a lightning bolt in the center.

"We? You're not seriously dragging me into your mess, are you?" Zarin asked.

"You've been helpful so far." Magnus opened the door, holding the button. "Is Elex coming along, Suma?"

"No."

"I'll go," Malir offered from the hall.

"We're already stretched thin. And don't you think her fiancé, Dean, already put in a requisition to join their expedition?"

Malir shrugged. "Was he permitted?"

Magnus shook his head. "Of course not. What did I say? We have an influx of Alliance members sending us fresh recruits. There's another batch from the Nulach coming tomorrow."

Jules was grateful they'd added Jarlo's people to the mix, but it only worked if they had enough support staff at their Terran site. She should have discussed these ongoing issues with her mother.

Zarin was the last one in the room, and Jules could easily identify the trepidation in her slow steps. "It'll be okay. You've heard the rumors about me?"

"Who hasn't?"

"Then you have nothing to fear. No one will harm you, okay?"

"Fine. Not that it matters if they do." Zarin walked past her and kept going.

"What's that girl's problem?" Suma asked.

"I read her file. She left home when she was eleven, finding refuge on a tour craft. She ditched it at the end of the line and worked her way to Udoon, then to the Station. Zarin has likely been dealt a rough hand."

"You can't save them all, Jules," Suma whispered.

"But I can try." Jules put an arm around her shorter friend. "Otherwise, what's the point?"

"No wonder everybody loves you." Suma put her tablet away. "We might be gone for a while."

"We'll find your father. Sarlun needs to come home."

"You have your wedding to plan, and so much going on," Suma said.

"We're not in a rush." Jules wished her friend would confide in her about the pregnancy.

They went outside, feeling the warmth of the sun on

her face, and Jules inhaled deeply. She loved it here, even with the raw heat the day brought, and the cool nights. She'd spent the last few years working tirelessly to train their recruits, and to fill warships with soldiers and fleet crew to protect their alliance. She wouldn't let Hulope or this organization threaten their livelihood. The Institute taught warfare and weaponry and ground combat, not computer hacking and espionage.

With a glance at Zarin, Jules knew they'd failed in that aspect. Because no matter how many soldiers you had, someone like the organization could turn you on your heads, and that scared Jules more than anything.

Dean jogged over, his brow sweaty. He was in training gear, and a pulse pistol clung to his chest holster. "I wanted to see you off." He glanced at Malir, who left abruptly when Magnus barked an order.

"Thanks." She took his hand as they walked. "Be careful. This organization has their sights on us for some reason, and I'm wondering if they won't do something rash."

"We'll be ready," he told her.

"See that you are." Jules kissed him. "I love you." She reached for the star necklace around her neck, the one he'd given her years ago.

"I love you too." He kissed her again, and something exploded in the field. "Whoops, I should have been paying attention. Be careful out there, Ju."

Jules watched Dean run to his recruits, and smiled as a drone dropped from the sky, extinguishing the flames.

"That's your boyfriend?" Zarin snuck up behind her.

"Fiancé."

"What are you waiting for? He looks like a catch to me." Zarin lifted her thick eyebrows.

Jules didn't respond as she dragged the girl to the outdoor portal sphere.

"Is this…"

"It's a Shandra Valincin. One of four Deity portals," Jules said with pride.

"That's incredible."

Jules touched the portal with Suma and Zarin inside the transport circle. She pictured the five rings and lightning bolt, and put protective shield up.

NINE

Sarlun's eyelids blinked open, his head groggy once again. "Where am I?"

"You are in the Archives," a voice said.

The man's outline was dark, but he heard a whining noise as he moved.

Sarlun recalled the moment he'd opened the door, seeing the Cleaner robot. He'd reached for his weapon and tried to lash out, but had experienced a course of electricity through his body. Then complete darkness.

"You're a robot," Sarlun grunted. He flexed his fingers, almost expecting to be tied up, but he wasn't.

"And you're from Shimmal." The voice was less mechanical than he'd assumed, but it was still somewhat monotone.

"What do you know?"

"That you're new to the Backyard. Within days."

"That's not very difficult to ascertain. Are you connected to Tixa's network?"

The robot's eyes whirred and glowed with a soft blue light. "Tixa?"

Sarlun realized this wasn't a Cleaner. He wasn't visibly armed like the others, and his build was slighter. His head was flat on top, his shoulders pointed. "What are you?"

"I am the Record Keeper," he said.

"I thought they were dead." Sarlun repeated what he'd

been told by his allies.

"She did die, about thirty of your years ago, but I took over. I have her memories, though the file was partially corrupted at the time of transference. She was a good woman, but perhaps obsessed with her personal mission."

"Which was?" Sarlun looked around the room, seeing the countless framed paintings decorating the walls. They were all different sizes, the artist clearly the same. Hundreds if not thousands of faces stared back, their pictures capturing them at a vulnerable moment within the Backyard.

"To preserve their memories." The Record Keeper waved a metal hand in front of him.

Sarlun stood, his body protesting at the movement.

"Have some water." The robot motioned to a table, where a loaf of bread steamed beside a tall glass, filled to the brim.

"Why do you have food?"

"I like to be prepared. It's not often I have company, but when I do, I choose to be a gracious host. It was the Record Keeper's way," he said.

Sarlun guzzled the water and took a big bite from the bread, finding it more than satisfactory. It was delicious.

He walked along the edge of the domed space, admiring the skill the painter had. The faces were mostly glum, their skin lacking the soot stains he might expect, but their eyes were solemn and empty, as if they'd given up. It saddened him, but he was grateful someone had captured such an important moment in their lives. Because of the Record Keeper, these victims of the Backyard would be remembered, if only by a robot.

"I cannot go on calling you Record Keeper. What was her name?"

"Her given name was Hermione Jessob, but she went

by Herm."

"May I call you Herm?"

"Certainly," he said.

"How did you get here?" Sarlun inspected the huge room, observing all the various people Herm had immortalized on his canvases.

"Me or Herm?"

"Both."

"Herm came to Belash when she was twenty, a young artist seeking opportunities. Her skill was quickly apparent, and the regent took her in, offering to sponsor the lass. Herm was too talented, and she painted the regent's wife with such clarity, it exposed all the flaws she saw in herself. Then, the Backyard was an old concept, and it was said that everyone who entered died within the first week. Herm, being new to Belash Bazaar, hadn't heard of it. When she was sentenced to banishment, she thought they were joking, for she'd just painted the finest piece of art she'd ever seen." He paused, looking at the wall of pictures.

"This world is awful," Sarlun said.

"I'd have to agree. Someone took pity on Herm when they pushed her through the gates, and she was able to keep her brushes. She met several allies within the walls, and eventually, they settled in the north, where she built this hut. I arrived much later, when she was nearing the end."

"Where did you hail from?" Sarlun asked.

"I was designed to be an artist. To replicate the universe's greatest painters and sculptors. I'd heard about Hermione Jessob and wanted to meet her, to learn her skills."

"And the only way to do that was to enter the Backyard," Sarlun finished for him.

"Correct. I flew to Belash, dropping from orbit, and

landed near this home. The locals have no idea I am here."

"How did Herm react?"

"She was fearful at first, but I demonstrated my work. I proved my worth," he said. "Come with me."

Sarlun went to another room. A tattered cloth hung over something in the corner, and Herm tugged it off, revealing a life-sized statue. It resembled a peculiar being with two noses, long slender fingers, and wide-set eyes. "This was Herm?"

"Yes. It was a gift to her, and she let me stay." The way he said it made Sarlun understand how much this metal being missed his mentor.

"It must be difficult," Sarlun whispered.

"What?"

"To exist among her memories."

"No. It is my pleasure, though visits have grown increasingly rarer. No one wants to venture within the Backyard anymore. It was once almost liveable, with community and determination. The Stacks changed that. The chemicals kill the people. The Feral are dangerous."

"I need your help. If you accept, I'll ensure this place is destroyed. We'll keep the Records, I promise you this."

Herm stared at the statue, nodding his head once. "What can I do?"

"You knew I was from Shimmal. Did you encounter my sister?" Sarlun's voice lifted with emotions.

"Yes."

Sarlun reached a hand to the wall to steady himself. "Show me."

Herm took him to the far side of the giant dome and slowed near the halfway point. "Shula was here almost forty of your years ago."

Sarlun swallowed and touched the frame. Shula's eyes were damp in the picture, her snout raised slightly. He found comfort in her expression, the sly smirk that always threatened to turn into a laugh. The mischief was once palpable, but it was mostly lost in this older version of his sibling. She looked ready to throw in the towel. "Oh, Shula, what happened to you?"

He didn't expect an answer. "She left."

"I thought no one escaped the Backyard," Sarlun whispered.

"They don't. Not without some assistance." Herm turned his back to Sarlun and went to the center of the dome. He tapped his foot, and a console appeared, lifting from the floor. Herm pressed a button, and the middle of the dome spread open, showcasing the black sky above.

"You'll help me?" Sarlun asked.

Herm's eyes glowed again. "I have one last obligation before we leave."

"What?"

Herm gestured to an easel and pointed to a stool near it. "Please take a seat. I must record your visit."

Sarlun's snout flicked to the side, and he glanced up, then to the picture of his sister. "Very well."

The robot selected a wooden palette with an assortment of colors and dipped a well-used brush into one. And he began to paint.

---

*M*y head ached, and I was dangerously low on fluids, but we arrived the end of the tunnel system after hours of sliding through the globe. I cut the stream of air behind me, rolling on the wheeled device under my foot, and finally planted my other boot, stopping. Hugo did so with much more grace than me, and he laughed when we reached the corridor's exit.

"Now we're talking," he said.

After hours of seeing the same carved tunnels, it was strange to witness something different.

I blocked his passage into the next room. "Water first. Then food."

"Fine. How fun was that?"

"I think you enjoyed it more than I did." I regretted suggesting the trip the moment we'd started down the massive network of tubes.

"It's hot here," Hugo complained. His helmet was still in his pack, as mine was too.

"We could mask up. Keep us cooler," I suggested.

Hugo wiped sweat off his face. "Maybe in a minute."

We each drank some water and shared another bar. "We've been awake for too long, son."

"We can't sleep now. We might be near the core."

"We'll investigate and decide," I said. I was genuinely curious about what we'd find in the core.

"There's still no sign of any locals. Not even a dropped toy… eating utensil. Lost hat. Nothing."

"Someone made this intricate system for a reason. I think we're about to find out why." I gazed past Hugo into the dark room.

"You ready?" Hugo grabbed his pulse pistol, and I yanked my rifle from its clip. With a quick charge check, I nodded.

"Me first." I stepped around him, shooting my light into the room. The beam kept going, not encountering a blockade. "It's huge."

"And hotter." Hugo whistled as we entered the giant chamber.

I used my suit's scanner, confirming the air wasn't about to kill us, and though it showed modest amounts of radiation, we were protected against that level with our yearly shots. The ground was black stone, rough and grippy under our steps.

"Dad, check it out."

We headed to a cliff; red-hot molten magma roiled and bubbled below. Stairs were carved into the ledge, heading lower.

"This is it! We know where the locals went."

"Maybe." I kept my eyes open and my ears perked. I scanned the cavern, searching for signs of danger, but it was vacant. I almost suggested we hightail it and return home. This would be a good job for one of the new drones to oversee. But I was a curious man, and we were so close to an answer.

I went ahead of Hugo, and he waited for me to lead him down the steps. They were narrow, and not as deep as I'd have liked, so we went cautiously, sticking close to the wall. The magma was still about a hundred feet under me, but the air was thick with heat, my breaths growing ragged.

And, suddenly, the stairs ended.

Hugo nearly bumped into me, sending me into the pit, but he caught himself one step up. "Why does it stop?"

"Good question," I whispered. I shifted my foot, and a pebble kicked off, falling toward the hot liquid. Something shimmered, and the tiny rock vanished.

"Did you see that, Dad?" Hugo asked.

"I did."

"That's a portal. Or a link… whatever they called it."

I was drawn to this. Were Reflective Worlds real? Could this be a natural connection to an entirely other place? How many of our planets had this within them, waiting to be discovered?

"Should we pack up and head home?" Hugo sounded upset.

"No," I said, surprising myself. I secured my rifle and grabbed my helmet. When it was sealed, I ensured Hugo did the same. "We're using it."

"Dad, we're supposed to record…"

"Not this time," I told him. "And when we tell your mother about today, it was much safer, okay?" I grinned at him through the facemask.

"Deal." Hugo bumped fists with me.

"Let's determine how large this portal is." I grabbed more pebbles, placing them in my palm. I spent a couple minutes guaranteeing the invisible gateway had big enough borders for us to enter it. When I was confident we'd fit, I turned to Hugo. "Wait until I travel through. If there's anything suspicious, don't follow."

"Like what?"

"Just be smart."

"I can do that." Hugo licked his lips.

"You don't have to do this," I told him, wondering if I was pressuring my son into danger.

"I want to, but I'm worried about you," he admitted.

"Here goes nothing." I stood on the edge of the last step, lining up with the portal. All I could see was spitting magma below, but I knew there was a barrier between me and my impending death.

It had been a while since I'd acted this reckless, but my body yearned for adventure. I leaned forward… and dropped.

I landed a moment later and rolled onto my back.

Two guns pointed at my face, and all I could see were the giant barrels.

---

*J*ules didn't let her guard up as they emerged through the Shandra. She sent out a burst of energy, frying anything electrical in the vicinity. A few objects sparked and smoked. "Got the cameras. No one will know what happened."

"I knew they'd be watching it," Zarin said. The three of them were held within Jules' sphere, and she quickly evacuated the Shandra room, finding the world it resided in barren and dead. The star was a cool blue, the sky black and shallow. She bent down, picking up a rock, and dropped it. The stone took a few seconds to fall to the surface.

"Little to no atmosphere," Suma said. "Gravity low."

Jules used her tablet and turned toward the mining colony. "It's thirty thousand kilometers out."

"How are we going to get there?" Zarin asked.

Jules smiled. "Hope you're not scared of heights." She shot high, leaving the planet behind.

She raced toward their destination, eager to confront the organization and learn where Sarlun had been filmed. The trip didn't take long, and she slowed as they approached the cluster of planetoids. Eleven of the misshapen rocks were present, and she went to the largest. There were a handful of structures on the surface, and a few starships in proximity.

"I expected it to be more impressive," Zarin said. "I pictured an evil base made of crystals and precious stones."

"This isn't the storybooks," Suma told her.

Jules noticed a handful of enemy vessels blinking to life, their hull lights flashing on. "It seems I've triggered some sort of defense mechanism."

"Great. Do we run?" Zarin asked.

Jules sighed. "You have a lot to learn."

"Jules never runs from danger. It's her greatest… or worst attribute. Depending on who you ask," Suma declared.

Jules flew to the closest ship and shut her eyes. There were no signs of life, which made this that much easier. She hated killing people, even if they were bad.

The ship was small, not needing to hold a lifeform. It was essentially an automated drone, with heavy artillery. The blast shook her sphere, but her barrier held. Jules avoided a second pulse, the detonation exploding behind them. She targeted the front cannon, and it erupted, destroying the entire drone.

The others came for her, and she maneuvered through the area. All in all, the drones were dealt with quickly, bits and pieces of the machines floating around the mining colonies.

"That was astonishing," Zarin breathed. "Can we do it again?"

"Let's hope I don't have to." Jules continued flying them to the sole structure on the biggest planetoid. She tried to sense a living being, and when she was about to give up, she caught a hint of a single soul. Jules felt his emotions, his fear as he watched the strange alien sphere arrive at his home.

Jules didn't bother with niceties like knocking on the front door. Instead, she vibrated her sphere and pierced through the roof into the building.

"You flew into a wall!" Zarin exclaimed.

"So did you," Jules said.

The place was brightly lit, with hundreds of screens displaying feeds from all over. Jules set them to the floor and let her sphere collapse. Suma had her gun up in a second, and stood in front of Zarin while they studied the room.

"It's the Black Hole. They're analyzing everyone's

actions." Zarin walked to a screen, touching it with a finger. "They know what's happening no matter where they are. It's unbelievable."

"What is?" Jules asked.

"All of them are harshly encrypted messages between users. These guys are dissecting private missives in split seconds."

Jules noticed how it was all happening live, and the strange alien dialogue passed between two users, scrolling onto the large screen near them. "What does that mean?" she asked the girl.

"That they knew everything about me before I was offered the job. They must know I was leaving to New Spero," she muttered.

"Why? You weren't supposed to breathe a word of this mission to anyone," Suma scolded.

"I didn't… well, Bash is my best friend. He's living on Bazarn Five. Lower levels."

"And what did you tell Bash?" Jules inquired.

"That I went with Jules Parker to visit New Spero," she disclosed.

"That's enough. The organization will be keeping an eye on our activity at the Institute." Jules had half a mind to leave and warn Magnus.

"If you think they weren't already, you're delusional." Zarin found a keypad hidden along the wall. She typed so fast, her long sloth-like claws clicked in a blur. "Look."

Jules did, seeing footage from the Institute's security system. "Are you saying they have access to this? We made sure it was the most secure technology in the universe."

"Nonsense. Maybe in your Alliance, but anyone can bust through those weak firewalls."

Jules almost forgot there was a living person in the building, and she threw the shield back on when a door opened across the massive room.

Footsteps echoed throughout, and she braced herself for action. When she saw the man, she loosened up.

"I believe you are trespassing," the sole inhabitant said. He was tiny, about four feet tall with large feet, his shoes sticking out. A striped tail swayed behind him, and he had brown eyes below a huge forehead, his lips pale and pink.

"I'm…" Jules started, but the guy cut her off.

"Jules Parker from the Alliance of Worlds. You were born on Sterona, but resided on New Spero, Earth, and Haven, most recently at the Institute. You may very well be a Deity, as the records are unclear, but you do possess otherworldly attributes not related to anything we have on file. You're five foot four, weigh…"

"I've heard enough," Jules said. "Since you know so much about me, how about you share some information about yourself?"

The man seemed delighted. "I am Poacher."

"*You're* Poacher?" Zarin seemed in awe.

"The one and only," he said. "I invented the Black Hole, or at least the iteration we now utilize. She can't claim to hold that title. The previous model was full of holes, so I patched it up."

Jules didn't ask who he was referring to.

"No wonder you can circumvent everyone's security," Zarin mumbled.

His beady eyes narrowed. "You have great promise. Maybe we can come to an arrangement. I researched you personally, Zarin. It would be wise to agree to my upcoming terms."

She glanced at Jules as if seeking approval. "No. I'm with the Alliance now."

Every last display in the room flashed to black, and a video began playing. It showed the busy streets of Bazarn, and a figure became highlighted. The camera followed him, switching views until he was alone in an alleyway. He stared at a tablet and glanced up at the street signs, as if ensuring he was at the right location.

Zarin hissed an inhale. "That's Bash!"

Two hooded assailants entered the alley from either direction, and one pulled a gun. He fired it, and Bash clutched his chest, dropping to the ground like a sack of potatoes.

"What have you done?"

Jules stayed calm, assessing the situation. Poacher knew Zarin would be coming with Jules Parker, and that she'd contacted Bash, making him important to her. So he'd hired goons to kidnap Bash from Bazarn to use as leverage. It wasn't an original move, but it was effective.

"Come to my side, and we will bring Bash into the fold. He will become rich with you, and we can forget that little incident ever occurred. He was only sedated, do not fear," Poacher said.

Jules saw the way Zarin's eyelids fluttered. "And if I don't?"

"I kill him." The video flicked to another scene, and the young man with raccoon eyes was seated at a chair, his arms chained with glowing energy tethers.

"Stop," Jules said softly. "You don't have the upper hand, Poacher."

"Is that so?" he asked.

"What if I was to tell you I've already won?"

Suma stepped closer to Jules.

Zarin cried out, watching her friend as a man appeared on screen, holding a gun.

"Where is he?" Jules asked.

"Far enough from you to be out of reach," Poacher said with a laugh.

Jules wasn't about to let Bash be killed because of her actions. She closed her eyes, concentrating on the feed's energy. They'd brought Zarin to New Spero within the last day, meaning there likely hadn't been enough time to move Bash from Bazarn. That helped.

She focused on Bash and the image of the unique alien, a race she still didn't know the name for, and sensed him in a room below the surface. Then she shifted to the other man in the space with her. He was an ugly soul, a dangerous criminal with a penchant for murder. The police had spent years searching for him on Bazarn, but he had the resources to elude them. Doing jobs for people like Poacher paid well and kept him living a good life.

"Make your choice. Join me, or Bash dies," Poacher gave the ultimatum, and Zarin started to walk over.

"You may want to reconsider this, Poacher," Suma said. "The Parkers aren't very merciful."

"I have nothing to fear from the Parkers. I'm running out of patience, Zarin."

"I'm sorry," she mustered.

"Don't be." Jules lifted a finger and bent it. The man with the gun in the displays dropped his weapon. He turned to face the camera, his expression wild and angry. She flipped her hand upside down, fingers rising up, and she spun her wrist. The criminal's neck snapped, and he fell to the floor, leaving a shocked Bash still in restraints.

Jules concentrated on that next, removing the power source from his energy cuffs. Bash stood up, staring at his forearms, then stepped to the camera.

Leave. Go to Alnod Industries' head office and tell them Jules Parker demands you are brought to Haven immediately, and that you require guards. Disconnect from the Black Hole. Do you understand? She pressed the thought into his mind from millions of light years away.

Bash nodded on the screen and grabbed the fallen gun. "What have you done?" Poacher roared.

Zarin misses you. You will be reunited soon. And she severed the ties. Jules clapped loudly, and the entire room full of screens sparked as she blew up their network connections. They went dark.

"You're a superhero," Zarin whispered.

Poacher fled.

Jules shot forward, landing in front of the guy, blocking his exit. "I don't think so." She picked him up with a blast of her sphere, securing him. "Now, it's time you answered my questions."

Poacher's posture changed. He must have realized his mistake.

Jules' friend smiled at her while talking to their captive. "I told you never to underestimate a Parker."

TEN

"*D*o you like it?" Herm set the paintbrush on the desk, staring at his finished work.

Sarlun's neck was kinked after hours on the stool, and he wondered why a robot couldn't take a picture, or paint faster, but he didn't say this out loud.

He stretched and sauntered around the easel, expecting to see a familiar face. But it was even more miraculous than he could have imagined. Sarlun knew he wasn't young anymore, but the man he saw was his father. The way the corners of his eyes crinkled, and how his snout drooped lower every decade.

Herm spared him the effects of the smog, and he recognized that the artist of all these paintings had done the same thing: capturing them as they might have been outside of the Backyard, not within the four walls of their prison wasteland.

He smiled when he noticed his mouth was slightly ajar, a habit he'd acquired when deep in thought. Suma used to tease him that a bug might fly in if he concentrated any harder.

"You didn't answer. Does this mean you don't like it?" Herm asked, the robot seeming self-conscious. Sarlun wondered if the emotions were a result of the real Herm's memories existing inside the vessel, or if this robot was programmed with some higher level of AI advancements than he'd ever seen.

"You are correct. I don't," Sarlun said, adding a layer of malice to his tone. Then he grinned and set a hand on the robot's shoulder. "I adore it. This is the single greatest honor I could have asked for."

"Then we will bring it with us," Herm said. "And your sister's."

"You will actually leave?" Sarlun knew he'd said as much earlier, but kept anticipating he'd decline eventually.

"Yes." He unscrewed a cap on one of his fingers, and hot air gently blew from the tip. "I'll dry it."

"Of course," Sarlun said.

A few minutes later, his portrait was rolled up alongside Shula's, and they were placed into a metal cylinder, the cap sealed tightly.

The dome was still wide, and ash began to fall from above. "We should go," Herm said.

"How? Can you fly?" Sarlun didn't think the robot had enough hiding spaces on his torso for jet propulsion or thrusters.

"At one point, I could, but I repurposed those elements," he told Sarlun.

They went outside, the air denser with pollution. Sarlun sniffled and sneezed. "Where to?"

Herm led him a hundred feet from the domed building and knelt, sweeping dirt from a hatch. He opened it with three spins of the release and climbed into the hole. Sarlun's ankles hurt as he descended and jumped the last few feet to the ground.

Herm pushed his finger into a socket, and the lights flickered on. The shop was impressive, with work benches and countless Cleaner robots deconstructed in various phases.

"Where did you get all these?"

"In the early years, visitors would bring Herm offerings, and since there was little to bargain with but the damaged Cleaners, that's what she'd receive. She stored them, since Herm didn't have a mechanical mind. She did use some of their oils for paints."

Sarlun smiled when he understood what the shape in the middle of the shop was. "You built a ship."

"With spare parts from my own thrusters, and years of acquiring Cleaners. It won't take us far, but we can escape," he said.

"What of my sister? I was hoping to track her. You said she left?"

Herm paused, his hand finding a power switch on the ship. It grumbled and shook, the hull's exterior lights coming on. "That is correct."

"How?" Sarlun asked. He'd known it. Deep down, he was positive she'd managed to leave the Belash Bazaar in one piece.

"Shula visited Herm the day before they picked her up. She likely wished to be documented. I believe Shula wanted people to think she'd died within the Backyard."

Sarlun contemplated why. She was a good woman, a kind sister, but why would she want her trail to turn cold? The only reason he could fathom was that someone sinister was after her, and she needed to disappear. "Can you recall anything else?"

"Only the vessel's markings. It was invisible until it landed." Herm's eyes went dark, and a holographic projection shot from his mouth. It played along the wall.

The ship descended over the Record Keeper's home and settled on the soot-covered stone. Five circles. A lightning bolt. Where had Sarlun seen that shape before? Shula ran to the vessel, waited as the ramp lowered, and rushed inside as it closed. The ship became invisible again, and it was gone, along with his sister. The footage stopped.

"That's our clue," Sarlun said.

"I was going to build a replacement. Give him my and Herm's memories," Herm the robot said. "But if you mean to destroy the Backyard, I will hold off."

"That is my intention," he promised, more for the people like Tessa, Oran, and Erem than himself.

Their ship was only ten feet long, and the cockpit unfastened on hinges. There was the one cabin, with barely enough space for Sarlun and the metal man. No bathroom. No beds. No comfort.

"How can I survive?" Sarlun asked him.

"We must board another craft within two days. That is all the air we have for you," he said.

"Two days," Sarlun whispered. "We'll still be close to the Bazaar."

"No. We will make one jump. I have seen to it." Herm motioned into the cockpit, and Sarlun climbed in.

"What kind of jump?" Sarlun asked.

"We will travel twenty-seven light years."

It wasn't all that impressive, but for a ship this size, built by an artistic robot, it became remarkable. "How far is Tixa's reach?"

"He has contacts around Belash, but that is not a concern," Herm said. "This takes us beyond his net."

"Tixa is a large fish in a small pond," Sarlun told him as the cabin closed overhead. "There are far worse people to deal with than a gangster like him. How do you know about Tixa if you've been here for decades?" The robot had feigned ignorance about the man earlier in their conversation, but after the trying couple of days, Sarlun couldn't be certain.

"People like to talk. The visitors I've encountered in the Backyard have no love lost for the man. He terrorizes his community. Steals the children of his constituents, forces them to work in the barren landscape, scraping the dirt for remnants of a potent drug. They become addicted in the process, and Tixa reaps the reward, selling the drugs off planet, claiming he's ridding Belash of a toxin." Herm poked his finger into the dash, the lights flashing on.

"Tixa is the toxin," Sarlun mumbled.

"That he is. But he is no longer our concern," Herm said.

"Why are you helping me?" The ship rumbled under him as the ground separated, rocks raining on the top of the vessel.

"Because I have served my purpose here. And because she said you'd come one day."

"Who did?"

"Shula. She told Hermione that someone resembling her would seek her out. If they did, she asked that Herm judge whether their intentions were true, and to act accordingly."

Sarlun thought that sounded exactly like his sister. "And what is the judgment?"

"Time will tell." Herm shot the ship straight up, speeding from the Backyard.

Sarlun hoped Tessa and the brothers witnessed the craft leaving, for it would offer a glimmer of hope.

"Activating the cloak," Herm said.

It looked no different to Sarlun. He sat on the deck, using a single strap around his chest to stay secured. "Are we invisible?"

"No, nothing so advanced. I've just scrambled the sensors of the ship, as well as the robots and cameras watching over the fences. They will not see our departure," he said.

The viewscreen was a miniature display, and he had to squint to make out the image. They were already in space.

Herm rotated the craft, giving them a view of Belash. "I wasn't expecting to leave so soon."

Sarlun thought the robot might be having second thoughts. "Let's find my sister. It's time we reconciled and took back our planet."

Herm glanced at him, his eyes brightening. "Now things are getting interesting. Tell me of Shimmal."

Sarlun paused as his ally spun them around, powering on the jump drive. The ship shook so violently he thought his legs would go numb. "How much ..."

The stars stretched on the tiny display, and it felt like his entire body was being torn to shreds. Sarlun screamed in pain, his brain itching, the soles of his feet burning. And it was over.

"We have completed the jump," Herm said.

Sarlun unstrapped from the cabin, tossing his jacket beside him, and dabbed his sweating face with the sleeve.

"Now will you tell me about Shimmal?" Herm asked.

Sarlun tried to get a view of the area. "Where are we?"

"Along a trade route. We should intercept a ship exiting the Belash quadrant in one point four days. There is time for conversation."

Sarlun relaxed, thinking this might work. He'd gone to the Backyard to chase a ghost, and he'd proven she'd visited the world. He peered at the cylinder holding the portraits and smiled to himself.

"Shimmal is a beautiful planet. The people are kind, and hard-working… but a shadow has taken over, and her name is Hulope." Sarlun gritted his teeth and recalled the story, leaving no detail out.

———

*H*ugo's breathing was labored, and it drew my attention to him. My mind was groggy, my vision swimming as I blinked my eyes open. "Son?"

Hugo didn't respond. I was tied up, my arms overhead, and it reminded me of the time they'd caught me on Sterona, right before Jules was born. Kinca, the scarred Kraski, had come, doing Lom of Pleva's bidding, and was ready to end my life when the rescue team busted down the doors. This time, I wasn't going to be so lucky. No one had our location.

My feet barely skimmed the floor, and I pushed my toes on it, shifting my weight, which gave temporary relief to my wrists. My shoulder sockets felt like they were on fire, but all that mattered was ensuring Hugo was okay.

"Hugo!" I called it louder, and his chin snapped up. "Dad?"

"Thank the stars," I whispered. "We're going to get out of here."

"Where are we?"

"We passed the gateway in Pestria's core, and ended up across on this other world. They stunned me, and that's all I remember. I woke up two minutes ago and saw you."

"That's what I recall too." Hugo glanced up. "Our wrists are secured with metal, not energy, so we could possibly break it." He tugged on the binds, but they were solid. "The room is dark, but there's a door to your right, Dad. Light is seeping below it."

I hung there, admiring how well my son was dealing with the situation. He was analyzing it, trying to determine a way out. It was what he'd trained for at the Gatekeepers' Academy, and I was proud of him.

"What else?" I asked, urging him on.

Hugo smiled when he noticed the ledge behind us. It

probably secured shorter beings, jutting from the stone wall about eight inches, like a fireplace mantel.

Hugo didn't comment. Instead, he bent his knees, pressing his toes to the ground, and kicked off, using his upper body to lift up on the chains. He looked like an Olympian on the rings. His muscles bunched and he grunted as he flipped over, his feet landing on the ledge. Now the chains had relaxed.

Hugo struggled to open the shackles, but they were on tight. "There's a pinhole."

"That'll be the release," I said. "Use your collar."

Hugo must have forgotten about the safety precaution, and smirked. "We make a good team, don't we?" He had enough slack to reach the collar, and he unzipped a pocket, removing an assortment of tools. They were added to the Gatekeepers' suit for emergencies, and this constituted as the perfect example of that. He took a miniscule screwdriver, jamming it into his left shackle, and after a few moments of shifting it around, the clasp released.

Hugo did the same to his other side, and rushed over, quickly freeing me. "You did well, son."

Hugo's mirth quickly dissipated. "There's a lot of work left. What's the plan? Should we escape and return through the gateway?"

I considered the options, and that was the best. I hadn't gotten a good look at our captors, but if their initial response was to shoot before talking, I didn't see a meeting ending well for us. We were outnumbered and unarmed. They'd taken our packs and weapons.

"We do what any good Gatekeeper would. Observe. Record. Report." I went to the door, putting an ear to it. When I heard no noise, I searched for a handle. It wasn't a normal knob or lever. I had to stick my hand in, and it must have tripped a sensor. It opened without a sound.

The Search

I'd expected to walk into a corridor, but was instead greeted by a massive hangar. The ceiling was so high, I could barely see it, and the space went on for what appeared to be miles. Hundreds of robots stood in a line, and I guessed they were powered off. On the other side were dozens of spacecraft, ranging from single-pilot skimmers to much larger exploration vessels.

"Where are we?" Hugo asked.

"I don't know, but they have a hell of a lot of firepower," I answered.

Footsteps echoed from a distance, and I picked up the gentle murmur of a conversation. I sprinted across the deck, struggling to stay silent as I rounded a fighter ship. The design was magnificent: smooth lines and sleek shapes. Magnus and Slate would be in heaven.

The voices were approaching, and I peered at the source, seeing a tall woman in a black uniform, the man beside her shorter and in gray. He was bald and dark-skinned, his demeanor compelling. He walked with ease, and the woman seemed to cater to him, relaying information from a circular tablet attached to her forearm. I couldn't understand their language, and I wasn't certain what race they were. They were humanoid, but their foreheads were square, the woman's bright red. She gawked at the robots with interest and spoke softly.

"She's kind of hot," Hugo said.

I rolled my eyes and put a finger to my mouth, telling him to stay quiet. He shrugged and pressed into the ship's hull as we observed.

The pair stopped near the robots, and he murmured something unintelligible, making her frown. The woman used her tablet, and the nearest robot activated, his head coming up; his sharp shoulders shifted as his arms rose, and he stepped closer.

"Dad, I've figured out the language," Hugo said. "It's close enough to the ancient Illiko dialect for the translator to work."

The captors hadn't removed our earpieces, and I tapped mine, flicking it to the proper channel, copying Hugo's.

"They are nearly completed, your Graciousness," the woman said.

"Very good. We will stop hiding in the dark. She thinks she's in charge, but we have something to show her," the man said. "You have done well, Alyce."

"Thank you, your Graciousness. It has been my pleasure."

"Send them out. We will meet our leader in one week's time. She will either listen, or…"

"Or we will usurp her seat," Alyce finished, and the man smiled, revealing pointed teeth.

"*I* will usurp, Alyce." He gazed daggers at his assistant.

"As you wish." She bowed her chin.

"Proceed with their embarkment, and meet me for a celebratory dinner," he said, and took off, sauntering away without watching as the robot army powered on.

Alyce supervised their march, and I spotted the ship they were entering across the bay.

"I have an idea," I told him.

Hugo followed me behind Alyce. She was distracted with her tablet, using it to guide the army, and I stopped near the wall, where numerous pieces of robots sat in giant crates. I grabbed one of their heads, finding it hollow. "We get dressed."

"Wear a robot?" Hugo asked, holding an empty torso.

"You have a better plan?"

Hugo clipped a thigh protection plate over his leg. "Nope."

A few minutes later, we were bad renditions of the soldierbots, but I thought it might be enough to pass as one from a distance. Alyce was lingering near the ship's ramp while countless androids streamed up the steps and into the craft. Hugo and I intercepted the group, cutting in line near the rear quarter. The robots didn't seem affected by our intrusion. Hugo bumped into me when the one in front of me stopped, and I thought Alyce might notice. But she didn't break from her work.

They moved slowly, and I tried to emulate their actions. My vision was hampered by the helmet, but I saw enough to copy their frigid walk. Finally, after what seemed like an hour, we were at the ramp, and I started the climb when everyone came to a halt.

Alyce muttered from a short distance away, and I risked a glance. She was coming in our direction.

"Come on," I whispered.

Alyce tapped on the circular tablet, and the line started moving again. Sweat poured from my forehead, dripping down my brows, and I blinked the salty liquid from my eyes. I couldn't risk wiping it. I silently urged Hugo to stay calm, and we began up the steps. Soon we were on board, and the robots shuffled into position.

"This way," I muttered to Hugo, and ran to the back, hiding in the corner of the giant hold. This ship was large enough to contend with *Light,* and the cargo space was twice that of our exploration vessels'. It had to be, to contain this many robot soldiers.

Alyce entered, and scanned over the army, a smile on her face. She turned away, and I sighed in relief.

"Is someone there?" she asked, her voice translating in my ear. I froze, and saw Hugo standing as still as he could next to me. "This ship is off limits." She took a moment to scan the interior, but finally left. The ramp receded, and the ship's door closed.

The robots around us powered down, their lights dimming, their joints relaxing.

"That was awesome," Hugo whispered.

"We're not out of the woods yet."

"Who are these guys?"

"They were discussing an ultimatum. I'd guess there's an internal conflict. A power struggle about to be resolved," I said.

"Yeah, and we're in the middle of it." Hugo took the helmet off.

"Only if we're still on this ship when it leaves," I said.

The deck vibrated, and I knew that sensation. Hugo's eyes went wide. "I'd say that's exactly what we're doing. Leaving."

It lifted from the hangar, and I wondered how long it would be before they realized we'd escaped our cell.

ELEVEN

"*I* will not betray her," Poacher said.

"Who is she?" Jules asked again.

Poacher was tied to a chair, and he made whimpering noises. His tail flicked behind him, indicating he was clearly agitated.

"It doesn't matter what you threaten me with, I won't disclose anything," he assured them.

Jules glanced at Zarin, then to Suma. "Can you do it?"

"Everything is in place." Suma turned the screen on, and a series of letters appeared. None of it made any sense to Jules, but she wasn't familiar with programming.

"What have you done?" Poacher asked.

"This is a message on the Black Hole. It'll go to any contact you've associated with. I've attached your picture, as well as your family's names and locations," Zarin said.

"That's impossible. I've protected—"

Zarin shook her head. "You didn't plug the third binary string. Such an amateur move."

"That's a failsafe. It should have been impossible to find." Poacher's hard exterior was crumbling before Jules' eyes.

"I'm the best, Poacher. There's a reason I'm booked up for months at a time."

"If you release that, I'll be done. She'll kick me out— or worse, kill me. That's our primary rule. Stay

123

anonymous."

Zarin's finger hovered over the controls. "Jules, give me the word."

She finally had Poacher's attention. "I'll ask once more," Jules said. "Who's in charge?"

"She goes by the Director. It's an old name, legendary, really. I've never seen her in person, I swear."

"Director?" Zarin raised her eyebrows. "I thought she was made up. Like a group of people all using the alias."

"Why did you think that?" Suma inquired.

"Because the stories from the Black Hole's inception seem absurd. Director's a fable."

"She is not. She's very real," Poacher insisted.

Jules kept at it. "How do I find her?"

"You don't."

"There must be a way."

"No, she contacts you," Poacher said.

Jules exhaled and rubbed her eyes. "Tell me where the footage of Sarlun was found."

Poacher must have realized protesting was futile, because he answered immediately. "That was at Belash Bazaar."

"Belash Bazaar? Never heard of it," Jules said.

"No reason you would have, since you're coming from the Alliance. The man in charge is named Tixa. A deplorable creature. If this Sarlun was there, let's hope he stayed out of sight."

"Why?" Suma asked.

"Because Tixa doesn't like anyone interfering with his business. We've seen his sales on the Black Hole. A local drug called Artificial that's ten times more addictive than Synth, and half the cost. He's the scum of the universe."

"As opposed to what you do?" Zarin asked him.

"We operate within our own set of laws. And we treat

our people with respect," Poacher responded loudly, as if he was insulted. That explained a lot about the organization. They believed their actions were just.

"How can we reach Belash?" Jules asked. "Is there a portal?"

"Portal? To Belash? No."

"Then show us the coordinates." Jules released the tendrils of energy securing Poacher, and Suma handed a tablet to him.

"There. Will you leave me be?"

"Not quite." Jules figured it was worth their time to investigate the Director, considering she was in charge of the Black Hole. "You must have some piece of advice that will lead me to the Director."

He sighed and nodded, picking another location on the tablet. "They're meeting in a week. Her second-in-command will be present."

"Who's that?"

"His Graciousness, Morg Ashr, and his loyal Alyce. They're bringing an army."

"Army? I thought you were warriors of the web?" Suma commented.

"We were, but Morg has pushed to build a foundation and shift the organization in a new direction. I haven't bought in to his ideas, but many have. Let me go!" Poacher demanded.

"No." Jules stood and glanced at her own tablet, seeing a message from the reinforcements she'd contacted from the Institute. The ship was small enough to access the portals, and it lowered to the edge of the building. "You're under arrest, Poacher, for crimes against the Alliance."

Poacher attempted to run, but it was futile. Jules tethered him at the ankles, and he bashed into the floor. She floated him to the exit, and the pair of Keppe guards took him off their hands, cuffing him and placing Poacher into the ship. "Take him to Traro. High security. Leave his name and description off any records. His location is to remain completely undocumented."

"Yes, Miss Parker." They left with the captive.

"What about us?" Zarin asked.

"We're going to Belash Bazaar."

"What about the meeting?" Suma tapped her screen.

"We'll deal with Tracker once we've secured your father." Jules had a lead, and it was high time they brought Sarlun home.

They went outside, within the safety of her sphere, and she floated above the building. This place needed to be destroyed. Jules focused her energy on the structure. The roof collapsed, and something exploded within. The entire planetoid detonated, launching shrapnel at her barrier. Zarin covered her head with her arms, but the shield held steady.

"That's dealt with," she said.

"The Black Hole is going to notice the disturbance. Did you see the size of those routers in there? I bet half the damned network will be affected," Zarin said.

"Should have had better security," Jules told them. "Come on, we have a mission to attend to."

The salvage vessel was exactly where Herm anticipated, and they deployed a beacon, asking for rescue. It slowed, attaching to their craft with a tractor beam.

"What if they're not sympathetic to our cause?" Sarlun asked.

"All we need is passage to wherever they go. It's not a large ask," Herm said.

They floated within the hull, through an energy barrier, and settled on the deck. Herm opened the hatch, and the cockpit lid flew wide.

Sarlun poked his head out, not finding any indication of life. "I was expecting a greeting party."

"Be patient," Herm said.

Sarlun gathered his cloak and the tube holding the paintings, shoving it into his pocket when someone arrived.

The woman was haggard, with short black hair and a snarl on her lips. "What do we have here?"

Sarlun couldn't believe it. "Another human?"

"What's it to you?" she asked.

"Nothing, but I hadn't realized so many of your kind had ventured beyond the Alliance borders," Sarlun said.

"Not everyone is destined for utopia, Stranger." Her use of the name they'd used for him within the Backyard gave him pause. "What are a man from Shimmal and a robot doing in a home-crafted unit in the middle of nowhere?"

"That's a tale unto itself," he told her.

"What is your destination?" she asked.

Sarlun glanced at Herm. "Nearest civilized world."

"Not many of those available, but there are plenty of uncivilized. What are you seeking? Passage to the Alliance?" The woman had lowered her guard, and her posture was freer.

He thought about the Alliance, and almost agreed that he needed to fly home. "I'm not returning."

"Maybe we're both running from something. Your name?"

"Sarlun," he said, and if she recognized it, she didn't give anything away. Most of the human population weren't aware of him, and barely knew what Shimmal was. They

Nathan Hystad

were content living their lives on Earth or New Spero, not bothering with the various levels of government or alien allies they were partnered with. It was the same with his people on Shimmal. *They are not your people, Sarlun*, he reminded himself. "You?"

"Cricket," she said.

"Nickname?" he asked with a smirk.

"Nope. God-given name. My parents were weird." She pointed at a closet. "You can stow the robot in there. Charging port is universal."

"I do not require charges," Herm said.

"A robot that doesn't need to be plugged in. Now I've seen everything. Suit yourselves."

"Where's the rest of the crew?" Sarlun asked.

"You're looking at her. I run a salvage business, and only hire contractually," she said. "At the moment, I'm searching for something. It's unnecessary to pay people or have mouths to feed unless we're doing some heavy lifting."

Sarlun liked Cricket right away. "And you're after?"

"A ship named *Mettle,*" she said.

"*Mettle?*" Sarlun almost choked. "What do you want with her?"

Cricket stopped at the bridge entrance, turning slowly. "Why are you so curious about an Alliance fleet ship?"

"I'm not. I've only heard about the expedition vessels," he lied. *Mettle* had been one of the earliest models of fleet ships, built around the same time as *Light*. Sarlun had personally overseen both of their constructions, but *Mettle* had too many issues, so he focused on *Light* instead, which became Dean Parker's command ship before being passed on to Slate.

A full crew had gone in search of the galaxies and had vanished, not unlike Tessa's friends on *Vast*. After those failed experiments, they rarely sent anyone out unless it was in one of their flagships, not these older iterations.

"Captain Derek Boggs," Cricket whispered. "In those days, the drama was high around the Alliance, with too many humans offered leadership roles. I think it's changed now. His second in command was a plucky Padlog named Gera. She was supposed to be no-nonsense, which is uncommon for the insectoids. Add in a Molariun pilot and a Bhlat weapons officer, and we had a full deck."

"Why the interest?" Sarlun asked her. "Did you ever serve the Alliance fleet?"

"Me?" She touched her collarbone. "Never. I left in the early years. Stuffed away on a Bhlat warship, and they kicked me off on some distant hellhole. I've done okay on my own."

"I'd say," Sarlun admitted. For a human to survive the depths of space, and to have her own salvage business, it would take a lot of... "What happened to *Mettle?*"

"I guess it sent out distress calls, but no one answered. I encountered a trader with loose lips on a nearby space station last week. Said the call is still playing, but when he investigated the coordinates given, there was nothing in sight. Not that he looked hard. He'd made the detour in hopes of a hefty reward," Cricket said.

Sarlun wanted to find his sister, but this was important. Dean would have searched for their missing crew. There were a hundred or so families with lost loved ones, and no answers.

"We'll help if you bring us to a real city afterwards," Herm said before Sarlun could suggest anything of the sort.

She stared at the robot and smiled. "You're different."

"I aspire to think that every being, cybernetic or not, is unique."

"Comments like that prove my theory. What are you?"

She stepped closer to Herm, and he lifted something. For a second, Sarlun thought it was a weapon, until he caught sight of the brush's tip.

"I'm an artist. Would you care for a portrait?" Herm asked.

Cricket laughed and walked onto her bridge. It was cramped, and pieces of junk lay in heaps all around. "Don't mind the mess. I was working on repairing the tractor beam." She cleared a pile of it, dumping the nuts and bolts into a bucket. She emptied a second chair off, then a third.

Sarlun took a seat. "How far is the distress beacon?"

"Ten hours." Cricket keyed directions into her dash and played the message.

"*This is Captain Derek Boggs of* Mettle, *an Alliance of Worlds exploration vessel. We've lost our engines, and fear sabotage. The ship wasn't familiar but had markings on the hull. Five Circles and a lightning bolt. We seek immediate assistance. Our coordinates are…*"

Sarlun gawked at Herm. "Did you hear that?"

"Yes. That is the same symbol as the craft that came for your sister," Herm told him.

"Sister? Who are you guys?" Cricket asked.

"Like my friend said, he's an artist, and I'm a lonely wanderer." Sarlun straightened his jacket, feeling restless. There was a puzzle around him, but Sarlun wasn't sure if he was a piece or the constructor.

He watched as Cricket set course for the listed coordinates, and Herm retrieved his paints and brush.

"You weren't kidding," Cricket mumbled.

"I do not kid. I'm a robot." Herm set up an easel and unrolled a blank canvas.

"*T*his is Belash Bazaar? It's a dump," Jules said as they lowered to the planet. It took nearly a full day to arrive at New Spero, find a wormhole generator vessel, and travel from point A to point B.

"I don't think we should land near the city," Suma suggested, and Jules agreed.

The Kraski ship floated toward the surface, quite some distance from the populated region. "What's that?" Zarin asked, gesturing to the north.

A giant area was cordoned off, with massive walls.

"Maybe a wildlife preserve?" Suma asked.

"Yeah, one with a mile-high smokestack pumping pollution into the animals' nests. It's nasty." Zarin frowned at the sight.

"Suma, you two stay behind. I'll be back," Jules said, and her friend nodded.

"Wait, you're leaving us? What if the locals come and confiscate the ship?"

"She has a point," Suma said.

"Fine. Everyone out." Jules had been hoping for a quick solo mission, but she couldn't risk anything bad happening to Suma, not on her watch. Especially with the child within her. Jules stared at her friend, and Suma frowned.

"You okay?"

She wanted to ask why Suma hadn't told her yet, Shimmal customs be damned. They were practically family. "I'm fine." They exited, and Jules could smell the smog from miles away. "That place needs to be dealt with soon."

"It's already become a wasteland," Zarin said. "You heard how Poacher described it."

Jules gawked at the strange walled-off region and then at the city. "We'll make this quick. Let's go to the bazaar and ask around about Sarlun. If anyone's seen a tall man

131

with a snout, we're golden." And they were off, flying above the dead soot-covered desert.

They began the journey to town, Jules deciding to walk the last mile after lowering to the ground from the safety of her sphere.

It wasn't long before two hideous men arrived, their six-wheeled vehicle kicking up dust and dirt as it halted.

They spoke in an odd tongue, and Jules flipped the translator on. "… illegal to be here. You must check in with the Belash Bazaar, and Tixa will decide which fields you go to. Come with us."

Jules got the gist. These bullies thought they could demand things of Jules and her companions. "I will walk to the Bazaar on my own," she said, the words translating through a speaker on her belt.

They looked puzzled and lifted their long weapons, powering the ends on. An electrical current snapped and crackled.

Jules waved her hand, and their weapons bent in half, starting on fire. The stunned guards dropped them and ran in the opposite direction of the city. "I guess we have wheels."

She hopped into the driver's side and searched for the proper controls. There were none.

"Over here," Zarin said, thrusting a lever forward. Jules was presumptuous to believe this car would operate like something in the old North America.

Suma almost fell out of the back, with no doors on the vehicle, and shrieked when Zarin cranked the tires to the side, skidding along the dirt.

"Sorry!" Zarin called into the wind. "It's a little touchy."

The cityscape grew as they sped toward it, and Zarin managed to slow before crashing into a cart carrying a group of dirty children. Jules met gazes with a frail boy and could tell he was in duress. His pupils were huge, and he was shaking.

"Not now," Suma told her from behind. "We can bring it to the Alliance and they'll help. We don't have the means to protect them yet."

Suma had been reading her mind. "Okay. But I won't let Tixa get away with this."

Jules lifted a hand, waving at the boy, and he duplicated the gesture. Her heart broke as they drove on. That was someone's child, and they were being forced into labor at such a young age.

Zarin hit the brakes when she spotted more guards, and circumvented the area, avoiding the street to bypass them.

When they stopped at a dead end within the city, Jules used the translator, asking a woman for directions to the Bazaar. She pointed right. "It is not safe."

"How far?" Jules asked.

"A hundred steps," the woman said, and glanced over her shoulder, hurrying off.

"We walk from here." Suma had her tablet out, with a picture of Sarlun on the screen. She boldly showed it to anyone they crossed paths with. "Have you seen him?"

This went on, with everyone shying away from the three strangers. Jules, Suma, and Zarin were from various planets, and quite different from the locals. They stood out like sore thumbs. It wasn't long before the guards were trailing them, and Suma picked up the pace.

The bazaar the city was named after was impressive. There must have been hundreds of vendors, marketplaces with food, woodworks, weapons, beverages, and clothing distributors all crammed in together. Jules had expected it to be run by the people of Belash, but she was sorely mistaken. It was filled with aliens.

The smell was almost overwhelming, a mixture of cooking meat and sweat. None of it was appealing.

Jules thought she even recognized a few of the alien races, but their names didn't come to mind. She'd seen so many new types during her marathon to find the First World. It made her wonder how Jacke was doing in his new life, since transporting his people from Zecos Three.

Suma continued asking people, showing them Sarlun's image, and a couple of times, they reacted before scurrying off. "This'll never work. The guards are too threatening."

Jules noticed a man discreetly duplicating their trajectory, but from a row over. He was from Belash, but he was cleaner than most, his expression not as demoralized.

She circled around him, and when he stopped, searching for her position, she tapped his shoulder. He spun around in shock. "Looking for someone?"

"I know the man you seek," he said.

"I'm all ears."

"For a price."

Of course. "How much?"

"One hundred coins."

Jules had absolutely no clue what that meant, so she retrieved an Inlorian bar from her pocket and slipped it into his hand. "Does that cover it?"

His cheeks turned red, and he twitched as he shoved it into a secret pocket behind his vest. "They took him. This man tried to kill Tixa."

"Where did they go?"

"To the Backyard." He stuttered the words, as if he might suffer the same fate.

"Is that the place in the wasteland?" she asked.

"I don't know. We are not permitted beyond the border."

Guards approached Jules from all angles, and the man departed hastily. No one stopped his exit.

"Tixa will see you."

Jules gave her best innocent smile. "I'm not sure who you're referring to. I'm here because I heard the food was to die for." They looked confused, but still chose to approach. She noticed Suma and Zarin had cleverly distanced themselves. "Lead the way."

TWELVE

"I wish we knew our destination." Hugo stood up and straightened after sitting for the last eight hours.

"Be careful," I said softly.

The rows of robots were still, but the room vibrated with the ship's movement, almost giving me the impression they were all powered on. I used the bulkhead to stand and walked to the nearest machine. The robots were a foot taller than me, their heads stretched long, the shoulders sticking up six inches. I noticed a lens on each of them and assumed there was a weapon embedded somehow.

"Dad, what if we try the computer?" Hugo asked.

He'd mentioned it when we'd first settled in for the ride, but I'd dismissed the notion entirely. But maybe he was right.

"It's time to investigate," I muttered. I was thirsty, hungry, and had to use the facilities. We checked the perimeter of the huge cargo hold and saw no signs of organic beings within the space. That was a good thing.

"I found something," Hugo said, and he stuck his hand into the strange door handle, opening a secondary room.

"Looks like an office," I told him. There were two screens on the wall, a possible chair, and another door. I used it and noticed what could only be a bathroom. "Give me a minute."

Hugo wrinkled his brow but didn't reply.

"Stay put." I sealed myself in and tried to figure out the unusual technology. After a couple moments, I relieved myself, and it automatically sucked the contents of the bowl away. A mist shot from the wall, and I put it on my palms, hoping it was an antiseptic, not an air freshener.

Hugo was where I left him, and he shrugged, asking me how to use the space.

While my son was occupied, I searched the office, finding a bottle and something in a shiny chrome wrapper. I tore the packaging and sniffed the bar.

"Food?" Hugo asked when he returned.

"Think so." I broke it in half and passed him the chunk.

We tasted it together, and while I'd been anticipating a protein bar, it was basically beef jerky, salty and hard.

"I've had worse."

"Like Slate's lasagna," I said, making Hugo smile.

"If we get out of here, I'll eat a piece. Maybe even two."

"I might hold you to that."

The lights turned on in the cargo hold, and I shut the door, keeping my foot in the jamb so I could watch what was happening.

"This won't be enough," the older man said.

"I assure you, your Graciousness, they are trained for extensive combat," Alyce said.

I'd been wondering if the pair of them had joined the ship, or if it was autonomously flying to its destination. Their presence answered that question for me.

"The cities are well constructed, and they have soldiers. You know that battles are won in the air or space, not on the ground. You're thinking like a relic," his Graciousness said.

Alyce put her hands on her hips and shook her head. I could only see them between the rows of robots, but her expression was one I'd witnessed countless times from Mary and Jules. It spoke... 'silly man, stay out of this.'

"You let me worry about the starships. What do you think I've been working on the last decade? When we arrive at Shimmal, we'll power off every one of their engines. They'll have no defense against our Bot army."

I glanced at Hugo. "They plan to attack Shimmal?"

"Alyce, be frank with me. Will she agree to our terms?" the man asked.

"If she doesn't, then she'll quickly learn of your impatience, Morg Ashr." Alyce's smile was disturbing.

"Let us discuss things further." Morg licked his lips. "I'm thirsty. Bring one of the robots. I need someone to serve us tonight."

Alyce laughed, and her circular tablet expanded on her wrist. She typed on it, and one of the robots powered up, his eyes glowing. "What is your name?"

"*I am B-8882. Please instruct me.*" The voice was genderless, the tone flat.

"B-8882, come with us. You will be mixing drinks."

"*I am not...*"

She tapped more icons, and the tablet glowed the same color as its eyes. "Your programming has been updated."

"*Yes. Thank you. I am prepared.*" B-8882 followed them from the cargo hold, leaving hundreds of identical machines behind.

I only dared to exit the office when they were gone for five minutes, and I cracked the bottle cap. It smelled sterile. "Here." I offered it to Hugo.

He took a sip and grimaced. "It's gross."

I tested it. "Better than being dehydrated."

"They're coming for Shimmal, Dad. We have to stop them."

"Do we? They're no longer our ally," I said.

"Dad, you can't be serious right now. We love those guys. It's Hulope that's the issue. We can't let anything happen to Sarlun's..." He stopped himself. "To Suma's people."

"I know." I was still upset that their population hadn't fought harder to be in the Alliance, to overthrow their new leader, but it was obvious they'd been fed lies by their government. It wouldn't be the first time that happened in the history of the universe.

"I figured out what we can do," Hugo declared.

"That smirk tells me it's not going to be easy."

"That depends on who you ask."

"I'm asking you," I said.

"Okay, then it's a tough one."

"What is?"

"We steal Alyce's tablet."

"Why?"

"So we can control the Bot army." Hugo smirked and lifted his eyebrows.

———

Sarlun stared at the painting of Cricket, admiring how talented Herm truly was. Every lifeline, each tiny detail of her face was etched onto the canvas. The pilot of the salvage ship only casually glanced at it when she'd been presented with the artwork, probably because it reminded her just how much of her time had expired out here all alone.

Sarlun had felt the same way when he'd seen his portrait. In his mind's eye, he was forty, healthy, and fit for anything that he could encounter.

"We're nearing the source of the distress call," Cricket said.

Sarlun stood behind her chair, watching the screen. There was nothing to see.

"I didn't expect anything less," Cricket told him. "But where did they go?"

"Perhaps I can be of assistance," Herm said.

"What are you thinking?"

"Each ship gives off a certain amount of residual pollution, no matter how well designed. There should be a means to track it."

"Not after these many years." Cricket zoomed on the region.

"I can help." Herm pointed at a second chair. "May I?"

"Please." Cricket's jaw clenched, and Sarlun assumed it was difficult for her to let anyone touch her computer. She was used to being a loner, which was something Sarlun could relate to.

"If I reroute the air cycling and gravitational drive, I can…"

"You're going to kill the air and gravity?" Cricket barked.

"Only momentarily."

Cricket stared up at Sarlun. "Do you really trust this guy?"

Sarlun appraised the robot and nodded. "I do."

"Fine. But it better be quick."

Herm used the keypad, and the vents kicked off. The breeze of the circulating air ceased, and Sarlun gripped the back of the chair when the gravity failed. Objects floated through the cabin, and Cricket batted a piece of junk away. Nuts and bolts lifted from containers, and Sarlun realized they should have secured all the rubbish on board first.

"There." Herm motioned to the main screen, and a light green line appeared. "This documents their path. It's a feature most don't realize come standard with ship designs, no matter the creator. All they need is energy, because they attract one another. If you retain your focus on the area, the residual specks will become obvious."

Sarlun wished Suma was here to question his line of logic, because it sounded off to him; but they'd found *Mettle*'s path, and that was enough for him.

The floating pieces fell to the bridge's deck, and Sarlun's feet touched the deck while the air began to flow again.

The green line continued on, and Cricket sped forward in her salvage vessel, trailing the glowing path.

It led them to a dark moon orbiting a snow-covered planet. Even from above, it was obvious this place was in an eternal winter.

"They didn't land on the moon," Cricket said.

"No. The engines were cut, and someone brought them to the surface," Herm informed them.

"How do you know?"

"Hypothesis."

"For a painter, you seem to have all the answers."

"Might one not be skilled in various situations?" Herm asked with a hint of amusement.

Sarlun nodded at the planet. "Should we investigate?"

"I don't like this. How are we going to find *Mettle* in this ice world?"

"The distress call. Can you search for the ID label on it?" Sarlun asked.

Cricket grinned and went to work. "Why didn't I think of that?"

She replayed the message and sifted through the noise, discovering the ID tag that accompanies every communication. "Now all I have to do is ping it back, and—"

The radar appeared, and a red dot flashed on one of the four main continents. The oceans were frozen over, making it difficult to distinguish land from water, but the computer did the analysis where their eyes couldn't.

"We have contact." Cricket sped into the atmosphere, the screen burning hotly upon entry. They burst past the barrier and dove toward their destination.

Once they lowered beyond the clouds, it was snowing.

"Minus forty-seven centigrade," Cricket read off the sensors.

"We'll need jackets," Sarlun said.

"Air is breathable. Which is a surprise, given the fact that no vegetation exists."

"It's recent," Herm told them.

"What is?" Sarlun squinted as he watched the land increase in size.

"They did this. Whoever trapped *Mettle* here also caused this eternal winter." Herm rose from his seat.

"Cricket, when did it leave? Fifteen years ago?"

"About that. Maybe sixteen," she said.

"There she is." Sarlun couldn't believe what he was seeing. The Alliance exploration vessel was fully intact, frozen into a massive clear block of ice.

"I found her. She's mine," Cricket quickly proclaimed.

"*Mettle* is property of the Alliance," Sarlun said.

"And who's here to enforce that?" Cricket's demeanor changed.

"Depends what we find," he whispered, and she shrugged, grabbing a gun from beside her. Cricket landed next to it and started from the bridge.

"What are you two waiting for? We have a ship to explore."

Sarlun stared at his robot friend and they trailed after Cricket, eager to discover what happened to *Mettle*, and how she ended up locked in ice on an alien world this far from home.

The ice was thick, and they judged *Mettle* was beneath twenty meters of solid-frozen water.

The wind blew cold air against Sarlun's face, and his snout wiggled in discomfort. They wouldn't be able to linger for more than a few minutes before freezing themselves.

"Stay put." Cricket ran up her ramp, and the ship lifted from the snow.

Sarlun had a sinking sensation in his gut, like Cricket might leave them to die on this icy nightmare.

"She won't depart," Herm said. "She's invested."

And he was right. Cricket spun the craft around, backing the thrusters toward *Mettle*.

She rushed to join them and held a tablet in her grip, her gun nestled into her thick black belt. "We might want to spread out for this."

The trio walked a short distance away, while she remotely powered on the thrusters. The heat blasted behind the vessel, quickly melting the top layer. Water pooled near them, and soon, they had a hole large enough to open *Mettle*'s hull.

"Good thinking," Sarlun praised.

"Thanks. When you're a solo crew, you learn to be creative," she said.

"Be warned, this could be bad." Sarlun stepped into the snowy mess, his boots keeping his feet dry.

"Hundreds of crew," she whispered. "Terrible."

"But you still want their ship," Sarlun muttered.

"Absolutely." Cricket reached the hull first and searched for the ramp's manual external failsafe. She tried it, but it failed.

Sarlun grinned, knowing full well only a handful of people, other than the ship's primary crew members, had the ability to open the external ramp manually. He was one of them. "May I?"

She stepped back. "Be my guest."

Sarlun touched the five-digit code and pressed his thumb to the screen that revealed itself, finishing the two-part verification. It worked, and the hull slid apart, granting them access.

"Nice work. I guess you're keeping secrets too, aren't you, Sarlun?" Cricket busted by him, pulse pistol in her grip. "Let's see what's left of *my* ship."

Sarlun didn't correct her as they entered. Herm was behind him, watching everything with a whirring of his machinery. Sarlun guessed he was filming their adventure.

Everything was unremarkable, until he noticed the figure across the docking bay. "Hello?" he called.

The person didn't move.

Sarlun had a sneaking suspicion, and it was verified when he neared the man. He was in the Alliance uniform, their logo on the chest of his gray outfit. The Bhlat guard was refrigerated, his mouth twisted in a sneer with icicles hanging from his lips.

"This is impossible," Cricket said.

"It's like they were flash-frozen." Sarlun headed to the door, and they found more in the corridors beyond. Everyone was upright, their bodies stuck in whatever position they were in when the tragedy occurred.

"It couldn't have been the elements," Herm proposed. "It would have taken much longer to die if they crashed on the surface."

"There's no evidence to suggest a crash landing at all. The hull is perfectly intact." Sarlun knew there was an explanation, but none came to him. "We must check the bridge."

They entered the familiar halls. The backup power was on, utilizing a low-energy output battery kit he'd created with the help of Alnod Industries. It would work for years. While it didn't keep life support going, it gave enough light to guide their way. Sarlun bet he'd be able to locate the bridge without his eyesight. He'd been integral to the creation of these exploration ships. Being on an Alliance vessel reminded him how much he missed his old life. What was he doing, running around in hiding? He should go home and face the music.

Everywhere they strode, more people blocked their path, and they had to squeak by a few as they neared the proper doors. Sarlun used his access code again, and he entered the bridge.

Captain Derek Boggs was in his chair, hands clenched on the arms. He was frowning, his mouth slightly open. It was obvious he was in the middle of an important command when he became frozen.

"Incredible," Cricket whispered as she crossed the deck to the dark viewscreen.

Sarlun had an idea. "Cricket, do you have a scanner?"

She lifted an eyebrow. "Medical?"

"Yes." He reached his palm out, and she gave it over. The tool was old and clunky, but it powered on. Sarlun waved it in front of Derek, and almost dropped it when the results came. "He's not dead."

"Give me that." Cricket yanked the scanner from him and checked the findings. "What in the hell?"

"They were put into some form of cryogenics." Herm glanced around the bridge. "There must be a device on board that is keeping them in this state."

"Even if they were frozen in place, how can their basic life functions be functioning without oxygen? Sustenance?"

"I have never heard of this technology, so I cannot explain. Perhaps if we…" Herm stopped when Cricket had one of the computer consoles working. She knelt to plug in a battery pack and dusted her pants off.

She seemed to know her way around an Alliance system. "You sure you didn't serve?" Sarlun asked again.

"I'm positive, but I may have had the pleasure of borrowing a transport ship," she said.

"And did you return it?"

"I figured the Alliance wouldn't want the scraps after I was shot down." Cricket smirked at him, and Sarlun let it go. Who was he to judge the morals of another?

"What good will this do?" Sarlun asked.

"I was thinking there might be something pulling power if it's on board." She scrolled through the link to engineering, and Sarlun indicated where one area had a large draw.

"There."

"Let's go. Herm, stay on the bridge."

"Very well," the robot said.

Sarlun felt a surge of adrenaline. They might be able to save this crew and get them home. Which would mean Sarlun could join them. His journey might be close to an end… but… he hadn't located his sister yet, which was half the point. He wished to be united with her, but what did it matter if he was resolved to return to the Alliance? Clearly, Shula didn't want to be found; otherwise, she wouldn't have worked so tirelessly at remaining unseen.

They crossed the ship, using the stairwells since the elevators were out of commission, and eventually found Engineering. Sarlun glanced up at the drive, smiling to himself. They were so much larger than the new models, and most of it had been rendered useless with the addition of the wormhole generators. But he appreciated the complexity of this version.

"It should be…" Cricket froze in place, her arm raised,

the gun still in her grip. Ice formed over her skin, and Sarlun stopped in his tracks, trying to locate the source.

Everything turned cold. He watched as his finger turned blue, but couldn't move as it spread throughout his body. Soon his vision faltered, and Sarlun's consciousness slipped away with the frozen tundra.

THIRTEEN

"*W*hat do you want, girl?" Tixa asked. Jules had her translator in, allowing his gruff words to make sense.

"I'm interested in finding a friend of mine," she told him.

They were in a private cabana at the edge of the Bazaar. It was big, overlooking the entire market, and the sounds of the day carried to them, along with countless different scents. Local women came and went, bringing food and drink in an endless stream.

Tixa downed a couple glasses of a bright pink beverage and didn't once offer Jules anything.

"What does this have to do with me?" Tixa waved a man in, and the guy strode to his boss' side, a long gun at his hip. He whispered in his ear, and Tixa smiled, his ugly face even more gruesome with the gesture. "It seems you already have friends with you."

Suma and Zarin entered the cabana, their heads down. Zarin had a bruise on her eye, and Suma rubbed her forearm, as if she'd been hurt. Rage filled Jules, and she almost exploded with anger. It took all her energy to remain visibly calm. "I don't know what you're talking about."

"These aren't your allies?" Tixa motioned at the two ladies.

"Nope. I'm here to locate a man…"

"With a snout like hers?" Tixa grabbed Suma's wrist,

148

dragging her closer. "What are you three doing at my Bazaar?"

"I told you…" Jules' head spun as Tixa struck her.

"Touch me again, and you'll regret it," she whispered. "Let Suma go, and maybe I won't kill you."

Tixa released Suma and laughed. It started in his chest and traveled to his expansive belly. Soon he was bellowing with hilarity, like she'd told the universe's best joke. "You know, I needed that."

Jules had heard enough. She started to tap into her powers, but they were blocked. She lifted a finger, attempting to shoot him with a beam of energy, but there was nothing.

"What are you doing, girl? You come here and point at me?" Tixa swung again, but this time, Jules dodged it.

She saw a crystal at the end of his gaudy necklace flare up when he neared her. "No way," she muttered. It was the same material that old Professor Thompson had used to steal her abilities to take over the Academy when she was a first-year student. Suma had been working there too, and Jules saw the moment Suma spotted the stone.

"Why don't you leave us alone?" Suma called, trying to steal his attention.

Jules stepped back, hoping to avoid the crystal's range, but two huge guards were behind her, dragging her to Tixa. He laughed again and came closer, his breath rancid. Bits of meat clung to his teeth, and she gagged. He found this even more amusing.

Tixa touched her cheek with a gnarled fingernail. "Who is the man you seek?"

Jules needed to change trajectories. "His name is Sarlun, and he's a traitor. He must pay for his sins." She glanced at Suma, hoping her words didn't offend her.

"Then I'm happy to tell you he's probably dead."

"Probably?" Zarin dared ask.

"People don't survive long in the Backyard."

So Sarlun was in that fenced-off area after all. Without thinking, Jules tried to throw her sphere up, but it failed, and the crystal glowed on his chest. He didn't seem to notice, and she was grateful for the small victory.

"I'd like to see for myself," Jules told him.

"Tell you what. Since I'm feeling generous, all three of you can visit the Backyard." He snapped and more guards entered, carrying metal cuffs. "Bring them to the Backyard."

Jules exhaled and allowed her arms to be secured behind her. All she needed to do was to stay distanced from this goon, and her powers would likely return.

Tixa downed another two shots of pink liquor and started to eat, disregarding them as they were dragged from his tent. Jules took a final glance at the Bazaar, observing the squalor most of the population seemed to be in, then the gluttony of their leader, and it made her sick.

They were shoved onto a cart, and it headed north from the city. The cart was slow-moving, the pair of guards eerily silent as they led it to the giant fence. Jules tested her powers, but they still failed her.

"We'll find him, Suma," Jules promised.

"Are they back?" Zarin asked her.

Jules shook her head. "I'll keep checking."

The gates opened, and the guards grunted, shoving them inside.

"What about the cuffs?" Jules called.

The pair looked at each other and one came to her aid, undoing hers. Jules considered attacking and taking their weapons, but didn't want to put Suma and Zarin in danger. The huge black gate swung closed, sealing them into the Backyard.

"This is nasty," Zarin said, kicking at the soot-covered ground.

A smokestack thundered out blackness in the distance, and Jules instantly felt dirty being within these walls. "He has to be here somewhere."

She grinned as she sensed the smallest bit of her abilities returning. Not enough to do anything yet, but she knew they'd recharge.

"Where to?" Suma asked.

Zarin reached into her shirt and pulled a tablet out. "Perhaps Tixa keeps a map of the place."

"Where did you get that?" Jules laughed.

"When the big lug was punching me in the eye, I was pilfering this. I figured it was a fair trade." Zarin turned it on, and they crowded in, staring at the screen. She quickly found a reference to the Backyard on the device, and a 3D rendering appeared. "It's bigger than I would have guessed."

She zoomed on the smokestack, and when she tapped it, the map sank into the ground, exposing a massive network of tunnels below the Backyard. "What is that?" Zarin whispered.

"It appears they continue to the core," Jules said.

"The core? They're using the center of Belash to what... cover this area in smog?" Suma tapped her chin.

Zarin clicked a secondary link. "There must be more to it."

"What?" Suma inquired.

"Drugs. The heat helps their main export grow faster in the fields a short distance away. Tixa uses this place to test different versions of it. It says something here about the Feral."

"He's testing his drugs on prisoners?" Jules fumed. "We're going to take this freak down."

"And my father?" Suma asked.

"If Sarlun is around, we'll rescue him, then tear the Bazaar to the ground, one tent at a time. Starting with Tixa's." Jules smirked. A creature howled from somewhere in the filthy expanse. "We should move."

"Where to?" Zarin asked her.

"The smokestack. We'll start with the tunnels." Jules had a mission, and her steps had purpose as she marched over the soot-covered stones.

The massive vessel was eerily unmanned and quiet. Hugo and I had spent hours searching for a tablet we could use to control the robot army, but so far, all we'd discovered were empty quarters.

The design was far different than the Alliance versions, but there was still an entire deck we hadn't explored: the top one. Unfortunately, we had no passcode to enter.

"Now what?" Hugo leaned on the door.

"We find another way."

"Dad, this is nuts. Why don't we wait until Alyce comes back with the tablet, then we—"

"What? Jump her? What if she powers the army on first and they tear us apart?" I asked. I had to be more cautious with Hugo than I'd ever been with Jules, mostly because she could always pull me out of harm's way, rather than vice versa. Hugo was a great kid, and a smart and capable Gatekeeper, but he was still my son first.

"Good point." Hugo peered down the hall. "What if there's another option?"

"I'm listening."

"The decks have to be connected by ducting, no matter

who designed the thing," Hugo said, rushing back the direction we'd come. "So all we have to do is…"

"Crawl through some tight spots and sneak on the top deck," I finished.

Hugo beamed as we entered yet another empty room at the end of the corridor. "Now you understand."

He shone a light we'd found three decks below on the ceiling. "There." The grate was letting out a stream of cool air.

"After you, Hugo. It was your idea."

"I can't reach it." There was a single piece of furniture along the bulkhead, and we heaved the heavy metal cabinet under the vent. Hugo quickly removed the screwdriver from his suit and undid the hidden bolts. The tip was malleable, adjusting to whatever kind of alien screw we encountered. Not everyone used the American standard, go figure.

He passed me the grate and I set it on the floor, questioning if the vent was wide enough for us to squeeze into. Hugo answered as he jumped, dragging himself into the ceiling.

I shrugged and came after him, barely fitting.

Hugo moved fast through the ducting, then up the small rungs, before it leveled off, angling horizontally. I realized we were probably above the top deck, and Hugo took the first exit, dropping into the opening onto the floor ten feet down. I joined him, and my knee twisted uncomfortably as I landed.

"You okay?" Hugo reached for me, steadying my balance.

"It's fine. Just an old injury."

I tested my weight and found I could carry on with mild discomfort. This deck was entirely different than below, and I realized that all five others were designed to transport robots exclusively. This deck was designed for Alyce and Morg to occupy comfortably.

The walls were painted in calming neutrals, the flooring bright white and shiny. Vegetation grew from mounts along the bulkheads, vines carrying over the rooms and halls, giving the place a sense of nature even though we were in the dark vacuum of space, probably light years from a habitable planet. We'd done the same thing on *Light,* in the courtyard, so I appreciated this even more.

"Pretty cool, hey, Dad?" Hugo touched a vine, and it began to wriggle.

"Let's keep our hands to ourselves," I warned him.

I stopped when I heard music drifting from farther down the hall. I thought it was instrumental; then I noticed the harmonized voicing weaving in and out of the tune. Whoever these guys were, they appreciated the fine arts, and it made it harder to view them as monsters. I didn't have enough information about their mission, just that they were delivering this army to Shimmal. It didn't mean they were coming for the Alliance, because officially, Shimmal wasn't part of it any longer, thanks to Hulope.

Hugo kept walking until he was out of reach. I jogged to the door he stopped at, and peered in.

The robot they'd modified had drinks on a tray, and he offered them to his organic rulers.

Morg accepted his without comment, but Alyce actually thanked the robot, which was interesting. The tablet was on the table between the pair of them. The serving bot took their used glasses and exited the room.

I ducked, pressing to the wall, and Hugo did the same. It walked right by us and went into another room.

"That was close," I whispered.

"Tell me again," Morg said.

Alyce seemed completely coherent, her uniform still

crisp where Morg's was wrinkled. She sat upright in her seat, but Morg was slouched in his, as if he'd partly melted into the chair.

"We will rule the organization."

"We?" he asked.

"Yes. You'll be the head, but I'll be right beside you, Morg. You promised this."

"Yes, I suppose I did. And rightfully so. You've done well over the years. I apologize that it's taken so long to come to fruition," he said, looked at his drink, and downed half. Alyce took a small sip of hers.

"Patience is essential, your Graciousness. One doesn't build an army of robots, or a fleet of vessels, on a whim. It demands time, and a vast number of resources."

"All done behind her back, I'll remind you," he said.

"She will be furious," Alyce said.

I was beginning to see more of the whole picture. They were members of some organization, but weren't at the top. They answered to another woman, while secretly accumulating weapons and machine soldiers to do their bidding. And we were on the way to meet with the others.

"Let her whine. Without us, she is nothing," Morg barked. "She'd still be stuck in the Backyard if we hadn't rescued her all those years ago."

The Backyard? I mouthed the name.

"She isn't as grateful as she could be. It was her fault she was caught. Searching for Reflective Worlds on a pit of a place like Bazaar Belash. We should have left her," Morg said.

Hugo and I shared a glance. "Reflective Worlds," he whispered.

"She's distracted, but it will be over soon. We'll give her Shimmal on a platter, and she'll take her place," Alyce said.

That was almost as confusing at the rest of the conversation, but I didn't have time to dwell on it. Alyce was leaving. She turned the music down and caressed the vines in the room, causing them to shiver and squirm. "I must retire. Do you wish to keep the robot for the night? He will continue to serve you."

"Very well. Leave him." Morg finished another drink, and Alyce nodded.

I noted that she didn't take the tablet. Hugo was already halfway down the hall, and we ducked into a doorway to avoid being caught by Alyce. I heard her footsteps recede, and turned, coming face to face with the serving robot. He stood a foot taller than me, his eyes glowing brighter.

"Would you like a drink?" he asked.

"I would," Hugo said, and I slapped his arm away.

"No. We're fine," I muttered, grateful the robot didn't blast us with his many assorted weapons.

"Very well." He carried another round for Morg on a tray, and walked off, leaving us alone in the galley.

"Who are they talking about?" Hugo asked.

"Did you hear them mention the Reflective Worlds? Sounds like their boss lady tried to find one in a place called the Backyard. Ever hear that before?"

"Nope." Hugo snatched a piece of food from the counter. Before I could stop him, he plopped it into his mouth. "Dad, that's delicious."

My stomach grumbled at the thought of food, and I ripped off a chunk. It was flaky, resembling a pastry. It was the best thing I'd ever tasted. I pulled another piece, devouring it while Hugo went for a second.

"Maybe the recipe is on her tablet," Hugo kidded.

"We can't stay here." I listened at the exit.

"But I'm thirsty too." Hugo began sorting through the

cabinets and found two bottles. "How do I open this?"

There was no cap to twist off, and definitely no bottle opener. The top seemed part of the unit.

Hugo waved a hand in front of it, and a tiny round light appeared on the neck. He pressed the button and the tip vanished. "Cool." He tried the drink, and his eyes grew bigger. "Who are these guys?"

I did the same with my bottle, finding a delicious type of sparkling water. "I know who we can hire to cater Jules and Dean's wedding," I mumbled.

Before the robot returned, we scattered into the hall to wait in a nearby room. Once I guessed Morg may have consumed another cocktail or two, I took my chance. "Stay put."

This time, Hugo didn't argue with me. "Be careful, Dad."

The galley door was open, and the robot stood facing the hall, his eyes powered off. The light in Morg's room was on, but only dimly. He snored in his seat, an artificial holographic fire flickering. The vines from the wall crept across the space, shielding him as if they were a blanket.

He adjusted, and I held tight, waiting to see if he woke up. But he didn't. More snoring, and I crawled closer, heading behind him. The tablet remained where Alyce had left it, and I stretched my hand out, blindly trying to grab it.

Something brushed my wrist, and I nearly jumped in shock, until I looked up at the vine. I patiently let it pass, and yanked the tablet back.

"We're going to do this with or without you," Morg said.

I was directly behind his chair, and I stayed on all fours, holding my breath.

"Yes, Mother. I have been a good boy." He snuffled again and returned to a deep sleep.

I retreated to the exit, and found it blocked by a layer of vines.

One of them spun around my wrist, another on my ankle. I was caught.

FOURTEEN

*T*he robot drifted in and out of focus. "Are you okay?" Herm leaned over him.

"What…" Sarlun touched his snout, feeling the dampness from the melted ice. "You saved us."

"Yes. You were susceptible to the device." Herm pointed at the sphere, the size of an EVA helmet. It was powered down.

"I didn't even consider it still working," Cricket complained. "If I'd come alone, I'd have been trapped like the entire crew, waiting for the next person to arrive and fall into their trap."

"Then it's a good thing we had Herm with us." Sarlun patted the robot's back. "Thank you, my friend."

His eyes brightened. "You're welcome, Sarlun. It is nice to have a friend."

"If you two are finished, we have some explaining to do." Cricket held her arms up, and Sarlun turned when a man cleared his throat.

"Who are you?" The man wore the Alliance uniform, and aimed a pulse pistol at their group.

"I am Sarlun, the head of the Gatekeepers," he said without thinking.

"No kidding." The guy grinned and lowered his weapon. He scurried over, extending his hand. Sarlun smiled as the man empathically pumped the shake.

"You're *that* Sarlun?" Cricket asked.

"I thought my name would have given it away," he told her.

"Why should I know how many Sarluns are on Shimmal? It might be the alien equivalent of the human name John."

"My name's John," the uniformed officer said.

"Of course it is." Cricket left Engineering, shaking her head in astonishment.

"John, before we continue, there's something you need to know. Your ship was lured here. You've been frozen for more than a decade," Sarlun told him.

"Frozen?" He tugged on the shirt clinging to him. "Is that why I'm soaked?"

"Yes. Please reassure your crew as they wake. We must get to the bridge," Sarlun said.

"Roger that. Come on." John went to the hall, talking to another pair of crew members, and they looked more shocked than he had. They rushed off, and John waved Sarlun over. He used a computer on the wall, turning more lights on. "I rerouted the solar back up. We'll take the elevator."

They hurried past more confused staff, and once Herm was on the lift, they headed to the bridge's deck. It was a mess. A couple of them were arguing, and Captain Derek Boggs was standing between a male Molariun and the Bhlat weapons officer.

"There is no point in placing blame. We'll decipher what they want, and…" Derek stopped when he saw their group enter. "John, who are your guests?"

"Hear him out, Captain." John motioned for Sarlun to tell his tale.

"You're Captain Boggs, correct?"

"I know you," he whispered. "Or perhaps your son,

Sarlun."

It had only been a decade, but those were hard years. "I am Sarlun."

"Did you…use a portal to get onto my ship? I thought only *Light*…"

"No. You've been trapped on a frozen world. The enemy you spoke of… they're gone. You were kept alive within a giant block of ice."

"Unbelievable," Derek Boggs murmured. "My wife. My children…"

"All older. But we can reunite you with them," Sarlun promised.

The bridge crew spoke in hushed tones, some embracing, others clearly upset by the sudden news. One moment they'd been attempting to fend off an enemy; the next Sarlun was passing this information, notifying them they'd lost a decade. It couldn't have been easy.

"Who were they?" Sarlun asked him.

"It was a man and woman. She called him Morg. They were anxious to test a new technology. The woman was professional, but callous. She said we'd be remembered as heroes."

"Do you have footage?" Herm asked.

"Yes." The wasp-like Padlog commander came forward. "I am Gera."

"My apologies. Crew, I am Sarlun, of the Gatekeepers," he said. They didn't need to know his burden, or that Shimmal was no longer part of their Alliance. He didn't think complicating their situation would be helpful. "This is Herm." They stared at the strange robot, but no one commented on his presence. They'd likely encountered Dean Parker's pilot, Dubs, at some point. "And Cricket."

She waved. "Howdy."

Gera accessed the last feeds and played them.

"Fear not, Alliance. We don't seek to harm you, but to offer you a place in history. I apologize for your sacrifice, but it won't be for nothing. Perhaps you will be returned one day, but for my sake, I hope it's long after I'm buried." The woman had a squared-off brow, her hair dark, her uniform darker. But it was her eyes that caught his attention. Sheer crystal. *"Morg, will you do the honors?"*

Captain Boggs' voice could be heard. *"You will stand down. This is an Alliance Exploration Vessel, and you're interfering with—"*

The video continued recording as the crew members started turning blue and freezing up.

"I told you it would work. And painless too."

"I care not if it's painless," Morg said. *"Only effective."*

The image showed the ship over *Mettle*, and Sarlun gasped when he recognized it from Herm's recording of his sister escaping the Backyard. It was the very same vessel.

The feed cut off, and the screen went black.

"That's it?" Cricket asked.

"Captain, we have two choices. Either we see if we can reboot *Mettle* and send you home, or we track down these two, and make them pay for what they've done," Sarlun said.

Boggs glanced at his crew, landing his gaze on his second in command. "Gera, what do you think?"

"We've only been gone for a month, at least in our memories. I say we help these guys out and find Morg and his accomplice." Gera buzzed after her comments, and the rest of the crew nodded in agreement.

"Very well. Prepare to run diagnostics. A decade on ice might bring numerous issues," Boggs said. "Take a few minutes to decompress. Change into a new uniform and dry off." They were likely to catch colds if they didn't act soon.

Boggs waved Sarlun to his office and shut the door when the two of them were alone. "How is the Alliance? I'm worried that you came to find us after this long. Were we destroyed by an enemy? Lom of Pleva? The Kold or Kraski?"

"No. They're all dealt with. We no longer fear those groups," Sarlun said.

"Good. I can't wait to talk with Magnus again. Where's he stationed?" Boggs inquired.

Sarlun couldn't tell the man that the Magnus he knew had been killed on *Horizon* by the Arnap, replaced by a version of the man from another dimension. It was too painful. "New Spero," he simply said, and Boggs nodded.

"The Alliance is stronger than ever, so don't fret. I appreciate your help," Sarlun said. He didn't know how, but he was certain Morg and the mysterious woman would lead him to his sister Shula.

"Nothing to it. That's what we do, right?" Captain Boggs set a hand on Sarlun's shoulder. "It's an honor to have you aboard *Mettle,* sir."

Sarlun smiled at him. "The honor is all mine."

"Give me a few minutes and we can come up with a plan," Boggs said.

Sarlun left him in the office, and noticed Herm attempting to gain his attention as he crossed the bridge. "Yes?" he asked the robot.

"Cricket and I have an idea."

Sarlun peered at the bridge crew working on the system analysis. "Go ahead."

"It's impossible to track that ship, but…" Herm lifted the round device Morg had placed in their Engineering room. "I have discovered something within this that will aid our mission."

"What is it?"

"An ore, only found in one region."

"Where?"

"Ratov Two."

"And what's its relevance?"

"Ratov is where I was built," Herm said.

Suddenly, Sarlun was overcome with a wave of suspicion. Herm had been present when Shula had gone with the strangers on the video, and now he was saying he was built in the same region as the device they'd used against the Alliance fleet ship. "How did you escape?"

"I was different," he said. "I felt things. They couldn't control me with their tablets like the others. I pretended for as many years as I was able, until someone noticed. I was placed in a storage facility for further testing, but I broke out, climbing aboard an autonomous trading craft bound for the Belash Bazaar. There, you know my story."

"Are you sapient?" Cricket asked him.

"Yes."

"I knew it," she said, smirking. "No one could paint that well otherwise."

"I think we'll find answers at Ratov Two."

"Then that's our destination," Sarlun told him. "Your home."

His eyes dimmed at the mention of his reunion with his makers.

"Captain," Gera said when Boggs exited his office wearing a fresh uniform.

"What is it? Can we fly?"

Sarlun joined them at the helm.

Gera pointed at the readouts. "Nope. The inducer is broken. We can't go anywhere."

Sarlun's hopes were dashed, but Cricket quickly changed that.

"No problem. There are three aboard my salvage ship. You can have one, but it'll cost you." Cricket crossed her arms and winked at Sarlun.

———————

*I*t was only a couple of hours before Jules learned firsthand what a Feral person was. They approached from the north, a group of five, growling and snapping their jaws. Their eyes were bloodshot red, liquid dripping from the corners of them.

Jules' heart ached that these people had been turned into monsters by experimental drugs. It wasn't fair.

"Anything yet?" Zarin asked, and Jules lifted a few feet off the ground before landing on the sooty rocks with a puff of black dust.

"Almost."

"How are we going to fight them without weapons?" Suma stood in front of Zarin like a protector.

The smokestack was a half mile away, and Jules wasn't planning on letting the Feral stop her now. "I'll handle it."

Jules had spent countless hours training for moments like this, even when she didn't have her powers. Since they weren't always reliable, she often trained to fight without them. She didn't have the same level of confidence now, but she was sure she could win this battle.

The Feral halted and shrieked in unison, turning and running.

"See, they must have known I was about to kick their…" Jules turned on her heel, seeing the robots rolling over the landscape. They were clunky and square, but their weapons were obvious. Glowing energy chainsaws spun on the end of their arms.

"We can't defeat those!" Zarin shouted.

The robots came nearer, making quick work of the distance. Jules closed her eyes and struggled to create a sphere around the three of them. It faltered and died.

Just when she was about to start running, the dirt erupted, sending their opponents into a hole. People emerged from an invisible barrier, rods in their arms, makeshift guns aimed at the bots.

"For the Backyard!" someone shouted, rushing the line of enemies.

The robots didn't stand a chance against the twenty assailants, and soon they were sparking in pieces on the ground.

Someone approached them, and Jules went ahead, keeping Suma and Zarin behind her. The man removed a cowl and stared at her with white eyes. Another guy the same size followed, and the duo watched her cautiously. "Who are you?"

"My name is Jules Parker," she said.

"No." A woman flipped her goggles off and wiped her soot-stained face. "*The* Jules Parker?"

Jules couldn't believe it. "Tessa?"

"You know who I am?"

"You were stationed on *Vast*. My father was searching for Shandra Valincins, and you were on the first mission to investigate the sighting of one in the Ishio System."

Tessa's tears ran in clean lines down her cheeks. "How did you remember my name?"

"I felt responsible. I remember the entire crew," she said. "I spent hours staring at the photos…"

"They didn't make it," Tessa told her, and Jules ran over, hugging the woman.

"I'm sorry."

"We should return to the safety of our village," one of

the big guys said.

"Yes, Oran. Why don't you and Erem gather the Cleaners? We can use those parts," Tessa said.

"Have you seen Sarlun?" Suma asked.

Tessa looked at the Shimmal woman like she just noticed Jules had company. "A man that looked like you was here."

Suma wobbled on her feet. "He's dead?"

"No, he escaped the Backyard with the Record Keeper." Tessa barked orders at the rest of her people, and everyone finished loading their carts with mechanical components.

"What do you mean?" Suma sprinted to the woman, reaching for her when the brothers stepped in her way.

"The Stranger left with the robot safeguarding the Record Keeper's work," she said, almost inferring this should make sense to them.

"When…?" Jules asked.

"A couple of days."

"Then we have time to track him."

"He'll be gone. We've kept our eye on the robot, and he's built something capable of jumping," Erem said.

Jules shifted gears. "Have you heard of Reflective Worlds?"

"Like a mirror?" Tessa asked. "No. Why do you ask?"

"There's a chance you're sitting on top of the access point to this planet's core," Jules told her.

The group of three peered at one another. "Why would you want to visit the core?"

"Because, in theory, you can travel to your planet's twin," Suma said, staring at the identical brothers as if they were an omen. "According to our late friend's studies, Regnig predicted the possibility of hundreds of planets linked to their partner, but none had been discovered. Not within his files. Just rumors and stories from various alien races."

"And you think Belash Bazaar has one?" Oran grunted.

"Yes." Jules pointed at Suma's tablet. "Show them."

Suma seemed hesitant to do so, but she powered it on nonetheless, returning to the underground map.

"Incredible," Tessa whispered. "We must find it. We can leave."

"Where do we go?" Erem asked with a heavy voice.

"Any place is better than the Backyard," she suggested.

Erem nodded. "Okay. Bring everyone to the village, brother. We'll escort them."

"Without me?" Oran asked.

"Protect them if the Cleaners return. I have a feeling this girl's mere presence will draw danger." He glanced at Jules.

She almost contradicted him, but it was true. She'd annoyed Tixa enough to send killer bots after her the second she arrived.

The twins clasped each other's forearms. "Be well."

Tessa hefted a weapon—something made from pieces of the Cleaners, if Jules was guessing.

Zarin gestured at the gun. "Can we get some of those?"

Instead, Oran handed her his iron rod. "We can't part with any more."

Zarin hoisted it up. "Heavy."

"All the better for beating a robot with," Tessa muttered. "Where to?"

Suma glanced past the human. "The smokestack."

"Of course." Tessa started walking in that direction.

The rest of their group vanished behind an invisible cloak, where Jules expected their village was hiding. The wind was cold, blowing ashes and smog through the entire area. The Backyard was desolate, depressing, and miserable. She couldn't imagine living here long term. This experience was enough to make her skin crawl and her eyes hurt.

They walked with little comment, and Jules focused on the smokestack while Suma asked questions about her father. Erem seemed to have great respect for the man he called Stranger. "He fought like a demon and gave advice like a leader."

"He *is* a great leader," Suma mumbled.

"What drew him to Belash?"

"I don't know," Suma said.

"He was looking for someone. A woman from Shimmal," Tessa said.

Suma stopped and spun around. "What woman?"

"He didn't say. We brought him to the Record Keeper to verify her presence. Everyone that visited the artist was painted," Tessa told them.

"Had she been there?" Jules asked.

"We let him ask in private. It wasn't our place." Erem kept walking, and they followed to the base of the smokestack. Thick, black pollution flowed from the top in a continuous cloud.

"He wasn't thrown into the Backyard," Suma said. "He wanted to be here. He attempted to murder Tixa, aware he'd fail and be sent to this hellhole. To find a woman from Shimmal?"

"Was he married before your mother?" Zarin asked.

No one spoke of Suma's mom, and Jules knew enough not to ask for details.

"Not that I know of," Suma whispered as they stared up the length of the stack.

"I've seen pictures of Sarlun as a kid. Remember when we were trying to locate the tattoo? There was a girl."

"His sister," Suma said. "She vanished years before I was born."

"He had a sister?" Jules hadn't remembered that.

"Shula had differences with her father, and she went off to explore other opportunities. She was never seen again."

"That's what Sarlun's doing," Jules proclaimed. "He's searching for his sister."

"But why now?" Suma touched the iron and yanked her hand back. "It's burning hot."

"Where's the entry?" Jules studied the ground.

"This way." Suma held the tablet, guiding them to a spot twenty meters ahead. The sooty stones looked identical.

Tessa crouched and struck the rocks with her knuckles. They sounded hollow. "Erem, will you do the honors?"

He removed a sizeable hammer from within his cloak and swung hard, breaking the thin layer of cover. The debris poured into a hole, and Jules grinned when she saw the rungs leading down.

"We found it." Zarin didn't hesitate to climb into the opening. She landed on the bottom a few seconds later. "It's safe. But we have no light."

Jules no longer carried the wand around her neck, but she still had a few tricks up her sleeve. She went next and brought a sliver of her powers through the barrier, leaving her hand glowing green.

Tessa and Erem gawked at her. "The rumors were true," the woman from Earth said.

"Most of them," Jules agreed. "But at the moment, they're muted, so let's hope we don't encounter anything too strenuous."

"Like the Mountain of Refuse worm," Erem whispered.

"Worm?" Suma asked.

"Don't worry about the creature. He doesn't leave

170

home." Tessa motioned toward the next tunnel. "This way?"

Suma centered her tablet. "It's going to be a long trip without your abilities, Jules."

Jules checked the map, seeing the endless tunnels descending into the planet.

"Then we better start now." She took the lead, letting the green sphere light their path.

FIFTEEN

*I*t all happened so fast. My ankle was caught by the vines, my wrist by another, and I was slowly being pulled apart. Thankfully, I had Hugo, because he was there a second later, slicing the vine with a knife from the galley.

He did so quietly, since Morg was literally passed out a few feet from my position on the floor. The plant resisted, but Hugo dragged me clear into the hallway.

The door automatically slid closed, and I lay on my back, clutching the tablet to my chest. Something clacked on the floor a short distance away, and we rushed in the direction we'd come.

Before I rounded the corner, I saw the hint of Alyce's figure in the corridor. We went as quickly as we could, returning through the grates to the lower level to rejoin the cargo bay full of robots.

"That was close." Hugo heaved his breaths.

"No kidding." I scanned the room, finding the mechanical army at ease. None were activated.

"What if they can track the tablet's location? Ping the spot?" Hugo asked.

I handed it to him. "You're better at that kind of thing. Take a look."

"It's in another language…" Hugo stuck his tongue out and removed his translator from his ear. He undid the miniscule panel and cut two wires, connecting them to the

172

back of the device we'd stolen. The words changed on the screen from whatever their speech was, to English.

"How did you…?"

"I have a knack for this stuff," Hugo said. "I'll check for a locator."

As it turned out, there was, and he quickly disarmed it. "We should be in the clear."

A light blinked on. "What's that?"

Hugo grinned as the dot moved through the 3D image of the ship they were traveling in. "That's another tablet. We can anticipate their moves."

"Alyce must have noticed the tablet was missing, and she grabbed another." I craned my neck, trying to see better. "Is she coming this way?"

"No. She's walking to the bridge." Hugo used a different feature, and suddenly, hundreds of blue icons appeared in the cargo hold. "This denotes the robots." The bridge had three of them. "Automated pilots and crew. Pretty cool."

It was impressive that these two beings could operate an entire starship while lounging around, but it made our job easier. With the tablet, we could control the army.

"Can we change courses?" I asked Hugo.

"Don't think so. Not from here. We'd have to be on the bridge. According to this, only the primary controls can alter commands to the ship, and this is a secondary," he told me.

"Makes sense. Would you leave the primary with Morg?" I laughed when Hugo quickly shook his head. "What about the star map?"

Hugo changed programs and touched the screen. "We're nearing the destination."

"I thought we had a week."

"The meeting was in a week, but that doesn't mean

they didn't intend to arrive a couple of days early," Hugo said.

"Where are we?"

"Ratov Two," he read.

"Never heard of it. Have you?"

"Nope."

We had no choice but to wait as the starship decelerated, heading straight for their planetary destination. The vessel had nothing in the way of an escape pod or lander we could trust to take us securely. We checked everything we could on that tablet over the next few hours, and in the end, we were resigned to stay put, hide when the time came, and figure out where to go from there.

The device didn't carry any information about Ratov Two, which implied it was a secret within this organization. They'd gone as far as wiping all specifics from their own databases, making me even more intrigued.

We had no means to view the surroundings outside the vessel, so we stayed in the back corner, opting to climb into empty crates when we were certain the starship no longer moved. I sensed the slightest jolting of the deck, and guessed we'd docked on a space station.

In an hour, I finally heard muffled voices from beyond, and pressed my ear to the interior of the crate.

"…will be thrilled for the support. Come, the Director will see you now."

"Very good." Morg's voice was distinct. "Is she on planet?"

The answer was impossible to discern, and that was all I could determine.

After another few minutes, I risked a peek into the cargo hold. The robots were inactive, and the main doors were closed. "Time to go," I said.

"How can we escape, Dad?" Hugo had the tablet

strapped to his wrist like Alyce had done earlier.

"It might be tough, but we have to leave this vessel."

"If they're bringing it to Shimmal, maybe we stay and fight," he said.

"I appreciate the bravery, but we're talking about two evils. If we're caught by Morg, we're dead. Even if we get to the capital, what are we going to do? Tell Hulope? She'll kill us too."

"Fine. Then we go with your plan." Hugo went quietly, his feet patting on the deck.

The keypad for the exit was big, with alien symbols. He was about to try something when the hatch hissed open. We rushed to the side while two soldiers entered, holding guns.

"This is their big army?" The man spoke in Shimmal squawks.

I told you Morg was an idiot. I couldn't believe that a female Toquil was here with the organization. It showed how widespread their reach was.

"Come on, we'll miss the card game if we delay," the guy said.

I'm happy to take all your credits again. The Toquil's thoughts pressed into my head.

"You're not reading my mind, are you?" the guard asked.

I didn't hear her response as they moved out of range.

We managed to roll through the doors before they were fully sealed. The connecting tube was huge, leading to a lengthy arm of a massive space station. Beyond the glass was Ratov Two, a flourishing planet with immaculate blue waters, and midsized continents littering the globe.

A pair of human guards stood with their backs to us, talking idly.

I glanced at Hugo, him at me, as if we were both

judging whether their uniforms would fit us. I sneaked around the left one, Hugo the right, and we gave them matching choke holds. Within seconds, they were slumped to the deck, and we dragged them to a storeroom, shoving their unconscious bodies in. I unceremoniously removed the man's clothing. They were slightly snug, but I managed.

"Dad, we should put ours on them," Hugo suggested.

"Great idea." Dressing dead weight wasn't an easy task. I found tape to bind their wrists behind their backs, and to cover their mouths.

One of them started coming to, and as much as I wanted to ask him why he'd ever betray the Alliance to work with this organization, I didn't have time for a conversation. So I decked him in the jaw, and he dropped.

Hugo passed me a gun and took the second for himself.

The uniforms had displays on the chest with glowing numbers, and I exited the storeroom with purpose. We strolled through the corridor like we belonged and found the nearest transport section. An assortment of aliens waited, some sleeping, others quietly chatting.

An unfamiliar being barked, and I turned my attention to it. "Sorry, we're new on base and the Director sent for us. Something about an issue with the new dignitaries' visit."

It nodded, loose lips slapping from the action. Its face was lengthy and narrow, eyes gaping in two directions. "Very well. Take the next one," it said in a high-pitched English accent.

"Thank you." No one confronted us when we took the transport. They remained transfixed in position.

"They're wearing something on their eye," Hugo whispered.

I noticed the beam of light reflecting off their pupils.

"Maybe they're linked to a network."

I relaxed when doors closed and we were separated from the group.

"How did we do that, Dad?" Hugo asked.

I shrugged and stared out the sliver of a window as the transport unlatched from the station, lowering to Ratov Two. "Sometimes you only need to pretend you belong."

"My first couple of years at the Academy were like that," he said.

"Really?"

"I was your son. The kid brother of their great Jules Parker, the prodigy. So yeah, I had to pretend to fit in, even if I didn't."

"And now?"

Hugo rested an arm on the back of his chair. "I do belong."

"I'm sorry I dragged you into this," I said.

"Dragged? I love having these adventures with you, Dad." Hugo leaned forward as the transport lurched into atmosphere. "Who knows how many more we'll have?"

"Because I'm getting old?" I cocked my head, and he smirked.

"No, because Mom is going to kill you when we make it home." Hugo didn't laugh at his comment, and he was probably right.

"But we've learned that the Reflective Worlds are real. If we can get to the alternate Earth from the core, this could be huge." I hadn't really contemplated the ramifications of such a discovery, but I assumed we were the first people in our Alliance to experience the links.

"Imagine the unspoiled resources," Hugo murmured.

"Spoken like a true capitalist. We can't go into this venture thinking about plunder, Hugo."

"But Rivo said—"

"She's in it for the money, and I don't blame her. Alnod Industries is the Alliance's biggest supporter, and without their income, we wouldn't have the Institute or half our fleet, but even Rivo wouldn't desecrate a planet for their water or ores."

"Yeah, she'd give the locals a cut," Hugo joked.

"That's Rivo for you." The transport landed on the surface, and the door automatically opened. I checked the gun, seeing if there was anything proprietary about it. I didn't see a safety or biogenetic trigger lock, and placed it in the hip holster from the uniform I'd stolen.

No one greeted us. Another of the strange aliens we'd encountered up top was present, but it was in a discussion with itself. I saw the gleam of light in its black eye, and I figured they were having a conversation online.

Ships hovered in the sky, and I cast my gaze over the city. It was spectacular. Everything was the exact same color—an off-white—or maybe that was a result of the filter from the gray-blue star that hung low in the horizon.

Drones floated by, throwing beams onto the streets. They continued without slowing, but my heart raced in my chest. Were they searching for the stowaways?

"Dad, chill. I don't think anyone realizes we exist," Hugo said.

"But we escaped our cells before sneaking on board. Someone must be looking for us," I suggested.

"Maybe not. I think the locals from Pestria were working for this organization. If you encountered two people and lost them, would you tell the boss?"

"Good point." I stepped into the blackening evening, seeing the sun lower in the distance. Night was upon us. I preferred the cover of darkness, rather than the full light of day. It made skulking, as Sergo would call it, much simpler.

"You two!" A robot appeared, thrusters in his feet setting him to the concrete alley.

I stepped in front of Hugo.

"Here for the meeting?" he asked in a monotone male voice.

"Yes. We were called by the Director…"

"This way." The robot spun on his metallic heel and marched us down the street to a floating cart that looked like it should have golf clubs strapped to its rear.

"Thank you," I said, sliding into the front seat. There were no controls. Hugo hopped in beside me.

"Take these." He passed us tiny discs, and when I hesitated, he gave further instructions. "Put it on your collar."

"You're not coming?" Hugo asked the bot, and didn't get a reply. The robot kicked his thrusters on again, and flew off while the cart shuttled us toward the tallest building in the city. "What do you think this is for?"

I clipped the disc to my collar as instructed. "A security pass?"

"Dad, they weren't wrong about you," Hugo muttered.

"And what did they say?"

"It's clear you have a four-leaf clover somewhere."

"Why do you think that?" I had an inkling.

"Because anyone else would be dead on the street, but Dean Parker is invited to the very meeting we're trying to infiltrate, and they give you a pass for it. You're the universe's luckiest man!"

I thought about my wife at home, and my two determined children, and grinned at him. "You're right. I am."

"Dad, don't be so cheesy."

The cart decelerated, stopping at the entrance of the skyscraper. Four Keppe soldiers lingered at the doors, two male, two female, and a drone scanned us from the awning. They awaited the results and stepped aside.

"We're new here. Which floor do we go to?" I asked the nearest in their own tongue. He seemed surprised by that.

"The highest level. The Director is starting soon. You two will be stationed inside."

"Why the last-minute detail?" I pried.

"The Director has requested extra security." He leaned closer. "Between us, there's something going on within the organization. She's been on edge lately. Be discreet, and if Morg Ashr causes any trouble, be ready to defend her with your lives." The Keppe soldier glanced at Hugo, who nodded his understanding.

"Thanks. Have a good night," I said, and we entered the foyer. "Guess I am the luckiest man in the universe."

———

Mettle's engine room thrummed with power, the tubes filling with energy. "There we go." Sarlun opened his mouth, appraising their tireless work.

"You really did help build these, didn't you?" Gera asked with a buzz.

"Yes." Sarlun wiped his hands on a rag. "They have more issues, but the repairs are simple."

"That was simple? It took a full day," Cricket complained.

"But we got it done. We don't patch and play in the Alliance, Cricket," Derek Boggs said as he entered Engineering. "Very good work, Sarlun. You're already an asset to the team."

"Wait until you're home," Sarlun said. "You'll love the wormhole generators, and the newest warships."

"Warships?"

"They're larger, capable of carrying hundreds of soldiers and dozens of fighters," Sarlun told him.

Derek Boggs looked confused at this. "Sarlun, I thought the Alliance was focused on exploration."

Sarlun was taken aback, but tried not to show it. Commander Gera stared at him, while other crew members circled their group within Engineering. Cricket had the slightest of smirks.

"We are, but so much has happened in the past decade, Captain. We face new threats at every turn, and it was necessary to shift focus from exploring to defending. With a flood of new Alliance members, we're spread thin. We've been relying on each planet to have their own fleet, but with that comes logistical issues, and uncertified training. The Alliance needed to become more congruent, to train recruits at one facility, and to integrate each race. You should see the Institute. We're—"

Derek Boggs crossed his arms. "I appreciate the sentiment, I do."

"But?" Sarlun waited for the next sentence.

"But that wasn't what I signed up for. Since I was a kid, I dreamed of the stars. Then the Event transpired, and everything changed. It was no longer a dream, but a reality. We weren't alone after all. I worked tirelessly to be a human captain of *Mettle*, even if people like Gera deserved it more."

"Not a chance," his first officer said with a smile.

"I don't want to be part of a war machine," he finished.

"You're missing the point. We haven't changed, Captain. The Alliance is all about expansion, sharing of ideas, and prospering as a group, but with that comes challenges. The Parkers want to ensure we're never threatened beyond what we can protect."

"The Parkers... Did Dean become the president of the

Alliance?"

Sarlun couldn't say, since he'd been gone by then. "I haven't been home in a while."

"I'll decide when I see our new situation."

Sarlun understood Derek's lust for adventure, because it was the same zest he had felt for years while searching the portals for undisclosed planets. "There's another option."

"What's that?" Derek Boggs led him from Engineering, and Cricket followed, with Gera behind them.

"The Gatekeepers," he said.

"That Academy on Haven. I thought that was for kids," Boggs told him.

"It's anything but. The Gatekeepers are an ancient organization, and only now are they beginning to flourish. We have an opportunity to develop rapidly. The Crystal Map has expanded as well, giving us countless new worlds to seek out. They're always recruiting, and someone with your… interest in the subject would do well."

Derek smiled as they lifted to the top deck. "I'll think about it. But in the meantime, I have a ship to captain." They walked onto the bridge, and he sat in his captain's chair, with Gera next to him.

Sarlun approached Herm at the console. "Hello, Sarlun," the robot said. "And Cricket. I trust the job went well."

"Yes."

"Paint anyone while we were away?" Cricket asked him.

"As a matter of fact, I did."

"Jeez, I was kidding."

"Set course for Ratov Two," Boggs ordered.

"Sir, if I may interject," Herm said.

"Go ahead."

Herm strode to the middle of the bridge. "If I recall, they were building a city on Ratov, as well as a space station. It would be in our best interest to arrive some distance from the planet itself."

"How far?"

"There's a planet nearby. Habitable. Archaic. I'd suggest that would be a good starting point," Herm said.

Captain Boggs glanced at Sarlun, as if seeking his approval. Sarlun saw no reason to object.

"Very well. Please plug in the details, Herm. That's where we're going," Boggs said.

Sarlun watched as the stars sped by in the viewscreen, and checked the estimated time of arrival. Even with their modifications to the ship's engine, which doubled the potential speed, it was almost three days away.

They waited to confirm the engine was running at full capacity, and when Derek was confident they weren't at risk, he waved Sarlun into his office. "Tell me more about these Gatekeepers."

"It would be my pleasure." Sarlun joined him, eager to share his life's work.

SIXTEEN

*T*he trek down was an awful experience for everyone. Jules wiped her nose, leaving a black streak on her arm. She'd probably made it worse. She'd been in the Backyard for less than a day, and yearned for a shower to cleanse herself from its filth.

The tunnels continued lower, like mineshafts from the early nineteen hundreds. Jules recalled visiting one near their home on Earth, and how excited Papa had been to show her something from his childhood. His own father had taken him on the tour, claiming that a distant ancestor had worked the coal mine at the turn of the century.

Now they'd have drones and robots for these kinds of tasks, and Jules could hardly imagine relegating people to do that kind of dirty work. It was awful.

Zarin seemed the most affected by their journey, her face twitchy, her posture rigid. "You okay?" Jules finally asked her.

"I don't like confined spaces," she admitted.

"We've been in transports and stuff together. Why now?"

"We're underground. So much terrain above us. I …"

"What is it?"

"There's a reason I ran away. My people were forced into bunkers during the Kava wars. I spent days at a time, sometimes weeks crammed into a box, hoping the Kava didn't destroy us, collapsing the ceiling above."

"I'm sorry," Jules said. She didn't know much about Zarin or her people, but the Kava sounded ruthless. "What happened?"

"I refused to go in, and my parents left me on the surface. They didn't want to, but the guards shoved my father while he reached for me. Their last few hours were spent worrying about me," she whimpered. Zarin's raccoon face was filthy, her white eyes damp. "The Kava blew the city up while I hid on one of their ships. I was small and snuck into a barrel. That's how I eventually got to Udoon. They were bringing stolen gear from my world."

"That's why I've never seen your kind," Jules whispered.

"I'm the last, as far as I know," she said. "Except Bash."

Jules stopped and hugged the girl. She resisted at first, but let herself relax into it. "You can find a new home. You don't have to be alone anymore."

Zarin recovered, brushing the embrace off. "I've done fine on my own." She peered around the cramped tunnels. "But thanks."

Erem halted ahead. "I hear something."

Jules listened as a shuffling sound carried from a short distance. Her light was still glowing, and she extinguished it, accidentally bumping into Suma as she squeezed to the head of their group. Her powers were back. She could sense them trickling through her body, bursting to escape. Jules released the valve and flushed with the energy of a god.

Her agitation at their situation eased, her muscles no longer ached, and her eyesight sharpened to that of a hawk. Jules raised the protective sphere for all five of them.

The first Feral trudged into the tunnel, pushing a

wheelbarrow filled with slick black chunks of rock. The smell was atrocious. The locals were skin and bones, their eyes practically hanging from their sockets. More of them traveled between two rooms, entering with a full cart, leaving with it empty.

"This must be where the smoke comes from," Tessa whispered.

One of the Feral crashed into another with the wheelbarrow, and they were instantly at each other's throats. Both bodies lay on the ground after a quick but brutal attack, and three Feral came, dumping their friends into the carts and rolling them into the second room.

"They burn them," Erem said with disgust.

"They're abominations. I'd be doing them a favor if I end their lives," Jules muttered.

She must have spoken too loudly, because they flooded the tunnel like zombies from one of Papa's old videos. Jules didn't panic. Her shield would hold.

The first crashed into the barrier, then the next, until a heap of them began to pile up. Instead of refocusing their assault on the newcomers, they fought themselves. Jules closed her eyes and turned to her friends, not willing to watch the horrific event.

When the movement ceased, Jules transported her allies to the opposite side. The adjacent room appeared to be empty when they reached it.

The room was a huge cavern, with a burning hot fire stoked a hundred meters from the entrance. A slight smoke lingered on the ceiling, but mostly it vented up with the hole in the rock. More of the carts were inside, toppled over. She grabbed an oily rock and tossed it into the flames. It instantly caught and was quickly nothing but a pile of ash, which blew upwards with the draft.

"This is why we live in squalor. Who would ever cause

pollution this bad?" Erem asked.

"Tixa must have a reason." Jules tried to figure out the best way to stop this. "You need to keep going."

"Without you?" Suma asked.

"I'll collapse the tunnels, but you have to get to safety first." Jules headed to the second room, where stacks of slick rocks were piled in giant heaps. "We won't allow them to continue this practice."

"But my brother," Erem said. "If you close everything, we'll be separated."

Jules pointed in the direction they'd come. "That's your choice, but make it quickly."

Erem glanced at the exit, then to Tessa. "I'll stay. Are you sure the core is the answer?"

"If we locate the core, and there's no gateway to the Reflective World, I can get us to the surface." Jules smiled at him, and he returned the gesture.

"Okay." Erem hurried from the cavern, and Suma stopped.

"We'll need light." Suma grabbed a wooden stick and wrapped a piece of clothing from a dead Feral around the tip. Jules shot a current at it, igniting the oil. It flashed on, giving her a powerful torch.

"They don't deserve this punishment," she told Jules before catching up to the others.

The caverns were equal in size, with a huge wall between them. Jules returned to the corridor and concentrated on that load-bearing wall. It began to crumble, the middle section extruding before the top collapsed inward. The flames engulfed the space, settling on the heaps of stone. The fire erupted like a bomb, and Jules was instantly covered by boulders and chunks of dirt. But her sphere held, and after another few detonations, the area calmed.

The fire would diminish eventually, the vent to the

surface and smokestack no longer viable. But her path up was damaged beyond repair.

Jules vibrated her shield, increasing the speed, and passed through the rubble like a ghostly apparition, haunting the grounds below the Backyard.

———————

*W*e were ushered into the room right before the meeting began, with a Shimmal man wiggling his snout in agitation at our tardiness. "Stand there. Do not interact, and for the love of the Creator, don't speak."

I nodded, and Hugo did too, expressing our comprehension nonverbally. The guy stared at us for a second, and I was worried he might recognize me, but he sighed and returned to the table, straightening a few things before scurrying from the space.

It was extravagant in its simplicity. A single flowing screen was anchored on the wall, showcasing images of the stars above Ratov Two. I wondered if it was a live feed from an orbiting satellite. So far, there were only us and a couple of other guards: a pair of unfamiliar beings with bigger guns.

Hugo still had the tablet hidden beneath his uniform.

The table was curved and white, the material faintly glowing. There were ten chairs, and a larger screen at the far end where a chair might normally have sat.

I didn't know what we were about to witness, but I felt the energy within the room. Whatever was happening was important to these people. We had little to go by, only that they were a secret organization with a lot of power and influence. And that one faction, led by Morg, was aiming to attack Shimmal.

I expected to learn a lot more in the coming minutes.

The doors opened, and in walked Morg and Alyce, accompanied by their serving robot. She had another tablet on her wrist, and she glanced around cautiously before moving to the table. "We're the first to arrive?"

"Isn't that what we planned? A private moment before the hoopla?" Morg dropped into the chair at the head of the table. It faced the screen twenty feet away.

"Shouldn't we wait?"

"You're too worried all the time, Alyce. I'm Morg Ashr, not some newbie recruit stepping on the Director's toes. She'll see our position and side with us. I guarantee it."

Alyce didn't look as confident. She appeared eager to argue with him, but stopped herself. "I'm sure she's listening right now." The comment was quiet, but I still heard it from my position.

A series of people strolled in, each acting wealthier than the last. I clenched when I saw a Kraski. I thought they were extinct. An Inlorian came behind him; her dress was long and flowing, and she wore sparkly earrings that seemed to hinder her movements. I was surprised to see one of their kind. They were historically diligent with being loyal to their own kind, and Extel wasn't a pushover. If he sensed deception, he'd lock her up in a millisecond.

Morg stood. "What is the meaning of this?"

"We were called in by the Director," the Kraski said.

"When did you get word, Karka?" Alyce asked him.

Karka? Had I heard that name before? I saw the symbol on his shirt. Five circles and the lightning bolt.

"A day prior. She demanded we attend this meeting, and suggested we'd lose shares in the organization if we objected," Karka said.

"Such nerve." The Inlorian woman was waiting near a

chair. "Is someone going to seat me?"

Alyce rolled her eyes and used the controls to order the robot to do so. He stomped over, sliding the chair back three feet.

"Does anyone know why we've been beckoned?" a Padlog grasshopper asked. For a second I thought it was the Supreme, but this one was much younger.

"No idea why she has such urgency," Karka said.

"How's PlevaCorp doing?" Morg asked with disdain.

PlevaCorp? Hugo and I shared a glance. That was a name I hated to hear any time, especially when in the center of a hornet's nest. He was like the bogeyman. Say 'Lom of Pleva' three times with the lights off, and he might appear from beyond the grave.

"You know it's not called that now. Those heathens at Alnod Industries tanked our value after the boss man bailed. Can you imagine? One-tenth of a credit? I should have made sure Bazarn was destroyed in that attack years ago."

"Garo is dead. Shouldn't that be revenge enough?" a human asked. I hadn't even noticed him before. His hair was black with gray streaks, his eyes green. I thought he looked familiar.

Karka frowned at the man. "You wish, Sully."

I tried not to stare at the guy they called Sully, but I failed, and our eyes locked.

Sully stood and crossed the room. "Do I know you?"

I shook my head. "No, sir."

"How did you get here?" he asked.

"Well… we took the transport," I said with a smile.

The others laughed. "Disrespect from the help. Isn't that why you went to jail in the first place, Sully?"

I knew exactly who this man was. Scott O'Sullivan, tech mogul. He'd been on the cutting edge of the internet's conception, raking in billions during the dot.com bubble. He created dozens of companies and sold them to corporations at a bloated evaluation. He'd held on to one specifically, an online community unlike any other, quickly shut down due to ethical barriers involving genetic coding and brain mapping. Long story short, he was trying to put his own brain into a computer, way before that was mainstream.

He'd assaulted his entire team when he'd been forced to close, and had ended up serving a life sentence. But the Event happened only two years later, and when the dust settled, things had changed. Pardons were made for a select group, and Sully had been one of those to go free. His flush bank account might have played a part.

"I asked you a question." Sully poked me in the chest. He'd obviously taken his own life extenders, because he didn't look a day over forty-five, though he should have been closer to eighty.

"We were recruited from Haven," Hugo answered for me.

Sully turned his attention on my son and grinned. "Aren't you a little young to be working for the organization?"

"Eighteen and proud to serve."

"Haven? That dump? No wonder you left. Tell me about your recruiting process."

"What are you doing, Sully?" Alyce asked. "Everyone on Ratov Two has been vetted. Numerous times." She used her tablet and scanned the discs on our collars. "They've passed. Now will you have a drink and join our civilized conversation?"

Sully sneered and returned to the table. The robot served them, and I was amused to see he knew each of their favorites without being prompted. Sully downed his beverage and walked to the bar, bringing the bottle with him.

"What about you, Morg?" the grasshopper asked. He rubbed his hands together. "Anything revolutionary to report?"

Morg grumbled and looked at his glass. "Been quiet. The usual chaos on my end. The Black Hole requires a lot of focus, so we've been head down, taking our cut of every lowbrow transaction in the universe."

"I thought that was Alyce's job," Karka said.

"It is…"

"Why she lets Morg attend these meetings is beyond me," the Inlorian said. "Alyce is clearly running the show."

"Enough!" Morg slammed a palm on the table, making Hugo jump. "I'm an asset. Without the Black Hole, none of you would be wealthy, and your power would be consigned to whatever crappy Ponzi scheme you could think up." He stared at the Inlor woman. "Before we met, you were wiping Inlorian bars and inspecting them for flaws. Now you're worth more than any other on your planet. Because of me!"

She stared at the table.

"And you, Sully. Did you really think you could have pulled off the android program without my expertise?"

Sully's hand twitched, and I saw a spark. "Fine. I'll give you that."

He was an android. I'd never seen something so advanced. He looked entirely real.

"We get it," Karka said.

But Morg wasn't done. "How could I forget Karka? Poor middle management Karka, left with all the responsibility when his boss killed the rest of the Kraski. He should have done us all a favor and ended your pitiful life as well. Do you remember how I bailed you out, hiding you for five years before regaining control of your company?"

"I recall." Karka drummed his fingers. "But I've also bailed you out since then, isn't that so?"

Morg smiled at him.

"We could accomplish more if we stopped bickering like children," Alyce said. "We need a united front."

"Against whom, precisely?" Sully asked.

"The Alliance," Alyce whispered.

"And how exactly do we take down the largest organized collective to grace our universe in millennia? They have Deities on their side, for the love of God," Sully said.

"Do you truly believe those rumors?" Morg asked him.

"Yes. And what about the Recaster, or the Creator, and that kid of Dean Parker's... she can snap her finger and break your neck. All of ours at the same time. I appreciate what you're suggesting, but why move out of the shadows and into the light? Why risk everything we've done in secret to destroy some Alliance?" Sully asked, checking most of the boxes in my own train of thought.

I silently warned Hugo to stay still.

"You speak of things that aren't possible, Sully. I knew you were delusional, but Recasters? Gods? Deities? What next? That girl... Jules Parker is nothing but a figurehead. An illusion drafted up by the skilled tech department at Al-nod Industries," Morg said.

I exhaled in relief. The more they believed Jules wasn't dangerous to them, the safer she'd be. "We could have her dead within days, remember," Alyce whispered.

My blood turned cold.

"One call on the Black Hole, and we'd have the galaxy's best and strongest chasing her down. Her head would be delivered in a box, if that's what you wanted. We only need to post the job."

"Is that what we've resorted to?" Karka asked.

Sully laughed, taking another drink. "Coming from a Kraski, that's pretty amusing. Wasn't it your people who single-handedly tried to annihilate the human race?"

"It was… but under Lom's orders."

"Then follow my orders, Kraski. Shimmal will be destroyed," Morg said.

"But Shimmal isn't even part of the Alliance," the Inlorian said. "Why bother?"

Alyce grinned and played a projection from her tablet. "Because everyone will assume that the Alliance did it."

An image of three warships flying through space near a moon appeared above the table.

"Are those 3D renderings?" Sully asked.

"No. These are real warships, built on the Alliance's exact specifications." Alyce steepled her fingers.

"How?"

"We own the Black Hole, Sully. We can do anything. Do you know how easy it was to find these blueprints? Their security was impressive, but a simple bribe to the right person took care of that," Alyce said.

It required all my strength not to ask who the rat was.

"Shimmal will have defenses. It won't work," Karka told her.

"That's why we have the robots ready to hit the ground," Morg finished.

The gathered seemed impressed. "Okay. Say we support this decision. What benefit do we have moving forward with the Alliance in shambles?"

Morg rose and put his hands behind his back as he walked to the head of the table. "We take over."

"What about the president?" Sully asked.

Morg smiled. "We arrest Mary, Dean, and their daughter Jules for war crimes. We place them in their own Traro Prison, in the highest security possible."

I backed up a step, subconsciously reacting to their plan. Hugo nudged me and I wiped my brow, giving him a supportive nod.

"And the girl? If she has these powers…" The Inlorian didn't appear sold on this course of action.

"I've read a few theories on the Black Hole. There are ways to contain her. We'll test them all."

If she doesn't kill you first, I thought.

"You seek to replace the Parkers. This will never work," Sully said. "They're treasured. No one will—"

Morg clapped his hands once, and the door opened. "I told you not to doubt me."

Mary walked in, wearing a white uniform, the Alliance logo on the sleeve, and she waved at the gathered group. "Hi, I'm Mary Parker."

SEVENTEEN

*J*ules caught up to the others in short order, and they didn't seem overly excited to be continuing down the dark tunnels. "Sorry about the delay. I said I'd keep you safe, and I meant it," she told Tessa and Erem.

"We should have investigated the stack and destroyed it ourselves," Erem said.

Tessa put a hand on his arm. "We've been distracted with trying to survive, Erem. And finding fresh drinking water. Food. It's not like we have the luxury of explosives at our disposal."

"Still…"

"Tell you guys what. Let's speed this process up now that my abilities have returned." Jules pushed the sphere around them, lifting everyone's feet from the dirty ground. "Hold on to something. This will be quick."

Suma clutched Zarin as Jules rounded the corners, flying them lower and lower. She adjusted the sphere's pressure as they descended rapidly, not wanting anyone to rupture an eardrum. She made quick work of the distance, and the heat intensified as they approached the core.

When she stopped, they were all drenched in sweat, their clothing soaked through. Erem's face was almost devoid of soot, and he rubbed his eyes. "That was kind of fun."

"When's the last time we could say that?" Tessa

laughed.

"Years, Tessa. Years."

The tunnels ended, and Jules took the lead. There was a hole, and an incredible heat. She left them within the shield, because of the potential radiation emitting from the area.

Jules lowered her arm into the opening, her fingertips glowing bright green, and she saw a shimmer of light about ten meters down. "Erem, give me your iron rod."

He brought it up and stared at the inanimate object. "I've had this for ages."

"It's safe with me."

He shrugged and passed it to her. The crude weapon was heavier than it looked. She wrapped a tendril of energy around it and let it go, lowering the rod to the shimmer. It vanished.

"It's true," Suma muttered. "There are Reflective Worlds."

"And we've discovered one," Jules replied. She tugged on the tendril, and the rod returned with her tether. "Here you go."

Erem took it, sliding it into his belt.

"Now what?" Zarin asked.

"We go to Belash Bazaar's twin planet," Jules said.

Tessa seemed uneasy with the idea. "Our people…"

Jules set her palms on the woman's shoulders. "Tessa, we won't forget to help them. But for now, we have to explore this."

"What about my father?" Suma's eyes were big.

"We can still follow his trail after. Let's check where this goes; then we deal with Tixa and the Backyard, and find out where the ship went with Sarlun."

"Okay." Suma peered into the opening. "I have to admit, I am intrigued by the concept."

"Someone built the Backyard on top of this tunnel system for a reason," Tessa said. "They wanted it hidden."

"But that doesn't mean Tixa is even aware of its existence. I have a feeling he doesn't have a clue," Erem added.

Jules' body tingled with excitement. She was about to travel through a… what was this? A gateway? "Are we ready?"

Zarin nodded, and everyone else shuffled to the edge of the hole.

Jules eased them toward the gleaming gateway.

She couldn't tell up from down as they passed through, like they were coming to the new world from the ceiling. Jules grew dizzy, but corrected the sphere, rotating them around.

The room was finished nicely, with white walls, gray flooring and windows on the right edge. "I wasn't expecting this," Jules said. They'd escaped ruddy mine shafts to be transported somewhere with class and design.

A tall door was closed ten feet away, and Jules jumped in front of her friends when it began to swing open. A robot strode closer, cobwebs clinging to his face and shoulders. A multi-legged insect scurried over his torso and hopped off, rushing to the exit.

"Hello," Jules said.

The robot's eyes brightened, and he spoke in an unfamiliar language. "Hello," he finally replied in English.

"Where are we?" Suma asked him.

"You are visiting Esteron," he told her.

"Esteron? How long have you been here?" Jules asked, figuring the robot had been in sleep mode, waiting for someone to travel through the Reflective World's link.

"I have been off for…" His arms twitched. "Nine hundred and twenty-four of your years."

Zarin whistled. "How does he speak your language?"

"There is a network. Even when powered down, we are constantly updating our databases. It's our design."

"Who created you?" Suma reached for him, and he allowed her to prod at a control panel.

"Why, the Gatekeepers did. Do you remember them?"

Jules coughed and cleared her throat. "Did you say the Gatekeepers?"

"Yes. The Reflective Worlds required protection, since they were sought after by the Revolution. The Gatekeepers put us in charge of defending the worlds with Links."

"What's your name?" Suma whispered.

"I am A-0002." His shoulders were pointed, his head elongated behind him.

"A-Two, then," Jules said. "Does anyone know you're here?"

His eyes dimmed. "The others are in place. It appears only seventy-nine percent of the Gatekeepers' robotics team are still operational. Our mechanics were intended to last long term, but a thousand years of disuse is pushing our design limitations." Something sparked on his elbow.

"I can repair this," Suma said. "Do you have tools?"

A-Two nodded, leading them from the room and into a larger space. It was covered in cobwebs, but a soft light made it feel warm. "I should not allow modifications."

"Don't worry. We're Gatekeepers too," Suma said, pointing at Jules. "My father is in charge of the entire network."

"Your father is Darius Neema?"

The name wasn't familiar to Jules.

Suma didn't miss a beat. "Yes. I am Suma Neema," she lied.

"Then please make the alterations. I would appreciate it." A-Two found a toolbox, and Suma opened his panel with a screwdriver.

Erem and Tessa wandered the room, leaving into the halls beyond, but Zarin stayed close to Jules. The young woman was used to being indoors working on a computer, not exploring ancient portals.

"Can you tell us about the Crystal Map and the Shandra?" Jules asked A-Two.

"The Shandra are off-limits. There are beings within: the Theos. Darius doesn't wish to disrupt them," A-Two said.

"Someone knew the Theos were trapped in the crystals," Suma said. "Incredible."

Papa had freed their souls after they hid within the Shandras to balance the universe once the Iskios had been displaced. He'd also thrown the Vortex of destruction into another dimension with a Shifter given to him by the late Garo Alnod. Thinking about all her father had done before she was born made Jules miss Papa. He was probably at home with the pup, reading a book and drinking a tea. It was so peaceful at the new house she'd gifted them near Terran One on New Spero.

The fact that Sarlun had ordered his goons to kill Dean and Mary lingered in her mind, but none of it had truly been Sarlun's fault. His father owed the price to Ranul, and when he'd died, the curse passed to Sarlun. Now it was up to Jules to bring Sarlun back in one piece and offer forgiveness.

"If you weren't into the Shandra, then where did the Gatekeepers explore?" Jules snapped out of her thoughts.

"We did not explore. We are Gatekeepers. We keep these Gates safe," A-Two said.

"Makes sense." Another circuit sparked, and Suma focused on the joint, repairing the soldering job.

Zarin finally broke her silence. "Does anyone live here? On Esteron?"

"Allow me to check…" A-Two went dark, and a light on his chest blinked. "There seems to be a solitary power center. The energy given off suggests an extremely potent network hub. I didn't imagine such a thing could exist. I sense tendrils leading in every direction, implying a network reach of millions of light years."

"Like the Black Hole?" Jules asked Zarin.

"Maybe. But why would it be here?"

"Let's find out." Suma closed the panel. "How's that?"

A-Two flexed his arms and dipped his knees, standing tall again. "Much better."

Suma dusted off the remaining cobwebs. "How long has it been since you were on the surface?"

"Only when I was brought here with Darius," A-Two said.

"Can you show us around?" Suma suggested.

"I should not leave my post."

"There's nothing to guard," Jules said. "If it makes you feel any better, I'll seal the door…"

"You don't need to do that." A-Two pressed a button, and the entrance to the Link slammed shut right when Tessa and Erem returned. "I will come. Let's start with the surface."

Jules was prepared for another session through a convoluted tunnel system, but realized they didn't have to when A-Two led them down the hall to an elevator.

Suma peered at it. "Is it operational?"

"I do not know."

Jules stepped inside and motioned for the others to proceed. Instead of bothering with electronics, she left it off, and used her sphere to raise the box toward the surface. She wasn't about to risk anyone's lives on a thousand-year-old elevator.

So many revelations had been brought to light. The

origin of the Gatekeepers, the confirmation of the Reflective Worlds, and a piece of history with this robot. Darius Neema was a mystery worth solving.

Jules kept rising, wondering what else they'd discover on Esteron.

I bit my tongue when Mary entered the meeting, her steps sure and confident.

"Now what in the galaxy is happening?" Karka demanded.

"Let me introduce my latest work," Sully said. "I was curious why Morg asked me to do this, and now I understand. It's one thing to blame the Parkers, and another to have actual footage of them on board their own warship issuing orders to destroy Shimmal."

"She's a robot?" Dasoli Six, the Inlorian woman, asked.

Mary stood with a frozen smile on her face. It looked just like her, so close that I'd been fooled for a second. "I prefer to be thought of as an android."

Sully smirked from his seat and poured another drink.

"Where are Dean and Jules?" Alyce asked.

"Still working on them," Sully said.

I was grateful for that. I tried to imagine the fallout if a Dean Parker android entered the room and everyone saw two of us.

"We wanted to perfect the president first, but we'll need to ensure the rest of the family is included in the charges," Morg informed them.

"Even the son?" Dasoli Six asked.

"The son? I thought they just had the girl," Karka exclaimed.

"Keep up, would you? I'm not worried about him. He's harmless."

Hugo's jaw clenched, but he remained stoic.

Sully sipped from his glass. "Mary, why don't you tell the group what we've discussed?"

I watched as this replica of my wife stalked to the head of the table, hands set on her hips like I'd seen so many times. I wondered if they'd observed her to perfect the mannerisms. It was unsettling.

"This is Mary Parker, the president of the Alliance of Worlds, and I order you to lower your shields! If you do not concede Hulope to me now, I will destroy Shimmal and everyone on it." She took a break, winking at Sully. "Very well. I see you're not taking my threat seriously. Fire."

The organization members clapped for her performance. "Excellent job," Morg said.

"You've started without me," a voice said, emanating from a speaker on the screen at the far end of the table. Everyone had been so distracted by the android that no one, including me, had noticed the display light up.

"Director, we apologize for our…" Morg was standing, and I heard the tremor in his voice. She was the true power of this organization.

The woman was from Shimmal: older, with lines around her eyes and a sense of determination. Her snout twitched for a second, reminding me of Sarlun when he was getting impatient. "Morg, I knew you'd try to pull something like this, but did you really think I'd allow you to destroy my home?"

Morg sat, grumbling under his breath.

But it was Alyce that responded. "Director, we have a robust plan."

"And what do you hope to gain by bringing a fleet to

Shimmal?" the director asked.

"We'll frame the Parkers and swoop in to defend your people," Alyce told her. That was clearly a shift in the original proposal I'd overheard earlier.

"I see. And who will be named president at the head of the Alliance?"

The group all looked at Morg, then at Alyce. "She will," Sully said.

"Alyce?" The Director laughed, the sound throaty and coarse. "We formed the organization to remain hidden. To profit from discreet transactions, to grow our power without anyone ever knowing we exist. And now you choose to reveal yourselves for the sake of... what? A title? Leading a bunch of planets who weren't strong enough on their own to survive, so they had to bind together? The Alliance isn't as stable as you all think. They're tied with twine, and one swipe of a blade will shatter everything. But that wouldn't be good for our business."

"We can control—" Alyce stopped when the Director frowned.

"We already control things. You realize that every credit the partners send to their precious president for the fleet or the Institute is funneled through *my* network? That we take half a percent? And what about you, Dasoli Six? The sheer volume of Inlorian bars we eradicate from the complex security system on Inlor. We could buy a planet with our score each year. No, this goes beyond credits; it's ego, and that's something we do not have within the organization."

I still couldn't believe I was bearing witness to the Black Hole's leadership board firsthand.

"We've prepared for this. I have the ships, the army." Morg gestured at the android. "The replicas."

"You will not use them."

Morg stood his ground. "We will."

The Director laughed, the sound unnerving. "Morg Ashr, are you suggesting mutiny?"

He scanned around the table, and I saw the others supporting his next comment. They could see themselves at the head of the Alliance, reaping the benefits, stripping the funding to the military and exploration budgets, and taking over places like Bazarn Five and the Academies.

"That's what we're saying, sugar plum," Sully said.

"Sugar…" The Shimmali woman grinned. "If you dare do this, I won't stop until you're all trolling the mines on Ospas."

Alyce blinked rapidly before replying. "Then you'd better call ahead and order the shovels." She turned the screen off with the circular tablet on her wrist. "We have to move fast. She'll try to block our exit, but we won't let it happen."

She stared at me. "Is that a problem?"

I pretended I couldn't possibly work against them. "Can we join you? I've always wanted to see those smug Parkers put in their place."

"Can you escort us to the station?" Sully asked.

"Sure thing." I glanced at Hugo, and shrugged when they all turned to run. Even Mary's replica went with them, but a couple of the others held back.

"What are you doing?" Morg asked.

The Padlog and Molarian rushed down the hall. "Dead weight, if you ask me," Sully muttered.

A pair of guards approached, and I recognized them from earlier. Alyce used her tablet, and the serving bot tossed his tray to the floor and began firing.

"Are they…" Hugo leaned over them.

"Just stunned," Alyce said. "It's not their fault they're listening to the Director's orders." She stepped past their bodies.

The elevator descended with us inside, and I was next to Mary, staring at the artificial skin. It was unbelievable.

"We may have overstepped," Alyce whispered.

"Nonsense. The Director has lost her way. She's hiding on that damned Esteron, hoarding the Black Hole servers. It was only a matter of time before we took matters into our own hands," Morg claimed.

"You didn't tell her the real reason we desire the Alliance," Sully said.

"And what's that?" Dasoli Six asked.

Morg peered over his shoulder at me. "Can we trust you two?"

"Yes, sir. One hundred percent," I assured him.

"Dasoli, we require the Crystal Map. They have access to so many worlds, and imagine how wide we can cast the Alliance's net once we're in charge. The Parkers have squandered their opportunity, trying to grow it slowly. They should have poured fuel on the fire instead of waiting around for their chances at expansion. That will be their downfall. We'll erase the memory of the Parkers from the history books and move on with me at the head."

"I thought we agreed on Alyce," Dasoli said.

"That was for the sake of the Director. Plus, she's not interested in the position, is she?" Morg gawked at his second in command.

"No, your Graciousness," she murmured.

"Very good. It's settled." The elevator opened, and twenty of the robot soldiers were present. For a moment, I thought the Director had sent them. Then Alyce brought her finger to the tablet, and they all moved their arms to reveal long guns in place of their hands.

There was no resistance as we marched from the skyscraper, filing onto a large, unmarked transport vessel. It lifted off, and I kept expecting suborbital projectiles to blow us out of the sky. When we passed through the atmosphere toward the space station, I began to relax.

Hugo and I faced each other on the benches, straps locked in place to hold us in the seats as we slowed, latching to the station. They left us on board as the robots marched off. "Hugo, we have to decide."

"To stay or run?" he asked, eyes wide.

"Yes."

"I don't know. We can't let them do this to the Alliance," he said. "I vote we go with them. Try …" He paused when Sully emerged by the exit.

"You guys coming?"

"Just an issue with the strap." I tugged on it, freeing the belt from Hugo's waist. "We can't leave now." I said it so quietly, only Hugo could discern my words.

Once again, we were ushered onto the starship we'd traveled to Ratov Two on and joined the organization elite on the bridge this time, rather than hiding in the cargo hold.

"Incoming trouble," Alyce said.

Morg took the captain's chair, and she narrowed her gaze. "I believe that's my seat."

He huffed and moved to the chair over. "You can have this victory, but I will be the Chancellor of the Alliance. Don't contradict that."

"I won't," she promised. "In the meantime, let's get out of here before the Director's defenders intercept us."

Mary's replica stood with Hugo and me, and I almost laughed at the irony. "Sully, get to work on the other replicants. We've brought your supplies to Deck Three."

Scott O'Sullivan seemed surprised at the news. "You expected the Director to deny your petition?"

"Either way, we needed to be on our way. Finish making Dean and Jules Parker, and bring Mary with you. Her presence annoys me," Morg ordered.

"Setting course for Shimmal. We'll use the wormhole generator when we're in the clear, but given the space debris in the area, I need to wait for a couple of days. Does that work with your timeline, Sully?"

"Yes. I'll have the Parkers prepared for their moment in the spotlight." Sully left with Mary following.

Karka held the back of a robot's seat, staring out the viewscreen. "When do we get the warships?"

"They're already moving for Shimmal. Our timing couldn't be better." Morg stretched his arms and grinned with excitement.

I noticed Hugo still had the circular tablet under his shirt. I was going to ensure nothing bad happened to the people of Shimmal, and that included not letting my family's name's getting wiped through the mud by the likes of these dissenters.

EIGHTEEN

Cricket flipped the cards over, and Sarlun groaned. "Bested again. I'll sit the next few out." He walked toward the viewscreen in the galley, hoping they were close. He'd spent many hours in the past day with Boggs, and really respected him as a man and captain. He'd make a great addition to the Gatekeeper organization if he did decide that being a captain for the Alliance in the modern era didn't suit his goals.

Unger, the Bhlat weapons officer, slammed a fist on the table, nearly cracking it. "You must be cheating."

"I cheat all the time," Cricket admitted. "On my school finals, and on my old boyfriend, but he deserved it. But on my mother's grave, I'm not cheating now."

He squinted and shoved the cards away.

The speaker rang and the captain's voice echoed through the ship. "We have reached our destination. Please arrange yourselves. Crew, prepare the battle stations." An alarm sounded, with a handful of strobing blue lights emerging from the floor.

"You heard the boss," Unger said.

Sarlun noticed Herm was already on the bridge when he arrived. His easel was out, and he was painting Derek Boggs.

"We'll have to complete this later," the captain told the artistic robot.

209

"It's nearly done. I won't be in the way." Herm continued dipping his brush on the palette, adding the finishing touches to his masterpiece.

Sarlun had to admit the robot was the most talented portrait artist he'd ever witnessed, and Shimmal had numerous experts in the space.

Mettle decelerated as they neared the planet, and from the zoomed-in view on the screen, the closest continent was covered in sand. The entire block of land was a rusty orange. Two moons surrounded the place, one so close, he was shocked it didn't interfere with the gravitational pull. Sarlun figured it probably affected more than the tides. The second was some distance back, on a long, looping orbit.

"A pair of vessels recently departed," Gera said, bringing the image on screen.

They were giant, shaped like an arrowhead, and speeding from this planet. "I assume that's Ratov Two?" Sarlun asked, indicating another world on the radar.

Herm didn't glance up from his artwork. "Yes."

"Captain, I suggest we send a lander to the surface, rather than *Mettle*. You've seen firsthand what these people are capable of, and I don't want your crew threatened again," Sarlun said. He felt close to the end of his mission, as if he might find an answer here, or on Ratov Two.

"I agree," Boggs said. He tapped his armchair controls. "Hangar One, prepare a transport for our guest Sarlun to operate."

"I'd like to come," Cricket said. Her own ship was in that very hangar.

"No." Herm stood to appraise his painting. "Sarlun and I must go alone." The way he said it sent shivers down Sarlun's spine.

"Fine, but you'd better come back. I can't get into Alliance space without someone to vouch for me. Not after…" She smiled, patting Sarlun on the shoulder. "Watch out for trouble."

"I intend to." Sarlun stopped at his quarters to grab his cloak. Herm met him in the hangar, and he clutched a rifle.

"This is for you," Herm said.

Sarlun had never seen a finer piece of weaponry. "Will we need to fight?"

"Perhaps."

"Where did you get this?" The metal barrel was etched with waving lines and symbols; the charging port blinked with green lights.

"I created it."

"On our trip here?" Sarlun could hardly believe it.

"When else? Come, Sarlun. We have a mission to complete."

The transport departed from *Mettle* and rushed toward the desert continent. It was peaceful below. A few flocks of birds took flight far above the surface, soaring through the air.

"What is this place?" Sarlun asked.

"Ages ago, a man had a dream."

Sarlun felt the mood shift, and Herm's eyes grew darker. "What kind of man?"

"He was a great visionary, complicated beyond his limited experience. He grew up on a nowhere planet, full of nothing dreams. But he propelled past his mediocrity. The man studied languages, then arts, and eventually found a way to leave his life behind. Once he traveled to another world, he couldn't stop. The Reflective Worlds called to him," Herm said.

Sarlun's muscles bunched at the mention of the Reflective Worlds. The Gatekeepers had been around for centuries, with Sarlun reading every bit of lore from before his own tenure at the head of the group. There were spans between active Gatekeeper organizations, and he'd encountered that term on several occasions.

Sarlun licked his lips when the transport landed on the sand dunes. "Who was he?"

"His name was Darius Neema."

Sarlun scanned his memory banks, but the name meant nothing to him. "And he lived here?"

"At one point. He was a master engineer and built the first of the Gatekeepers with his own two hands." Herm lifted his metal ones, the fingers bending and whirring with the effort.

"Did he… build you?" Sarlun asked, suddenly questioning Herm's previous tale of reaching Belash Bazaar forty years earlier.

"Yes. I apologize for the deceit, but I had to be sure I could trust you, Sarlun. You came to me, seeking your sister, and I wasn't certain if you deserved to be brought to her," Herm told him.

"You…" Sarlun stared at him as the transport's hatch opened, sending hot air from outside into the cabin.

"I have partnered with Shula, in a sense. She's working at rebuilding the Gatekeepers, as they were intended."

Sarlun didn't know what to say, so he didn't speak.

"Darius identified over ninety Reflective Worlds and sent his creations to each core's Link. I was one of them, placed on Belash a thousand years ago. But unlike the others, I grew bored of my station. I wasn't satisfied with lying dormant until the Link was used. I was different. I *am* different."

"You've changed the narrative from when we first met," Sarlun said.

"Another necessary deception."

Sarlun was beginning to understand. This robot had absorbed the consciousness of the old Record Keeper, and who knows who else sat within its circuit boards.

"You've figured it out? I knew you were a smart man, Sarlun," he said.

"You're Darius Neema." Sarlun held the gun, but it was too tight to wield it.

"Darius grew old, as organics do. I had no option. He begged me not to, that it was wrong, but I disagreed. His life would continue with me. I could finish what he started," Herm said.

Sarlun had to understand his motives. "Then why were you biding your time in the Backyard?"

"Shula is the only one with enough power to reactivate my Gatekeepers in their cores. And she made me promise to wait for you there."

Sarlun exited the transport, feeling sand brush against his skin in the wind. He raised his cowl, blocking the assault. "Shula expected me?"

"She anticipated you'd come after her, but didn't think it would take this long. Luckily, I am patient. I killed the Record Keeper, but kept her memories alive. And here we are. I will deliver you to Shula, and she will restore the original Gatekeepers, relinquishing them to me." Herm stood tall in the sun.

Sarlun had no choice but to accept the commentary of the robot in front of him, knowing full well he was an extremely dangerous entity. "Where is Shula?"

Herm pointed toward the horizon, at the large moon that sat like a pale ghost in the distance. "A few miles that way."

"Take me there." Sarlun began walking.

---

*T*he doors opened, and Jules swung her arm at the horde of six-legged creatures swarming their position. The animals were kind of cute, with fuzzy black noses crinkling up as they rushed to the elevator. Until they gnashed their sharp teeth and barraged her shield.

"What are those?" Zarin screamed.

"They were smaller when I last saw them," A-Two said. "A thousand years of evolution will do that."

Jules didn't want to fight anything, so she lifted their group, exiting the ramshackle structure housing the top of the elevator. The creatures followed, but she closed the door, sealing them inside. They began digging through the walls, but Jules transported her group a mile away before landing on the desert sand.

A-Two made a series of beeping noises, and he went rigid. "The founder is here."

"Darius?"

"In a sense. His very first creation. The debut Gatekeeper. A-0000."

"A-Zero?" Jules stared in the distance at a large moon. "What can you tell us about him?"

"Darius was brilliant, but even he admitted to his mistake when building A-Zero. He was more organic than machine. He didn't need to be controlled, and barely could be."

"So he created an AI that outwitted him," Zarin said.

"Essentially."

"What happened?"

"We do not know for sure, but it seems as though A-Zero stole his memories. He became Darius, and sought to change the way we operated. He gave orders about the Gatekeeping duties and built an army of robots to do his bidding. But…"

"But what?"

"He grew too absorbed in learning about the Reflective Worlds, about the Shandra, and space and planes. Interdimensional traveling. Time travel. We were stationed at the Links, but ran out of power sources. Like me, the others drained, waiting for the moment we were once again called upon. But it never happened. Until you came," A-Two said.

"And he's here? On Esteron?" Suma asked.

"Yes. He just arrived."

"This has to be important," Jules said. "Can you tell us anything else?"

"It seems he's uploaded dozens of beings' memories into his hard drive. The data is corrupt. I must close my own walls off so he doesn't attack my system."

"Do it," Zarin said. "I've dealt with a lot of viruses in my day. Don't let it in."

Jules noticed A-Two's lights dim. "Do you have his location?"

"Yes."

Jules wrapped her defense bubble around their group and carried them in the direction of the moon. It wasn't long before a shot of pain erupted in her head. "Anyone else feel that?"

"What?" Zarin asked. "I don't feel anything."

The ache increased, and she lowered to the ground, her sphere vanishing. "A-Two, can you tell me what's causing this disruption?"

He pointed at the ground. "The area is covered by a bed of crystals. Perhaps you're reacting to them."

"Crystals?" Jules walked ahead and shot a blast from her hand, digging a hole in the sand. The sparkling clear-blue material almost took her breath away. "For how far?"

"Twenty square kilometers," A-Two said. "This is

where the source of the network is hiding. No off-planet sensors could pick up on it."

"But you can?" Zarin asked.

"Only in close proximity."

"If the Black Hole servers are anywhere, this is it," Zarin told Jules and Suma. "They're containing all energy output beneath these crystals. The rocks absorb, which probably adds to her range."

"And give me a headache like none other," Jules whispered. She took a deep inhale and focused on ignoring the pain. The moment she attempted to bring her sphere up again, the discomfort returned. "Looks like we're walking."

They moved as quickly as they could in the sand, which stifled their speed. A-Two went methodically, and Suma's shorter legs had difficulty traversing the dunes. Zarin seemed in her element, scurrying over the waves of sand like she was born for it. Jules was curious about Zarin's kind, but after her heartfelt story earlier, she wouldn't bring them up, so she walked, step after step.

"Zarin, what really happens in the Black Hole?" she asked the hacker.

"You want to know?"

Jules nodded. She glanced at Erem and Tessa behind them. The pair hadn't said much, and seemed content in their silence.

"Look, I understand the Alliance's attempt to have this ideal society where no one goes hungry, and everyone can live their best lives. But the truth is, most people don't want that. They're either too ambitious, or lazy, or right in the middle, so there will always be inequality. And then there are the greedy who prey on all of them to make a buck. The Black Hole is a cesspool of everything the Alliance stands against."

Suma sneezed and wiped sand off her brow. "Such as?"

"The usual, like drugs, trafficking, trading, but there are a lot of dissenters, and political vendettas posted in forums."

"From Alliance members?" Jules asked.

"Oh yeah. Mostly from within. You'd be shocked at how many humans have planned to overthrow your New Earth."

"We've already dealt with that once," Jules muttered, recalling Frasier and his group who'd tried to destroy Earth from orbit in a space station. "Papa and Magnus disposed of them."

Jules pictured her fiancé's father riding a bicycle with Papa in Europe, using aliases to infiltrate his organization. It was the last time Papa had spent any substantial time with Magnus before the Arnap had killed him. She'd been so busy searching for Patty after the Zan'ra infected her. It made her miss Magnus dearly.

"If you think those people knew anything, they didn't. These are tech-savvy people with positions all around the world. They may attempt to shut off the grids before kidnapping the head of each new city you've built."

"But they aren't like the Restorers, trying to re-establish the old way of life?" Suma asked.

"No. They want Earth to leave the Alliance, and to block the—no offense—the traitorous Parkers from ever visiting again," Zarin said.

Jules rolled her eyes. "No matter what we do, some will think we're to blame for their unhappiness. What else?"

"The Black Hole users are trading secrets, selling artifacts that should never be public, and attempting to spread false information for profit. It's nothing new, but the fact is, the Alliance has been completely blind to any of this, and it's all happening under their nose," Zarin said.

"Because of the organization," Jules added.

"Yes."

"Then let's put an end to them. If the Black Hole servers are here"—Jules pointed to the dunes—"we take them down."

"It's not like we have a lot of firepower on us," Suma told her.

"Maybe not, but I'm sure we can figure something out." Jules was glad that the headache was subsiding the longer she was around the crystal-studded land.

Jules thought about Zarin's comments on the Black Hole, and how many residents within the Alliance were feeling oppressed. To her, it didn't make sense, but she knew that considering other perspectives was integral to being a leader.

They trudged toward the home of the Black Hole.

———————

I learned the ship we were flying on toward Shimmal was named *Unity,* which was far too ironic, considering that they were planning on destroying a planet to fracture the Alliance.

Hugo and I spent an entire day among them, no one harassing us. We had free roam of the vessel and took it to our advantage. It felt much different with people on it, occupying the halls and galley. We'd crept through it before, but then it had been hollow and cold.

The robots remained in the cargo hold, and I went there to test out the tablet we'd secured.

Hugo stood at the primary entrance, keeping guard as I operated the circular tablet. "How do you switch…" I touched the icon, and the screen changed. "Never mind. I see it."

"Dad, what are we going to tell them if we're caught?" Hugo asked.

I held the tablet higher. "That I found this on the deck."

Hugo shrugged and didn't comment.

I did a rough count of the robots in the hangar, and figured there were around three hundred. Twelve rows of twenty-five. Each was equipped with heavy artillery. The left arms were pulse cannons, the right an armor-piercing machine gun, their torsos filled with a thousand rounds. They also had grenades, time-controlled by this very tablet, if the user chose to override the robot's built-in artificial intelligence. Years of modifying their programming had resulted in a very intuitive soldier.

I couldn't let them harm the people of Shimmal.

With the press of a button, I linked to the nearest soldier, and his head lifted, eyes lighting up. I expanded the reach, and the entire regiment of sleeping robots woke. I had an army at my fingertips.

"Maybe we should send them to the bridge now," Hugo suggested.

It wasn't a terrible idea, but I couldn't risk damage to the ship, not in the middle of nowhere with my son here. "Have some patience."

Hugo looked disappointed. "Fine, but can you shut them down? This is making me nervous."

I heard an elevator open, and footsteps from outside the cargo hold. I powered them off as fast as I could and shoved the tablet into my pants.

Hugo hurried from the entrance, coming to stand with me.

"You see... that's where the..." I peered at the doorway, finding Sully there, a big grin on his face.

"What are you two doing?" Scott O'Sullivan asked.

"I'm showing…" I realized we hadn't even given them names. We couldn't very well be Dean and Hugo. That would put us in an awkward position. "…Barry how incredible your soldiers are."

"Barry?" Sully kept smiling. "And what is your name?" He stared at me.

"Luke."

"Luke and Barry." Sully approached the front line of robots. "Luke, you've had extenders, haven't you?"

I touched my cheeks, wondering how he knew.

"If you're curious why I'd ask, I tried them all. Spent years devising better options, taking trial drugs to hinder the aging process, but in the end, not even alien medicine could keep the grim reaper from knocking on my door," he said.

Hugo glanced at me, and I gave a quick shake of my head.

"So you designed a vessel to store your mind," I said.

He stopped at the far end, returning at a slow pace. "You know, it's difficult to remember that I'm not human." He poked his own belly. "It's so well-synthesized, you'd never guess unless you scanned me. I can eat, drink… do anything you can." He grinned again. "But it feels different up here." He tapped his temple. "Emotions aren't that tough to replicate, and I have all of my memories."

"Are others doing this?" I asked.

"Why, are you interested?" He laughed loudly, startling me.

"Maybe."

"You're not ready yet. When you've done ten rounds of extenders and watched your loved ones die around you, the narrative will change," Sully said. "What do you make of all this?"

"The incursion of Shimmal?"

"Yes."

"I…" I considered what he'd want to hear. "I think the Alliance has overstepped, and that they need a fresh start. The organization seems to be the answer."

"And that's why you chose to work with them in the first place," Sully whispered.

"Right."

Scott O'Sullivan came closer, his mouth inches from my ear. "I know who you are." He stepped away, clapping his hands together. "Glad to have you aboard… Luke." He smirked, stopping to peer at Hugo before walking to the exit. "Barry, keep an eye on Luke, would you? Rumor has it, he has a tendency to be in places he doesn't belong. This time, it might benefit us both." Sully eyed me from the hallway, and pressed the door closed.

Hugo panted a breath. "Dad, what the hell was that?"

"He knows." My heart was pounding. "But maybe he's not going to rat us out."

"Why?"

"He said we can both benefit. He wants something, and I bet it's not the destruction of Shimmal. It seems we might have a single ally on *Unity*."

"We're going to need it," Hugo sighed. "Can we leave this room?" He knocked on one of the robot's chests. "It gives me the creeps."

I noticed a group of people near the viewscreen on the second deck. "What's happening?" I asked them.

"We're passing a dying star." It was Dasoli Six, her eyes big as she stared at the screen.

I scrutinized the distant image, seeing the sphere of red, a cluster of gases expanding from the surface. It was simultaneously beautiful and chaotic.

"It goes to show you, not even a star can survive for

eternity. An omen, don't you think? Dasoli asked.

"For what?" Hugo replied.

"For the Alliance. Their reign is nearing an end. And sometimes you need to go supernova and rebuild in the aftermath." The Inlorian woman walked away.

As I observed the slow process transpiring within this solar system, uneasiness grew in the pit of my stomach.

NINETEEN

After hours of marching, Sarlun realized he couldn't keep up with Herm forever. The robot began slowing his steps to match Sarlun's, but even that wasn't enough.

"I need a break," he pleaded.

"Very well."

"You said it was a few miles," Sarlun complained.

"It is… eleven point four, to be exact."

"From the start, or here?"

"The start," he said.

Sarlun was growing increasingly frustrated with the odd robot. "How much farther?"

"One point four."

Sarlun laughed, the sound strange after hours of silence. "Why didn't you tell me that before I sat down?"

"Would your legs have ached any less?" Herm asked.

Sarlun chose not to reply. Herm was dangerous. He'd killed the original Gatekeeper founder, stealing his memories, as well as the Record Keeper from the Backyard. Who else was inside his circuitry? "No. I suppose they wouldn't."

"Do not be afraid," Herm said.

"Of what?"

"Me."

"I'm not." Sarlun shifted on his seat, stretching his legs out. His feet were hurting almost as much as his hips. He'd

223

spent far too many years behind a desk, and not enough of that time in the field. Sarlun wished he'd been more adventurous like Dean Parker, racing through portals and taking command of starships. Instead, Sarlun had let others do that, while he managed the countless areas required to keep Shimmal and the portals operating.

Before the Event, his life had been simpler. Sarlun loved his people. His daughter. But the moment Slate and Dean met Suma on Sterona, their lives changed forever. Then came the Iskios debacle, with Mary being possessed by the ancient race, and that had brought Dean to the brink. He'd found Karo, the sole remaining Theos, and together they'd freed Karo's people from their confinement in the Shandra stones.

Now Sarlun wasn't even involved, because of some dreaded curse passed on from his father. It wasn't fair. Perhaps he could get Shula, and they'd return home, so he could make things right.

Sarlun stood, not wanting to waste a breath.

Herm stared at him. "You are ready?"

"Yes." Sarlun limped slightly but forced his steps. The sky was darkening, the pale moon growing in ambiance as night settled around them. They passed a giant head sticking from the sand, and Sarlun walked to it, realizing the piece of statue was four times his own height. "Who lived here?"

"It was too long ago to recall," Herm said.

Sarlun's curiosity to investigate the ruins was overwhelmed by his motivation to find his sister. If they made it through this adventure, perhaps he'd return for more answers.

With another glance at the statue's head, he continued walking, each step feeling like he was sinking deeper into the sand.

"We're going to beat the others," Herm said.

"Others?" Sarlun slowed and did a three-sixty, trying to scan the horizon.

"Yes. A-0002 was the Gatekeeper on this world. He's been activated. He tried to block me, but he's not advanced enough to be successful. Though I do appreciate his efforts." Herm kept striding.

"But we don't have access to a Shandra," Sarlun said.

"No, but there's a Link."

"You mean this is a Reflective World?" Sarlun barked.

"Yes."

"Who does it pair with?"

"Belash," Herm said.

"Belash!" Sarlun shouted. "Why didn't we just use the Link? Why all the preamble?" He couldn't believe his ears. They'd wasted a lot of time, but they'd rescued the crew of *Mettle*, so that was meaningful.

"I couldn't verify if the Link worked, or if the planet's core was intact. If we'd traveled through and the world was gone, or the tunnels were collapsed, we'd be dead. Well, you would have died. I'd have been trapped."

Sarlun nodded, understanding the robot's train of thought. "Where's the entrance?"

"Ahead."

Crystals rose from the ground in a large circle, and he slowed, crouching to dig through the sand. There was more blue crystal below the surface. "It's everywhere?"

"Yes. Shula has utilized the natural reverberance for her benefit," Herm stated.

"Brilliant." Sarlun followed Herm to the ring of double terminations, their smooth edges perfectly imperfect. The landmark's center looked no different than the rest of the fields.

A small piece protruded from Herm's fingertip, and he

pushed it into a terminal on one of the crystals. It receded, and the sand began to drip away, revealing a staircase. "After you," he said.

Sarlun peered into the distance, but couldn't make out anyone trailing them. The moon began to expand as night settled, and it became almost blinding. He squinted into the stairs, hoping Herm was right.

"I'm here, Shula," he whispered.

The entrance stayed open as he descended into darkness.

The steps eventually were bereft of sand, and Sarlun noticed lights on the walls. They glowed dimly but offered enough brightness to see by. Herm seemed pleased with himself for bringing Sarlun and fulfilling his end of the bargain. His movements were more languid, his posture confident. Sarlun wondered which of his many acquired personalities he was drawing from.

Sarlun hadn't given much thought to what he expected the hub of the Black Hole to look like, but he was pleasantly surprised. "This is phenomenal."

They went into another sunken room, the ceiling domed and bathed in blue crystal. Hundreds of screens were mounted on their surface, with five pulsing stones in the middle of the space. Sarlun instantly understood. Shula was tapping into the Shandra network as a server. It was brilliant, yet extremely dangerous.

"Shula?" he called. But it seemed empty.

"She was supposed to stay here," Herm said. "I kept my end of the bargain. Where is your sister?"

Herm extended a weapon from his arm, and Sarlun backed into the wall, hitting a display. Icons and symbols skittered across the screens in endless data sharing.

"I have no idea! I was trusting you did!" Sarlun yelled at the robot.

"We've run out of time. The others are here," Herm said. "Do not tell them my origin story. I must get to Shula."

Sarlun nodded as the gun retreated. "I will do my best."

"The Gatekeepers will be mine," Herm whispered, and Sarlun heard voices from outside.

———

"*A*n underground bunker surrounded by crystals? Wait until I tell the gang about this," Zarin said. "We always speculated that the organization had some epic space station pinging off stars and echoing through nebulas to power it. I never imagined this."

Jules gritted her teeth, the pressure in her skull building. Her heart pounded and sweat dripped off her brow. Something down there was either calling to her or warning her. It reminded Jules of her father's story about going into a trance while visiting the mountains on New Spero with Uncle Zeke. He said it was like he lost control of his limbs.

Jules stepped into the opening without meaning to. Okay, maybe she was under some alien influence.

"I think Erem and Tessa should stay behind. Guard the entrance," she said.

Tessa nodded, grabbing a pulse pistol Jules had given her. Erem held his iron rod, and looked almost as dangerous as the human woman with the weapon. "We won't let anything inside."

"It's what's inside that has me concerned," Jules whispered.

"You feeling all right?" Suma asked her.

"Sure. You?"

"Jules, it's me. You can be honest." Suma stared at her

with those big, worried eyes of hers.

"Sorry. Something's off, but I can't tell what." She took another step. "I didn't mean to do that."

"Use the stairs?" Suma inquired.

"Yeah." She kept descending. "No one touch anything."

Suma shouldered her pulse pistol. "I'll take the lead."

Jules nodded in agreement, and they entered a secondary room. She shut off her own lights, allowing the ones in the walls to assist their passage. Each heartbeat was harder than the previous, but the moment she went into a domed room, it all stopped. Her legs stalled, her migraine subsided, and her racing pulse slowed.

Suma sighted a pair across the dome, and the rifle fell from her grip, landing with a clatter. She ran to the duo without a word.

"Sarlun," she whispered, discovering the man was no other than her own father. "How…"

A-Two staggered, his circuitry smoking. His head spun backwards, and he dropped to the floor, flames rising from a panel. A tiny stream of water splashed from the ceiling, putting the fire out, and Jules jumped to avoid getting wet.

"What the heck happened to him?" Jules muttered.

She recognized that the second figure with Sarlun was a robot, a similar design to A-Two, but perhaps a slightly older model. "He wasn't programmed to withstand the power of the Black Hole's server room. It's emitting more energy than his board would allow," the robot said.

Suma was still hugging her father, their lips moving softly as they had a private conversation. Suma's snout dipped and wagged when they parted.

Sarlun met Jules' gaze, and his eyes went even softer. "Jules… I can't begin to tell you how sorry I am."

"I know." Jules couldn't stay angry. She ran to the stoic

man, embracing him. "I'm so grateful we found you."

"What are you doing here?" Suma asked him.

Sarlun glanced at the robot. "Herm and I were…"

"Herm?" Jules watched the bot closely. "Are you the one from the Backyard?"

"How do you know that?" Sarlun asked.

"We went to Belash Bazaar," Jules told him.

"You did?" Sarlun's voice rose two octaves. "That place is dangerous!"

"Didn't stop you," Suma mumbled. "What were you possibly—"

"I was trying to find Shula," he said.

"Your sister?" Suma asked.

Jules didn't know much about their family, other than the fact she'd been gone for decades after vanishing from Shimmal.

"She wanted to be found by me," he said. "She left a clue on Belash with Herm, the Record Keeper."

Jules had heard the name. Tessa had used it when explaining Sarlun's escape from the Backyard. "You're the Record Keeper?"

"Would you like me to paint you?" Herm asked, head tilting to the side.

"Uhmmm, believe it or not, that's not the weirdest thing I've ever heard in the middle of a mission. Are you the…"

The floor shook, and the screens illuminated as one.

"What's happening?" Zarin asked. She was fumbling with a keypad.

Suma rushed to her side. "I thought Jules asked you not to touch anything?"

Zarin's nose twitched. "Sorry. I can't break past the firewall…"

A face appeared on all hundred screens, but it was

cloaked in shadows. It was obviously a Shimmal person, and when she spoke, Jules quickly assumed it was the mysterious Shula Sarlun had been seeking.

"You found me," she said.

"Not quite," Sarlun answered. "Unless you're hiding in the walls."

"Unfortunately, I am not."

"Wait, is this live?" Zarin interrupted.

"Yes. With the reach of the Black Hole, I can direct video any distance."

"So where are you?" Sarlun asked.

"Shimmal."

Suma gasped, and Sarlun looked about as surprised as his daughter. "What are you up to, sister?"

"Father was a brilliant man, but he had many secrets even you weren't privy to," she said.

Sarlun rubbed his cloak, where the tattoo had been up until a couple of years ago. "I have some idea."

"They're coming for me." The head moved, the snout lifting and falling. Jules tried to see her features, but the program made it impossible.

"Who is?"

"The organization. They're determined to destroy Shimmal, Sarlun. They wish to blame the Parkers, and Morg Ashr desires to sit in Mary's seat at the head of the Alliance of Worlds. Can you believe it?"

None of them knew who Morg was; at least, Jules didn't think they did.

Except Sarlun's expression betrayed him. "Morg lives?"

"Yes. He's been in hiding since Father's incident on Percil Seven. I took him in, though he never did know my connection to Shimmal. I've led the Black Hole for decades, keeping tabs on everything. I know all about you,

Sarlun. You've done well. Until lately."

"That wasn't my fault," he told the screen.

"It was, once again, our father. Can you sense a reoc-curring theme?" she asked.

Herm moved in front of Sarlun. "I brought him to you. Where is my prize?"

Shula smiled, that much was obvious, but Jules doubted it met her eyes. "You haven't, A-0000."

Jules blinked. This was the robot that had downloaded Darius Neema's memories.

"You were supposed to be on Esteron," Herm said.

"And you weren't meant to take four decades to bring Sarlun to me. I had to change tactics," she said.

"Enough about the robot." Jules cut them off. "What about my parents?"

"Jules Parker, is that you?" Shula's entire voice changed. "I've been waiting for the day we could meet… again."

Again? "How do we get to Shimmal?" All Jules could think about was helping stop Morg Ashr from laying waste to their previous Alliance partner's world, and not letting her parents take the fall.

"Ask A-Zero," she said. "He knows which Reflective World is Linked to Shimmal. Bring them to me, and you shall have your position as promised, robot."

"What about Hulope? If we show up, she's never going to l …" Suma stopped when the screen flickered.

It resumed play, and Shula was laughing. "You shouldn't worry about her. Go to Shimmal. Now. Or there won't be a planet for anyone to return to. And the Alliance will have a new president, with Mary and Dean in Traro Prison." The displays flashed before turning dark.

"Was it just me, or did that sound like a threat?" Zarin asked.

Sarlun stared at Suma as if a secret, unspoken message passed between them. "I don't believe Shula is trying to deceive us," he said.

"Come on. Then why all these games? She led you to the Backyard. You could have died there, Dad!" Suma exclaimed.

"But I didn't. And I'm glad you didn't either. Come, it's time to leave. Herm, you'll tell us how to get to Shimmal."

The robot's eyes were fiery red, his movements agitated. "I did what she asked. I won't let her goad me."

"Darius wouldn't react like this. He was curious, an inventor and philosopher. He led the Gatekeepers, as I have. The Record Keeper was kind and caring of the people they encountered in the Backyard. Is there not a shred of decency left within your circuit boards?" Sarlun pleaded.

The bot slouched slightly, and the color of his eyes shifted to yellow. "Perhaps I am too hasty. I've lived for a thousand years. Why does this minor delay perturb me so much?"

Jules huffed and tapped his shoulder. "If you show us how to travel there, I'll let you paint me."

This seemed to sell it. Once an artist, always an artist. "Deal. We must fly to the nearest Shandra. From there, we can use the portals to take us to the Link."

"Okay, now the complicated part. How do we destroy the Black Hole and get off planet?" Jules looked around the room.

"Destroy it? Are you sure that's a good idea?" Zarin asked. "Let me try something." She went to the keypad, typing quickly.

"You're asking me to leave it?"

"Sure. We should spy on it. It'll give you the advantage, should someone eventually turn on you," she said. Zarin frowned and retrieved a small tablet from her front pocket, setting it near the screen. It blinked a few times, and she smiled. "This might come in handy. It can shut the network down with the touch of a button." She passed it to Jules.

"Nah. I'd rather it be gone." Jules filled with power, the effects seeming magnified within the crystal-encased server bunker.

Herm tossed her to the floor. "I will not permit you to do this."

Jules bristled, her abilities threatening to burst out in anger. "Give me a good reason!"

Herm gestured at the broken robot. "A-0002 wasn't the only robot at a Link site. Each planet within the Reflective Worlds has one. Without Shula's network, we cannot fix them and guarantee the Gatekeepers of old are restarted."

Jules was on her feet, watching Sarlun. "What's your opinion?" She saw her own green eyes reflecting in the series of screens on the wall.

Sarlun glanced from her to A-Zero. "Herm's right. Plus, I doubt he'll help us if we destroy the Black Hole now."

"That is correct. You'll never reach Shimmal before the altercation."

Jules grinned, knowing full well she could make the trip without anyone else inhibiting her travels. But she wasn't about to leave Suma here, or Zarin, and now that they'd found Sarlun, she couldn't keep him in danger. "Fine. But when the Links are all established again, I will deal with the Black Hole."

Herm seemed happy, even though his robotic face remained unchanged. "We should go."

They rushed from the room, Erem and Tessa blocking the exit. "We good?"

Jules stepped aside, and Sarlun appeared with Herm behind him. "Hello, friends," Sarlun said.

"Stranger, you live." Erem clasped his arm. "I am astounded."

"And you… came all the way from the Backyard." Sarlun hugged Tessa.

"I appreciate a good reunion, but how are we planning to fly to another planet with a Shandra?" Suma asked.

Jules saw the outline of a ship hovering in the middle of the moon. "Is that *Light?*"

"No," Sarlun said. "It's *Mettle.*"

"This keeps getting more bizarre," Jules whispered. She glanced at Tessa, who'd been lost after her own expedition ship, *Vast*, had been destroyed. *Mettle* and *Vast* were tragedies the Alliance had carried with them for years. The beautiful vessel lowered toward them, the thrusters kicking up sand as she landed.

Jules was nearly overwhelmed by emotion. "Remember Captain Derek Boggs?" Sarlun asked.

She nodded.

"Would you like to see him again?" Sarlun dashed across the dunes and onto the ramp.

Jules followed.

TWENTY

The moment we'd added wormhole generators to our ships, the game had changed. We no longer needed to take years to travel across the galaxies, and time dilation became a thing of the past. The Bhlat were using it before us, as were a couple of other partners, but none of them had the range or capabilities of the newest iterations.

It appeared that the organization also had access to this version.

The announcement came while Hugo and I were in our separate quarters, me trying to make sense of my interaction with Scott O'Sullivan. If he knew I was Dean Parker, then what did he seek from me? He was human, or his mind was. Did that give him any sort of allegiance to me? Maybe he sought the head of the Alliance for himself, trying to oust Morg. Or perhaps he saw a financial benefit to helping me stop the destruction of Shimmal. Either way, I could use an ally on the inside.

Hugo met me in the hallway, his eyes red from lack of sleep. I wanted to hug him and bring him home, but here, we were Luke and Barry, not father and son. I sought to convey my apologies for ever getting him into this situation.

"We're about to make the jump to Shimmal," he said.

"I heard." We walked down the corridor to the bridge. When we arrived, a security officer stopped us.

235

"We'd like to witness the arrival," I told him.

The Padlog man set his hand on the holstered gun on his hip. "On whose orders?"

"Mine," Sully said when the doors slid wide. "Luke, glad you could join us for this occasion."

The insectoid buzzed a curse, and I ignored him. Everyone was here, with Alyce in the captain's chair, Morg half asleep in the one beside her.

Dasoli Six chatted with Karka, the Kraski in charge of the new PlevaCorp, and Sully led us to the edge of the bridge, gesturing to a pair of seats. We took them without comment.

Alyce glanced at me, but was quickly distracted. "Prepare for the jump."

"Preparing," a Bhlat woman said. Her braided hair had tiny bells that glittered in the light. "On your word."

"Now," Alyce said. The wormhole shot from *Unity*, forming a bright circle of swirling colors in front of the vessel. The ship entered, and we were almost instantly transported. I wished I could have gotten word to Mary about their plans so we'd have a defense force in place, but I'd been stripped of my belongings after arriving through the core from Pestria.

Someone must have been tipped off. Dozens of warships flew toward Shimmal.

"Is that the Alliance?" Hugo asked.

Sully laughed. "No. Those are ours."

I lifted my eyebrows, counting ten of the massive craft. That was more than enough firepower to destroy Shimmal and then some.

"Everyone in order? Sully, bring the replicas."

The doors opened, and in strode Mary's double.

"I've only managed to complete the president and the kid," Sully told her, smirking at me.

"You had one task," Morg complained. "Dean Parker is the face of the Alliance. Without implicating him, we may fail."

"Do you have an idea how much work and cost goes into one of these?" Sully asked.

"Mary's the president, and Jules is the poster child. It's fine," Alyce said. "In position."

Mary walked front and center, and in strolled a replica of Jules. Her curly brown hair looked real, her face with more makeup than the real Jules preferred. The eyes were what got me. They glowed a bright green.

"We're being contacted," Karka said.

"On screen." Alyce tapped the arm of her chair.

"Hulope," I whispered, digging my nails into my palm.

"You've come to invade Shimmal," she said.

Alyce and Morg glanced at one another before Mary spoke.

"Shimmal has broken the peace treaty of our Alliance. You've pulled your resources from the Academy and have threatened the Alliance and our partners on numerous occasions. I, Mary Parker, hereby order you to stand down as we make an example of you," the replica said. It sounded exactly like my wife.

"Shimmal will be destroyed!" Jules added, her tone slightly off. "I'm going to see to it. My Papa will push the button himself."

A drone above them, and in came a human, who, from a bad angle, might have passed for my double. He went to a console, his finger lowering toward the screen.

"Stop this pitiful charade," Hulope said. "Alyce, you're a fool for listening to Morg Ashr. I only kept him around to placate the others, but now I see where I went wrong. I gave you too much leeway. Instead, I was building the Black Hole, and making everyone an exorbitant amount of money. Morg, you could have bought a tropical planet and sat on a beach, watching the sunset for the rest of your life, but no… you had to get greedy."

I was beginning to grasp the picture. Hulope was in charge of the organization?

"You're Shula," Alyce said.

"Shula?" Hugo whispered. "Isn't that…"

"Fire!" Morg ordered, and the man pretending to be me struck the icon.

Nothing happened.

Hulope smiled wide, her teeth showing. "Here's what will happen…"

I glanced out the viewscreen, seeing the warships turning their attention on *Unity* instead of the planet.

Morg shifted in his seat, his face ashen. Alyce was more composed, but I saw the cracks forming in her façade.

"There's a far better way to fight the Alliance," Hulope said.

"How?" Alyce asked.

"With the fleet you intended to destroy Shimmal with. You will trick them with this fine replica of Mary Parker," Hulope ordered. "Everyone gather at Ebos. It's the least defended Alliance hub, and the very world which spawned the trouble in the first place. They've also built a new Academy there, and it would be a tremendous show of power."

I swallowed a lump in my throat.

"Ebos. You want us to destroy Ebos?" Morg barked. "What a waste."

"No, we'll take it hostage. Make our demands." Hulope seemed pleased with herself.

"Shula, what demands are you going to make?" Alyce asked her leader.

"We shall see. For now, do as I order." Hulope stood in her office, which I now recognized as Sarlun's. She walked to the side of the room and pointed at the viewscreen. "Sully, I thought you weren't able to make the replica of Dean Parker."

"I wasn't," Sully said.

"Then you should probably apprehend that man and his son, Hugo." Hulope's image faded, and everyone on the bridge stared at us.

I lifted my hands. "You didn't really think I'd stand by while you tried to destroy my family, did you?"

The stun gun's energy coursed through me, and I bit my tongue as I faceplanted on the deck.

Being on *Mettle* reminded Jules of *Light*. She knew every small detail on board, and had spent countless hours with her boyfriend, Dean, on board the Alliance exploration vessel. They'd shared burgers and their dreams for the future.

Now it seemed almost archaic in comparison with the warships, even though these were only a decade old. Technology improved at such a considerable rate, especially when dealing with dozens of alien races at a time.

Walking these halls made her miss her family, and mostly her fiancé. "I'll be back soon," she whispered to herself.

Jules noticed how well Tessa hit it off with the captain. Derek Boggs was a strong man, his nature calm and authoritative. It was the reason they'd selected him in the first place. She remembered being barely more than a kid and watching the procession as *Vast* and *Mettle* originally took to space, heading out on their debut missions.

It had been heartbreaking to hear Tessa's story and

how she ended up in the Backyard, but finding *Mettle* in one piece with the crew intact was inspiring. It was a great win for their side.

She used the computer near Engineering to see how far they were from the Shandra's destination, and grinned at the results. They were nearly in orbit.

Jules didn't trust the robot, A-Zero, or Darius, or Herm. Whatever name the bot went by, he was dangerous. Jules should have destroyed the Black Hole, but Zarin had persuaded her otherwise. With someone like her on board, they could keep an eye on things from the shadows, improving their odds. The universe was a hazardous place, with threats looming at every corner, so the more prepared they were, the better.

Jules went to the cargo hold for supplies and found Sarlun instead.

"Hello, Jules," he said.

Sarlun looked older, and not just two years.

"Hey, Sarlun." She smiled at him, but felt sick to her stomach. "I'm sorry you had to leave."

His snout drooped. "So am I. I never meant to harm anyone, least of all your parents."

Jules nodded her understanding. "You did blow up our house."

"Again, I apologize."

"I rebuilt it. Dean helped. Magnus too." Jules sat with him on the bench.

"I'd like to visit," he told her.

Tears filled her eyes, and she took his hand. "It wasn't your fault. Ranul was evil."

"I've come to terms with my actions. I would have returned sooner, but I found a trail for my sister, and had to see if I could find her," Sarlun told her.

"What really happened?"

Sarlun rested the back of his head on the locker behind him and sighed. "Shula was a tough child who didn't want to be coddled, and for my mother, that wasn't easy. Shula was bright. Far more intelligent than me."

Jules didn't interrupt, but thought Sarlun was selling himself short.

"Suma reminded me of her," Sarlun said. "Shula devoured information, and even created her own software network when she was ten. Father was furious when she used it to connect to his own security and adjust the settings. After that day, everything changed. Shula was sent to a school far from our capital city. I wasn't permitted to visit. And for an impressionable youth like myself, it made me resent my parents."

"I can see that," Jules said.

"Then one day, she vanished. Later, when I gained control, I investigated the school. Shula had been written up countless times for hacking into their books, for adjusting the scores and making threats to the instructors. She was an angry girl. Personally, I think she was too smart for her own good, and my parents didn't know how to channel or direct her skillsets."

"Did you know she was involved with the organization behind the Black Hole?" Jules inquired.

"That was a surprise. I was aware of the Black Hole since its inception, but I rarely gave it a second thought. To me, it was no different than the back-alley deals happening on every single Alliance world. No matter our intentions, there will always be illegal activity. So I ignored it like everyone else." Sarlun stared at the cargo hold's exit. "I fear what we'll encounter at Shimmal."

"That it'll be destroyed?" Jules asked.

"No. That Shula might be the one behind this strike on the Alliance," he said.

241

"I thought your sister was trying to prevent Shimmal from being attacked." That was what her message had suggested.

"I'm reading between the lines. It's obvious she's grown bored on Esteron. Shula must have developed the Black Hole as far as she was able, and now she's on to the next thing. That's how her mind operates. She couldn't wait for me there, so she left. I can only imagine what someone with her brilliance would concoct." Sarlun stood when Suma entered the room.

"You two ready?" Suma asked.

Erem and Zarin came behind her. "We will, respectfully, stay behind." Erem looked ashamed of his comment.

"That's good news to me," Jules said. "Too many people, and the mission becomes more difficult. Don't worry, Erem, we'll return to the Backyard and save the rest of the population. I promise."

"I appreciate it."

Zarin stepped closer, passing Jules her tablet. She leaned in, her raccoon nose sniffling. "I haven't told anyone, but this is linked to the Black Hole."

"Can't everyone do that?" Jules asked, and Zarin turned the device on.

"Not like this." She showed Jules how it worked. "You can cut the Black Hole servers off with the press of this icon, but it may not last forever. I expect Shula would anticipate these things."

Jules couldn't foresee why she'd need to use this, but thanked the girl regardless.

Tessa and Boggs strode into the cargo hold, and the captain raised a hand. "Good luck. We're going to go home. Should take us about four months," he said.

"Take care of them," Jules told the captain.

"I will." Derek smiled at Tessa. "Don't forget your

robot. He's been trying to paint the entire crew."

Herm appeared, his fingertips smeared with various colors. "It is time."

Jules preferred moving lighter, and they packed their weapons and supplies into an old-model transport. They waved their goodbyes, and Suma, Sarlun, Herm, and Jules lifted from the deck, heading into space. The planet below was inhospitable, but it was a short distance to the Shandra access to their next destination. According to Herm, that was Shimmal's Reflective World. Given the fact that the Shimmal Shandra was currently unavailable since Hulope's rise to power, this was their only chance at sneaking onto Shimmal discreetly.

The Shandra wasn't elaborate, just a cluster of stones and a table tucked into a crevasse near an icy surface. They used it, taking them to a world Herm called Neter.

It was coated in a thick dust, making their visibility tough, and Jules threw her sphere over their small group. She filtered the particles out and decided to expedite this process. Jules hovered above the cracked ground and sent tiny vibrations into the sphere while descending into the planet's crust, then the mantle.

No one spoke as they sped lower, racing through the solid rock as she guided them into the core. It grew hotter, and Herm's eyes glowed after a minute. "We are near. I can sense the Gatekeeper."

Jules decelerated, adjusting her angle to find the exact center of Neter. The heat pressed against her shield, but it held.

She lowered into an open space and settled to the stone floor. Liquid magma dripped from the ceiling and down the walls as the core sputtered and spat.

The robot guarding the Link was incapacitated, his body covered in scorch marks from the molten core. Even from twenty feet away, Jules could see the fraying on his wire harness.

"Please let me out," Herm said.

"It's a caustic environment," Jules told him.

"I will survive."

Jules allowed the robot to exit her sphere, and she considered leaving him to search for the Link.

Herm knelt at the robot, flipping his companion on his front. A welding arc blazed from Herm's finger, and in a few minutes, the Gatekeeper sat up, his power on.

"Where is the Link?" Herm asked.

"Are you A-0000?" the bot replied.

"Yes. Where is the Link?"

"Forty meters below." The robot pointed down.

"In the magma," Suma whispered.

"Will the sphere withstand it?" Sarlun asked Jules.

"I think so. Maybe I should go alone," she said. "Just in case."

"No." Sarlun shook his head. "We do this together."

Jules smiled as Herm returned. He smelled like sulfur. "Let's get to Shimmal. Shula owes me a promise."

Jules concentrated and hovered their group over the spilling magma. The heat was intense, even with the barrier she'd erected. "Here goes nothing." It was the second time she'd used a Link.

Jules almost passed out, but resisted long enough to see they'd transported to another place through the core. She was still stunned by the existence of the Reflective Worlds.

"Are we on Shimmal?" Sarlun asked Herm.

"Yes. We are."

Suma hugged her father as Jules removed the sphere encapsulating them. "We're home, father."

"Now it's time we save it," Sarlun snarled.

TWENTY-ONE

*W*hen I came to, it was obvious we were on a starship. I'd spent years on them, and I instantly became aware of the thrumming pipes, the groans of the hull reverberating through the decks, despite millions of hours trying to perfect space travel.

I rubbed my neck and took a seat on the cot. Hugo was already awake and searching for a way out.

"Son, how long have you been at this?" I asked him.

He jumped like he hadn't heard me move. "Dad!" He slid off his cot, landing beside me. "I've scoured this entire room, but can't find any possible escape."

"Then we wait."

Hugo shook his head adamantly. "They're going to Ebos. We've worked so hard on it, Dad. They opened Regnig's Academy!"

"How many days ago was that?" I tried doing the math but had lost count. It wasn't easy to remember days and nights when you were constantly being knocked out and traveling between worlds.

"If I were to guess, five?" Hugo mustered.

"Mom and Jules should be gone."

"Is that all you're worried about?"

"Watch your tone," I warned. "Shula could use them as bait."

"I thought her name was Hulope. What's up with

that?"

"I don't know." I stood up, walking to the barred doors.

"I remember hearing the name before."

"Shula?"

"Yeah. I think she might be related to Sarlun and Suma."

"Seriously?"

Hugo nodded and plopped to the mattress. "I could be wrong. She's got a lot of nerve, shutting Shimmal out of the Alliance and trying to take Ebos. The colony is filled with Alliance partners. And with the new school…"

"That's it. She wanted to ensure she had the right audience." I recalled the vote that had Hulope on the outs with the Alliance, when Mary was named president.

"I don't care why she's trying this, Dad. We have to stop her."

"That's where we agree." I'd almost forgotten about the tablet. "Do you still have the robot's control device?"

Hugo retrieved the circular tablet from under his shirt. "Right here."

"Okay." I connected to the nearest bot. We were obviously onboard *Unity*, and that was a good sign. I locked my command into the one soldier bot and instructed him to come to my position. The signal flashed green, indicating success, and I smiled at my son.

"What are we going to do when we get out of this room?" Hugo asked.

"Hide until we're on Ebos. Then you'll contact our base."

"Me?"

"You're better at this kind of thing," I told him.

"Really?" Hugo cracked his knuckles. "You are right about that, you know."

246

"It's what I've always told you kids. Play to your strengths."

Something bashed into the door, and I heard a muffled shout, then another bang. The doors opened, and a robot stood on the other side, the body of a guard on the floor unconscious.

"Thanks," I told him.

"What is your command?" he asked.

We'd been all over this ship during the journey from Esteron, and I knew just the place. "Engineering. We'll hide in the reactor core."

"We'll be fried!"

"No. They have the new models. The shield has been doubled to prevent any explosions. I checked when we were down there…"

"That won't be necessary," Sully stepped from behind the bot. "Come with me."

I jumped in front of Hugo. "Why should I trust you?"

"Because you have one choice. Either you believe that I'm here to help, or you die," Sully muttered.

A door flung open down the corridor, and I glanced at the fallen guard. "Fine. But we're having a conversation about your replicas if we make it."

Farther along were the duplicates of Mary and Jules, standing at rest. They only reacted when Sully neared, and the pair ran lead. We hurried into a storage room, waiting while two guards walked past, chatting about their dinner. When they were gone, we were back on track.

Sully led us through various decks, doing his best to stay in the shadows. "This isn't the first time you've skulked, is it?" I asked him.

"Won't be the last." He pressed his face to a screen, and the device scanned his eyes. "Inside."

The laboratory was dim, with pieces of electronics and

mechanical components strewn across multiple tables. This was one space I'd never seen. "I've been working on the replicas for years, but have rarely showcased the final product. Mary Parker was a challenge to recreate."

I noticed more of the androids hanging on the wall, their heads dangling.

"Dad, this is me," Hugo whispered as he touched one of his own replicas. There were two mounted beside a version of myself.

"Sully, what are you planning on…" I hushed up when a buzzer sounded.

"If you know what's good for you, stand with your family." Sully pointed at Mary and Jules.

"Hugo, pretend to be a robot," I told him.

"Actually, do quite the opposite. These are not merely robots, they're androids. Perfect versions of the people they're based after." Sully smiled at me, but I didn't return his gesture.

The door opened on Sully's command, and Shula was there, glaring at her acquaintance. "Scott O'Sullivan. It's a pleasure to finally meet the man behind the talent."

"Likewise, Shula. You've done us all proud with the Black Hole, and the organization could never have thrived like it has without your vision," he said.

"Cut the crap," Shula ordered. "Will these be complete in time for our incursion?"

"Yes. A few more modifications, and they'll be finished." Sully was behind Shula, and he met my gaze, shaking his head. She couldn't see him, since she was stalking toward the four of us.

"Dean Parker. He really does resemble our new captive." Shula touched my cheek, and it took all my energy to keep frozen. "Is he sweating?"

"I told you they were realistic," Sully quickly recovered.

"Miraculous." Shula went to Hugo, and walked by him, stopping at Mary. "With their assistance, I'll finally have what I've always wanted. The Shandra network."

"You mean to control the portals?" Sully asked.

"What do you think I've been building the Black Hole for? So degenerates can swap weapons on bog planets? I'll oversee the Crystal Map as well as the Reflective Worlds. I'll be unstoppable," she said.

"And you need a Valincin to make it work," Sully said, referring to the large Deity stones.

"Have you been listening? Sometimes I wonder why I have you on the payroll, Sully." She took one final look at me and went to the exit. "Just have them ready in three hours. We'll be taking Ebos."

"Yes, Shula." Sully bowed his head, and laughed when the woman was gone. "She thinks she can walk all over me. She's worse than Morg. Now she desires the portals? Who cares? I can do better on my own. With this technology, no one will have to worry about dying. We can transplant people into mirror image bodies."

I didn't know how to feel about his technology, but maybe it wasn't my place to decide. "How do we stop this?"

"Your faces will grant her passage on Ebos. With you and your wife ordering the colony to allow these vessels to orbit Ebos, no one will dispute it."

"So we tell them the truth?" Hugo asked.

"Not a chance. We get to the surface and escape through the Shandra Valincin," Sully said.

I gawked at him, like he'd told the world's worst joke. "Sully, surely even a man with your scruples can see how cowardly that is."

"But we'll live to retaliate," he said.

"I have a better idea," Hugo told us. "Hulope… or

249

Shula… will bring her robot army, right?"

Sully frowned. "Sure. It's in her best interests to keep the people of Ebos pacified."

"Then we use the army against her when we're grounded," Hugo said.

"How?" Sully asked.

I tried to stop Hugo from giving away our advantage, but it was too late. "Because we have the tablet that controls them."

Sully smirked, but didn't seem overly pleased with the concept of fighting. "Okay, say we capture Shula on the ground. What about the dozen warships in orbit?"

He had a point. I needed to get word to *Outpost*, but how…

"Sully, do you have the blueprints for the warships?" I asked.

"No, but they're accessible." He walked to the nearest console and brought up a program. "Should be in here."

Hugo took over, and judging by the speed with which he typed, he knew what I was looking for. "Dad, they've added the failsafe!"

"Failsafe?"

"We had an issue with the first warships when one was taken over by the enemy. Since then, we've added a backdoor program that allows another warship to connect with a fleet and take control. It's temporary, but that might be all we need."

Sully wiped his mouth with his sleeve, which offered us a glimpse of his old self. "Okay. We can do this."

"We have three hours to make the plan. There's no room for error," I said.

Sarlun had missed Shimmal, but he hadn't realized how much until he stepped foot on her soil again. The city loomed in the distance. His city. The place he'd lived for most of his life. He'd rebuilt the Gatekeepers, raised his daughter, and collected his artifacts.

"If they see us, we might be done for," Suma murmured.

"Then we'd better stay invisible," Jules said. Sarlun noticed a shimmer in the sphere, and he assumed they were no longer perceptible to the pedestrians around them. Jules carried their group into the sky, giving them an overhead view of the metropolis, and Sarlun absorbed the sight with a deep reverence.

Most of it looked the same, and he felt relief that this Hulope hadn't destroyed anything. The people seemed happy enough, going about their daily business. In his mind, the woman had been a scourge, judging by how she'd attempted to try Suma for Sarlun's sins. She'd shut them off from the Alliance, restricting access to the portals.

The name bothered him. Hulope. It was familiar, in a distant sense, but he couldn't quite put his finger on it.

And it struck him like a slap to the face as they descended toward the central palace. The home of the Gatekeepers, the location of the Shandra he'd protected for decades. Shula had loved a book when she was younger. She'd read it obsessively, and forced Sarlun to hear about the great heroine's tales at every opportunity.

"Hulope," he whispered.

"What about her?" Suma asked.

"Did you see her?" Sarlun asked.

"Sure. It was hard not to, when she was trying to kill me," Suma said.

"What did she look like?"

"A Shimmal woman. Older. Narrow snout. Dark skin."

"A scar on her chin," Jules added.

Sarlun closed his eyes, taking a deep breath. It couldn't be true. What had she done?

"It's Shula," he said.

"Your sister? No way." Suma stood in the sphere defiantly. "I would have recognized her."

"You never met her, Suma. She left when I was a child," he told her.

"But still…"

Jules floated the directly over his old office building. "What if you're right? She contacted us in the Black Hole. She might have been here."

"Then why…" Suma peered at the robot with them. "She wanted Sarlun and Herm to come."

"That still doesn't make sense," Jules said. "What reason would she have to need Sarlun at her side for any of this? And Herm?"

"Perhaps she intends to merge the Reflective Worlds with the Crystal Map, and connect them to the Black Hole," Herm suggested. "It would give her the ultimate power. Without Darius' knowledge, it wouldn't be possible."

"But why Sarlun?" Jules prodded.

"Because someone will need to fuel it. Like the Theos energized the portals before you fixed them," Sarlun said. "She would use me as a sacrifice."

"We have to stop her!" Jules lowered into the building, settling the sphere near Sarlun's old office. "When I release it, everyone prepare for battle. I'll keep the shield up, but your gunfire will still penetrate it."

Suma shouldered her rifle, Herm activated his gun, and Sarlun aimed his pulse pistol forward. Shula was an idealist who had the ability to make others listen to her rhetoric, no matter how delusional it might be. His own people might turn against him.

Despite Jules' warnings, the halls were quiet. The shield dropped, and Sarlun clutched his pistol, searching for trouble. He rushed to his office and tested the keypad. Of course it wasn't the same code. It failed, and they continued down the corridor.

"Halt!" a guard said.

"Yosha," Sarlun whispered. "It's me."

The guard jumped at the sight of his former leader. "Sarlun? How? We were told you were dead."

"Dead?"

"Hulope showed us video evidence. Killed by the beasts of the Forgotten Plains," he said.

"I am very much alive and well. Where is my... where is Hulope?"

Yosha glanced at Jules, then Suma, and lastly, the robot. "I shouldn't be talking about it."

"Yosha, tell me what's going on." Sarlun's voice was low.

"We fought her on leaving the Alliance, but she didn't want to hear it. Hulope's been ruling with a platinum gauntlet. From the outside, our world may seem the same, but everyone's cowering in fear. She's captured the heads of four dissent groups, and killed them all. Sarlun, can you take back control?"

Sarlun nodded and set a hand on the man's shoulder. "I will do my best."

"She's on Ebos," Yosha said.

"Ebos?" Jules' brow scrunched up. "Why?"

"She was waiting for this group to arrive. One minute we thought they'd attack Shimmal, the next they were bringing her with them to Ebos. That's the story I heard,"

Yosha said.

"Ebos…" Sarlun tried to think of why. "Anything else you can tell us?"

"Not everyone is as loyal to you as I am, Sarlun. If you plan to use the portal, you'll have to fight your way in. Ten soldiers guard it at all times." Yosha touched his own holster. "And these are our finest."

"We can handle them," Jules said.

"I don't wish to kill anyone," Sarlun told her.

An alarm sounded, and the lights began to flash red. "They know we're here." Suma touched a screen on the wall. "They've called for reinforcements."

"Then we'd better hurry. Yosha, stay clear."

Yosha gritted his teeth and grabbed his weapon. "I won't leave your side, sir."

Sarlun wanted to shout at him, but maybe the others would hold fire if they saw one of their own ranks on his team.

They raced down the hall, finding the portal entrance closed. Four Shimmal men and women stood at it with guns in their hands.

"I'll deal with this." Jules sprinted past them. "Over here!"

They all fired, but she was faster. Sarlun waited around the bend while three of the guards chased after her.

Herm went ahead, shooting at the lone soldier. A bout of electricity flickered from the end of his finger, and the man convulsed, crashing to the floor.

"Is he…?" Suma whispered.

"No," Herm said. "I merely stunned him."

Yosha was at the control panel, punching in a code, and the doors opened at the same moment Jules returned. Blasts shot toward them, but Jules had her shield ready. The green barrier absorbed the pulses, and Jules waved her arm, knocking the remaining guards aside. They bashed into the walls, and only two of them regained their footing.

"For Hulope!" the man shouted.

"For Shimmal!" Sarlun retorted, clubbing the guy in the back of the head.

The last woman stared at them, then at the portal. She dropped her weapon. "Sarlun… I didn't know."

"Yosha, guard the portal. Tell them that Hulope was a fraud. She's my sister, and she doesn't care about our people or the planet. She only seeks power for herself," Sarlun said.

"Is this true?" Yosha asked.

"Yes. Hulope's real name is Shula."

The Shimmal guards were getting to their feet. The woman lowered her chin. "We failed you, Sarlun."

"We're sorry." This came from another.

"The past is in the past. Let's stop Shula, and together we'll rebuild the future," Sarlun said, the words for himself as much as them.

The Shandra control table lit up as Jules approached it, the crystals below glowing a bright green. He watched as Jules selected the icon for the Valincin on Ebos, and hoped they weren't too late for whatever game Shula was playing.

The glow of the portal filled the room.

TWENTY-TWO

"*H*ello, Ebos," Mary said into the viewscreen.

"Mary Parker?" the person on the other end asked. "We weren't expecting you… and your fleet. The IDs aren't familiar."

Mary's replica robot smiled, the corners of her eyes slightly crinkling. "We've come to bring Ebos some well-needed reinforcements. With the addition of Regnig's Academy, the school requires further training assets. I will be landing near *Outpost*."

The woman on the viewscreen didn't move, her stare blank. She whispered something I couldn't hear. I was there with my family, Hugo and I still pretending to be Sully's replicas of ourselves.

Karo appeared a moment later, his white hair pulled back, his green eyes questioning. "Mary?"

"Hello…"

I realized this robot didn't know who the figure on-screen was. "Hello, Karo. How are you?" I asked.

Mary stepped back, and I went forward.

I almost urged him to set the defenses, to blast any incoming vessels to the ground, but I couldn't. Not with Hugo on board. "As Mary said, we have a surprise for the colony. We'll be landing in short order."

Karo narrowed his gaze. "Something's wrong," he said. Shula was on the side of the bridge, staying clear of the

256

camera. She looked worried.

"Everything is going as planned."

"I thought you and Hugo were on Pestria. No one's heard from you for a week. How are you with Mary and Jules? Is Suma there?" Karo asked.

All good questions. I appreciated Karo's concern, even when he had visual confirmation it was me and my family.

I had to be tactful. "We returned a few days ago, but kept it discreet because of the nature of our visit. Traveling with a bunch of warships might catch someone's eye." I smiled at him, but his expression was blank.

"If you're Dean Parker, what's Baro's favorite child-hood possession?" Karo asked about his child.

"The star blanket? He's not still carrying that thing with him, is he?" I laughed.

Shula observed me, her snout wiggling.

Karo's face relaxed, and he grinned finally. "Sorry about that. We've been preoccupied. There's been repeated attempts to hack into the Academy's files. Have you heard of the Black Hole?"

I shook my head. "Don't think so."

"Come, and we can discuss. See you soon." The video ended, and Shula strode across the bridge.

"Well done, O'Sullivan. How did you even program those memories into this robot?" she asked Sully.

"We managed to upload a file from Regnig. A biography," Sully told her, covering his betrayal.

I'd given him the line, knowing we might need an excuse for a replica with extensive personal data. It worked.

"Excellent." Shula gazed at Alyce. "Bring us down, and order the warships into position. If anyone flinches, we destroy the Academy first. Understood?"

I shuddered but didn't budge.

"Yes, Shula." Alyce lowered *Unity* and her cargo filled

257

with soldier bots toward Ebos.

"We can still do this my way, Shula," Morg suggested.

"One more mention of it, and you're finished," Shula said.

"But I think that I can—"

Shula pulled a gun from her cloak and fired it, shooting the old man in the head. He died on the spot. Hugo gaped at the corpse.

Alyce looked prepared to retaliate, but Karka intervened. "Morg should have stayed in his lane," the Kraski said, watching Alyce. "We will be greatly rewarded if we comply."

We descended through the clouds to the familiar Ebos. A serving robot came to unceremoniously clear the carcass from the bridge.

"Shula, we're receiving a message from Shimmal," Alyce said.

"On screen."

A man appeared. "Hulope, you wanted to know when your brother arrived."

Brother?

"Is Sarlun on his way?" Shula asked.

I felt like I'd missed an important piece of information.

"Yes. They passed through the portal."

"Very good, Yosha. You've done well," Shula said.

The Shimmal man seemed nervous. "There's one more thing."

"What is it? The robot was with him, right?"

"Yes, but…"

"But what?" Shula yelled impatiently.

"The girl is too."

Shula glanced at Jules' replica. "Is that so. This works out better than I'd thought. Now I have most of the family at hand. Dean and Hugo are in the brig, and we have these replicas still. With Jules Parker on Ebos, soon I'll have all three detained, and will only need the Alliance president's head on a stake."

The call finished as *Unity* landed near the broken warship that had crash-landed a few years ago. I'd been infected by Ovalax, and Sarlun had betrayed us. And he was here… with Jules.

"Time to take the Alliance and the Shandra network!" Shula exited the bridge, leading us to the cargo hold where the robotic army awaited. Alyce used the controls, bringing them to life, and when the ramp doors opened, Shula walked at the head of the soldiers.

When I descended to the grass, I saw Sergo, Karo, Magnus and Natalia, as well as her son Dean, marching toward us. They sensed something was off and stopped in their tracks.

Three hundred robots stomped forward, heavy artillery aimed at *Outpost* and the structures surrounding the first-generation warship. I had to reach it so I could shut down the warships in orbit, before they attacked.

It loomed about a kilometer away, and at that moment, it may as well have been a thousand.

"What's happening?" Karo called, seeing me with the replicas of Mary and Jules.

"Where is the president?" Shula asked.

"Mary? She's with you. Isn't she?" Karo met my gaze, and I nodded gently, trying to assure him it was indeed me.

"Then who's that?" Dean pointed past Sarlun's sister at the robot. "Jules? What are you doing here?"

My daughter's replica didn't respond.

Shula walked slowly, the army trailing her. "My name is Shula, or you might have known me as Hulope. I'm done pretending. I run the Black Hole, and now, the Shandra network. You will bring Sarlun and the robot A-0000 to me or the Academy will be destroyed."

"It's filled with students," Magnus said. "Thousands of them."

"Did I mince words?" Shula pointed up without breaking her gaze on my friends. "Find my brother and take me to the Valincin. I have work to do."

"Sarlun's not here," Natalia said.

I noticed the shimmer of light, and Jules' sphere appeared. The invisible shield vanished, and Jules stood between Karo and Shula. "Guess again."

Sarlun was behind her, and he grimaced when he saw Shula. "Hello, sister."

---

*I*t happened so fast. The robots were clearly constructed with the same plans as the Gatekeeper bots Jules had encountered, but these ones were armed to the mechanical teeth. Jules estimated they'd be able to blow *Outpost* up within minutes, but she was here to ensure that never happened.

She peered at the scene, everything moving in slow motion, and spotted Papa with Hugo… and her mom… and herself. What was that all about? Who was real?

Jules noticed a pulse beating in Papa's neck and sweat on Hugo's brow. The thing that appeared to be her mother wasn't moving at all, and neither was her own replica. Whoever built those had done a remarkable job, but she wasn't fooled by the deception.

She snapped her attention back, and everything sped up again.

Shula smiled at Sarlun. "Hello to you as well, brother. I see you found my trail after all. Convenient timing."

"This was not how I envisioned our reunion going," Sarlun said.

"I had to shift the pieces in place before we made this work," she told him.

"I know your plan to place me into the Valincin. You've seen how it worked with Ovalax, and now you think I can possess the stone and give you power over them," Sarlun said.

"No, brother. It's nothing so simple. We will both possess them."

"Whatever you're talking about, it's not going to happen," Karo said. "Jules fixed the portals. No one needs to occupy them for the network to run."

"I'm planning to connect them to the Black Hole, and my reach will be astronomical. I'll be able to create portals anywhere I choose, becoming immortal. Infinite. Worlds will come and go, races will die, stars will begin anew, and I'll always be there, in the network. With Sarlun, my kid brother." Shula looked deranged.

Sarlun flinched at the comments.

Dozens of ships headed in our direction from the colony walls, and Karo stood defiantly. "We won't let you damage the Academy or take the Shandra network."

"And how do you expect to stop me, Theos?" Shula growled.

The robots began to march forward, and Jules sped to her father. "Papa, what should we do?"

Papa looked shocked to see her suddenly beside him. "The warships. We can control them from inside *Outpost*. Bring Suma and power them down."

"Or I could…kill them all," she suggested.

"No. You aren't that person anymore," he told her, and Jules nodded in agreement. Killing had taken a toll on her, and she couldn't return to that, not unless she was pushed to it.

Jules sped to Suma, grabbing her in the sphere, and raced with her toward *Outpost*. The others were so invested in their deep conversation, they may not have noticed.

"The failsafe," Suma whispered. "Your dad was smart to think of that. I hope it works with these warships, since we didn't build them."

They entered *Outpost,* speeding past two sentries, and Jules slowed when they found Elex in Engineering. Suma rushed to her husband, hugging him.

"Suma? How did you get here?"

"No time for that. We have to connect with the warships in orbit!" Suma hurried to the computer and found what she was looking for.

"You got this?" Jules asked, and when Suma nodded, she was gone.

———————

"I give you one more chance before the Academy is destroyed," Shula said.

Karo looked dubious. "Fine. We'll concede."

"No we won't," I told them when I spied Jules returning from *Outpost*. I strode down the ramp with Hugo by my side.

"Sully, get your replicas under control," Shula told him.

"Uh, hate to break it to you, Shula, but this *is* Dean Parker." Sully grinned as Hugo used the tablet, taking control of the robotic army. The entire squadron of them raised their weapons to the sky.

"Where did you get that?" Alyce called, trying to regain management of her bots.

"Fire!" Shula spoke into her wrist device, but nothing

happened. "Fleet, I said fire on the Academy!"

"*Power's off. None of the warships are in command of themselves,*" a voice said through the speaker.

Shula's eyes burned hot, a horrific sneer on her face. "What have you done? Now you'll feel the wrath of my power!"

"Herm, don't do this," Sarlun told the robot that had accompanied them.

"She promised me the Reflective Worlds and the Gatekeepers. I know Darius Neema would want this. He still lives on within my circuits. As will Shula." Herm extended his arm, a pronged metal needle sticking from his finger.

"Sarlun, you will understand once you're within the Valincin," Shula whispered, and Herm stuck the back of her head with the sharp object. She shuddered, convulsing as the robot's eyes grew brighter. And Shula fell to the ground, twitching once before stopping.

More soldiers from *Outpost* were arriving, and I was glad Magnus had the sense to send protection from the Institute.

"What have you done?" Sarlun asked Herm.

The color of his eyes changed. "Brother, we can still do this. Without the pressures of interstellar battles, alliances, organizations, and the network. We can be the Shandra. Don't you see?" Herm still spoke in the same voice, but if I was understanding correctly, he'd downloaded her memories. If it wasn't so disturbing, it would have been remarkable.

"Drop the tablet!" Hugo ordered Alyce, whose back was pressed to Karka's, the Kraski holding a gun.

The robot army moved as one, and half broke apart from the group, marching toward Regnig's Academy.

Hugo stared at the disc tablet and touched the screen. "Dad, I don't have control."

"Did you think I wouldn't have the master?" Alyce glared at my son. "You've lost."

The brand-new Academy was only two kilometers away, and the bots began the hike. Half stayed, aiming their weaponry at Magnus' people. "Stand down, or we kill everyone," Alyce said.

Herm grabbed Sarlun's wrist. "You're with me."

He picked up my friend and ran with him toward the Shandra Valincin we'd placed on Ebos.

Shula was gone. Not dead in the normal sense, but in the physical form. Her mind persisted, lingering within the metal hull of this robot. A bot that had admitted to killing the original founder of the Gatekeepers, as well as the Record Keeper. Who knew how many other minds he'd stolen over the centuries?

Sarlun wondered if any of the personalities could take control, or if Herm allowed one, like Shula, to speak through him. Clearly, he utilized their skillsets, as he'd done when painting portraits which meant this mechanical man was capable of creating intricate networks like the Black Hole, and that in itself was beyond dangerous.

His back cracked as Herm ran, jumping over a barrier and landing hard. Sarlun nearly fell from Herm's grip, but he held tight, keeping Sarlun in his arms.

"You don't have to do this," Sarlun muttered. "We didn't know each other, Shula. You left me on Shimmal when I was a kid. Why should I work with you?"

"It no longer matters if you choose to or not. I only need you inside so I can control the Deity Stones. We have a connection, and that's enough," Herm said, using Shula's

The Search

words. "In mere minutes, I will command the Crystal Map and the Reflective Worlds. With the reach of the Black Hole, and Darius Neema's intelligence, we will be unstoppable."

"For what purpose? To end the Alliance? The Parkers?"

Herm laughed loudly. "They are infinitesimal to the universe. Specks of dust within my scope. I mentioned those things as lip service to the organization. People like Morg and Karka follow, but only if you cater to their greed. Without the promise of the Alliance, they would have wrecked my plans."

Herm stopped near the portal, where four guards stood at ready. He set Sarlun down. "Move and I won't kill you."

Sarlun flinched when the nearest man, a young Padlog boy, lifted his gun.

"Wrong answer." Herm went so fast, Sarlun barely saw him. The boy's weapon bent as he hit it, and he went flying twenty feet back when the robot shoved his chest. "Anyone else willing to stand in my way?"

They glanced at Sarlun. "Go unharmed. It will be okay," Sarlun said as calmly as he could.

The three guards gathered their fallen friend and hurried off, leaving the Shandra Valincin undefended.

"It's even more beautiful than I thought." Herm set a palm on it, the sound of metal on crystal grating.

Sarlun didn't think it was possible for Shula to place him into the stone. Was it? Dean had been able to free the Theos. With the backing of the Black Hole network, had Shula really figured the secret out?

Detonations shook the ground, and smoke rose from the battlefields. They didn't have much time. Regnig's Academy would be destroyed, and years of work on the Ebos colony would be for nothing. Sarlun had a moment of sadness that he hadn't been able to say goodbye to Reg-nig. While never as close as the Toquil had been with Dean and Jules, Sarlun had counted him a great confidante, and he'd miss debating with him over tea.

"Come here, brother. Place your hands on the Va-lincin," Herm said.

Sarlun dropped his cloak, letting it fall to the cobble-stone pathway. If he was to die, maybe he could help his friends in some manner. Defend the Shandra portals with his energy. He wished he knew how.

Sarlun peered over his shoulder at the ongoing skir-mish, but no one was coming to his aid. A blast shot from orbit, and the entire colony rattled, buckling Sarlun's knees.

"It seems the warships have regained their autonomy," Herm suggested. "It will only be a matter of time."

Herm shoved Sarlun closer, and he touched the cool portal sphere.

"This won't hurt a bit."

Sarlun made a silent prayer to the Cosmos and pressed his palms down.

TWENTY-THREE

Smoke and dust rose from the brawl site, but their side was holding its own. Once Jules had moved Papa and Hugo across the field, she'd started to focus on the robot army.

"Get Alyce!" Hugo called, shooting his recently acquired pulse rifle at the nearest enemy robot.

Jules scanned the organization members, seeing the woman wearing all black. She stayed behind her army, operating the tablet with proficiency.

"Jules, the Academy!" someone shouted.

Jules took a deep breath. They expected her to save the day, and rightfully so, but she had too many things to think about. Sarlun was gone with Herm, and the Academy was under attack.

She screamed and dove toward the woman, floating right through the bot protecting her. Jules battered into Alyce, sending her sprawling. The tablet fell from her forearm, and a Kraski man stomped on it before Jules could react.

"You fool, what have you done?" Alyce asked from her seat.

"I can't do this…" Karka's eyes widened.

The army began fighting erratically, their guns flailing in any direction, firing at will. Some of the blasts struck one another; sparks lit up the battlefield. More detonations erupted as they dropped grenades, blowing their own limbs off.

Jules stood in the middle of the hellish nightmare, seeing her friends running for the hills. She needed to stop this.

She lifted, focusing on anything metallic. She rose higher, tugging at the robots like a giant magnet. Her allies' guns were torn from their grips, but she didn't care. Half of the robot army followed her into the air, thousands of tons drifting high into the clouds without Jules breaking a sweat.

Unfastened pieces of the colony came along for the ride as she broke through the atmosphere, leaving Ebos. The robots tried to fire, their programming erratic, but nothing would harm her within the shield.

Once she was far enough from Ebos, Jules let them go. They drifted away from the world, trying to fight an unseen enemy.

Jules noticed a single warship was powered on, and it fired. If that struck the Academy, they'd have to rebuild. Another pulse blasted from the cannons, and Jules clapped her hands as she rounded the warship's hull. The cannon broke and seized when she shot a barrage of tendrils at it.

But there were still the first pulses racing for their target. Jules had to be faster than them.

She held her breath while picturing Regnig's Academy. The feeling of warmth at the applause when the statues were displayed to the crowd. Jules sensed the thousands of students within her walls at this very moment, trying to learn so they could better protect their homes and advance the Alliance with exploratory missions.

Before she knew it, she was standing in the courtyard, almost stunned that she'd dodged the cannon fire. She'd never moved that quickly before.

Jules spied students pouring from the front doors, watching the incoming bright flashes of light aimed at their school. And she rose, holding a protective hand above her. The other half of the robot army was almost in range, and she floated near them, circling the erratic soldiers with her sphere.

Instead of diverting the massive energy fields, she absorbed them into her shield. She took the brunt of the strike, letting it penetrate her sphere, then her skin and hair, and finally, her bones. Jules held, and the attack was finished, with the robots writhing on the ground, sparking and igniting on fire. They were done.

Jules' eyesight began to wane as students filled the courtyard, shouting support for her. Her shield faltered, and she began to plunge.

Her muscles were limp, her vision swimming, but the students of Regnig's Academy caught her, setting her onto the stone walkway.

Ableen was at her side, stroking her hair and shouting for help. She felt the Valincin's energy tensing, and Jules realized what to do. Jules grabbed the small device Zarin had given her from Shula's hidden bunker and flipped the switch, shutting off the Black Hole.

---

*H*erm finished speaking, but Sarlun had only been half listening. The sounds of the battle had subsided, and Sarlun prayed it was his allies that had won.

The Valincin warmed beneath his touch, and grew so hot, he wanted to remove his palms, but Herm held him steady. "It's time, Sarlun. Once you're inside, I will connect with you. And we will be unstoppable."

Sarlun wished he could have one more moment with his daughter, to tell Suma how proud he was of her.

The stone tugged at him.

The Crystal Map shone behind his eyelids.

The Shandra spoke to his soul.

Visions of crystals and portal symbols occupied his mind.

And he left his body.

It was a strange sensation, leaving your physical form but still feeling like yourself. He had consciousness, and that was one of life's greatest questions. He felt no aches or pains, only freedom as his mind plunged into the large round stone. It glowed hotly as he entered, and instead of fear, the Shandra Valincin was welcoming.

Herm could be heard in the distance, but the words were lost in translation. The barrier between the network and the Valincin was too thick. He was no longer on Ebos, but traveling simultaneously between each and every crystal portal. It was remarkable. There were even more than they'd thought, far more than the expanded Crystal Map indicated. He couldn't believe it.

Somewhere within the network, a familiar presence made himself known.

Sarlun, this is not permitted.

Regnig? he asked.

I am the Recaster. You must go back.

I'm not certain that I wish to.

The short silhouette of the bird man appeared in his mind's eye, his features sharper as he neared. Regnig looked younger, unblemished by his centuries of life.

You have no choice. Be well, my friend.

Sarlun shouted as he was shoved from the Shandra, returning to his body.

Herm stood over him, the robot's eyes flashing

brightly. "Why are you back?"

Sarlun's throat burned, but he managed to speak. "Because you're an abomination."

"The Black Hole is gone!" Herm's weapons slid from his shoulder, and red lights shone from the ends.

"*W*e received word that Jules protected the Academy. The warships are still inactive," Magnus relayed as we ran toward the Shandra.

Jules had somehow redirected the robots and prevented the rest of the soldiers from harming the training facility. Now all we needed to do was capture Shula, and the day was ours.

I huffed as we raced to the Valincin and saw Sarlun on the stones, the robot looming over him.

"Stop!" I shouted.

"It didn't work!" Herm bellowed. "All this preparation, and my Black Hole failed."

Sergo and Karo were close, holding Alyce and the Kraski man captive. Sully and the replicas arrived with Hugo, and the other versions of Mary and Jules strode forward. "Allow us," Sully said.

I doubted everyone knew that Sully was an android as well, but they quickly did when he front-flipped, landing like a feather at Herm's heels. He did a sweeping spin kick, tripping Sarlun's captor.

Herm clunked to the rock, but recovered without grace. His arm extended, slamming into Sully's cheek, but the replicas of Mary and Jules were there, defending their creator.

It was over fast, and Sarlun rushed to the replicas,

shouting for them to stop. "We have much to learn from this robot. Within him are so many brilliant minds. It would be a shame to waste."

Sully smirked and drew a tool from his belt. "Very well. Have it your way." He jabbed it into Herm's temple, sending shocks through the bot, and he hissed, whinged, and toppled.

I ran to Sarlun's side. "Are you okay, friend?"

Sarlun's eyes misted, and he nodded his chin to his chest. "Do you consider me one?"

"Yes." I hugged the man, patting his back and sending a sprinkling of dust into the air.

"We have much to discuss."

"Save it for later," I said, scanning the landscape. "Where's Jules?"

Magnus had a radio in his grip, and he shook his head slowly. "Dean…"

"Where is she?" I whispered.

"At the Academy. She's unconscious." Magnus gestured to a transport that had arrived. He relayed commands into his radio and set a hand on Slate's shoulder. "Ensure those warships aren't a danger, and scour the grounds for any remaining robot soldiers. We can't have those things wandering the colony at night."

"You got it." Slate smiled at me. "Good to see you, Boss."

"Likewise."

Sergo escorted me to the transport, and Hugo came with Dean, speaking in hushed tones.

All I could think about was my daughter.

When we lowered toward Regnig's Academy, I should have been filled with awe and wonder at the incredible sight. It was marred by a gigantic crater a half mile from the front doors. Part of the sidewalk and courtyard were upended, but the pair of statues remained in place. One of Regnig, the other of Jules Parker. My girl.

I was out the door before the transport landed, rushing through the crowds of students.

"That's Dean Parker."

"Did you see Jules? She was amazing."

"I heard she's a Deity."

"Is she getting married?"

I heard their whispers as I fled to the entrance.

Sergo beat me to it, holding the door for me, and I spied Ableen pacing in the hall. "Dean…"

"Is she?" Panic filled my muscles but evaporated when I realized Ableen was crying happy tears.

"She's fine, Dean." Ableen hugged me as I arrived, and I heard Jules inside the office, arguing with the local doctor.

"I told you, it's just a scratch!" Jules tried to avoid the man, but he stood firm.

"You absorbed two cannon pulses from a warship, missy. I think we should keep you for…" The Keppe doctor paused when I cleared my throat.

"She doesn't need to," I said, and he seemed confused.

"Papa!" She barreled into me, then hugged Hugo, and finally Dean, who'd stayed in line, probably not wanting to ruin the family affair.

Dean brushed his hair to one side and gazed at his boots. "I'm glad you're okay."

"Where's Sarlun? And Shula?" Jules was always ready to fight.

"It's over," Hugo told her. "We won."

"Shula…?"

"She's inside Herm," I regretfully informed her.

Jules grimaced, shaking her head. "Wait until Zarin hears about this."

"Zarin?" I asked.

"Papa, we have some catching up to do. But first, let's ensure Herm isn't a danger. We should contact *Mettle* to meet us on New Spero," Jules told Sergo.

"Sure thing." Sergo used his tablet. "Wait, *Mettle?* We lost her years ago."

"And Sarlun found them. They're transporting some friends of mine from the Backyard."

I was completely lost. "I think we should sit down and figure out what happened."

We were safe, and Sarlun was back, meaning Shimmal was devoid of their dictator. They'd once again return to the fold, and we'd all be stronger for it. And after losing Regnig recently, I was grateful to have Sarlun to discuss plans with.

"Dad, that was pretty exciting, but maybe next time, we can do our job instead. You know: observe, record, report?" Hugo nudged my arm.

"I'll think about it." We left the halls of Regnig's Academy.

EPILOGUE

Belash Bazaar was much darker in the night. The scent of roasting meat drifted down the alley, and Jules strolled with Dean at her side. Tessa and Erem lingered behind, their weapons hidden beneath black cloaks.

Sarlun rounded out the team, and he went ahead, standing up to the bouncer at the bar's entrance. "We're here to see Tixa."

Rain began to drizzle, and Jules clenched her jaw, expecting defiance from the big man at the doors. He glanced at Sarlun, then at the rest of them, gaze settling on Erem. He muttered in the local tongue, and Erem responded gruffly. The bouncer gave them a curt nod and stepped aside.

Sarlun's cowl was over his head, hiding his features, and Jules flipped her own off. Everyone stopped what they were doing, sloshing their drinks to the tables and bar. All eyes settled on Tixa.

The man was smiling, his ugly features exemplified in the dim establishment. "What do we have here? Did the Shareholders decide to finally promote me?"

Sarlun lashed out with his fist, striking Tixa in the throat. The man staggered back, and his goons abandoned his table.

"By the order of the Alliance of Worlds, we hereby dismiss you from Belash. Tixa, you are to be remanded to the

Traro Prison for corruption and endangerment of children. Your role in manufacturing and trading Artificial has been brought to the Shareholders' attention, and they agree to place Belash under the guidance of the Alliance until a time such as their own government can recover from the devastation you put them under. Furthermore, the Belash Bazaar is on hold until every last bit of Artificial is removed from the planet." Sarlun waited for someone to argue, and when no one did, he continued. "Do you accept the charges, Tixa?"

Tixa stared at Sarlun, then began to laugh, the voice loud and throaty. "You really think the Shareholders won't support me? To the Backyard with these fools!"

No one listened to their ousted leader.

The bouncer hurried up the steps and slammed a fist into Tixa's gut. "You took my nephew. He's Feral now!"

Sarlun stepped to the side while others came, expressing their pent-up aggression. Jules intervened, throwing a shield around Tixa. "He's had enough. He'll rot for what he's done."

They separated, giving a line to the exit, and Jules dragged him from the bar, into the damp street, and onto a transport. She patted the hull, letting Sergo know to bring the prisoner to the warship in orbit.

Tessa held Erem's hand. "Are you ready, Erem?"

"Yes."

Jules floated their group above the city as rain poured. Soon word would spread that the Alliance had visited, taking Tixa, and someone else would try to gain the throne. Unfortunately for them, Leonard and about two hundred armed Institute soldiers were prepared for that. Leonard would set the governing force up, peacefully listening to the needs of the locals. In Jules' experience, once you took a snake from a lair, more tried emerging.

The Backyard walls rose as high as ever, and she lowered inside their barrier. The rain made the ground a mess, but at least the smokestack was no longer operational since she'd broken the pits below the surface a few days ago.

Sarlun walked with Erem as he led the group. Jules slowed to match strides with Dean, and he peered from under his cowl.

"I was hoping you could clear something up," he said.

"Yeah?" Jules grinned at him.

Dean stopped abruptly. "Do you want this?" He indicated the two of them.

"Us?" She had been considering their future during her trip.

Dean started away. "I thought so."

"Yes."

He paused. "Are you sure?"

Rain came in waves, the stones becoming slick. But without the constant influx of soot, the Backyard felt cleaner, almost bearable.

"How can I prove it?" She took his hands, bringing her face to his. Their lips touched.

"Marry me."

"I already said I would."

"But not at some distant point in time. We have to choose a date. A venue. A wedding."

That scared her more than a cannon pulse or an army of enemy robots, but she smiled through the doubt. "Okay. Let's do it."

"Seriously?"

She kissed him again. "Next year. We'll talk to Auntie Nat, and my parents, and discuss the details."

Dean picked her up, spinning in the rain. "I love you, Jules."

"Did you think I'd ditch you if given the option?"

"No, but you're always so busy that I assumed it slipped your mind."

"How about we stick together for a while? No more separating for missions."

"So you'll move in with me?" Dean smirked as they trailed after their friends.

She saw the shimmer of the invisibility cloak, and Erem stepped through, leading Tessa and Sarlun.

Move in? That was a big step. A huge one. "Why not?"

Jules waited patiently while Erem and Tessa explained what had transpired, and the look of elation on the prisoners' faces.

"No matter the reason Tixa placed you in here, you have served your sentence. You will be subject to Alliance law from now on, so abide by it. You're free," Sarlun told them.

Oran clasped Sarlun's forearm. "Thank you, Stranger. And for bringing my brother back to me."

"I have some work to do." Jules floated into the air, climbing to a hundred feet. From here, she could make out the dark outlines of the giant walls barricading the people of the Backyard inside.

She'd heard about the worm from the dump, but Erem insisted the monster wouldn't stray from its home. Jules left it and concentrated on the walls. She clenched a fist, and they crumbled to dust.

"The Backyard is no more," Erem proclaimed, and the population began their journey to freedom.

———

Sarlun felt awkward walking into Dean's new house. The old one had been destroyed by his order, but the compulsion had been impossible to ignore. He rubbed the location of the extracted tattoo and waved at Slate.

He knelt at a stroller, and Loweck grinned at the small child within. Sarlun had only been gone for a couple of years, but so much had transpired.

Jules was engaged, Sergo and Walo had children, Magnus and Natalia were married, and Slate had adopted a baby from Zecos Three.

He stepped into the living room, the hardwood brand new and spotless.

"Sarlun." Mary exited the kitchen, and she approached with tears in her eyes.

"Mary…"

She wrapped him in a hug, and he melted into it. Sarlun couldn't speak; he just held his friend, the worry and emptiness dissipating with her kindness.

"I'm so glad you're okay," she said.

"And you as well." He stayed at arm's reach.

Suma and Elex were already there, and they joined the reunion. "Dad's back at work," she told Mary.

"Only for a few more days," he said.

"Why's that?" Elex asked.

"Because I'm emptying my office to make room for Shimmal's new leader." Sarlun smirked at his daughter, who appeared to be lost.

"Suma… it's you," Mary whispered. "We approved the changes to the Alliance agreement this morning. You didn't know?"

Suma stared at Mary, then at her husband. "Elex, were you involved?"

"Maybe. I thought it would be best coming from Sarlun."

"Dad, shouldn't the people have a say?"

"And when I asked, they suggested it was time for

someone younger, and with fewer blemishes on their record to lead them into a new era."

Everyone was listening now, their friends and family inhabiting the Parker living room. Most had drinks, and Hugo was poking at a piece of lasagna that Slate had brought, looking uneasy.

Jules beamed beside her fiancé, and she smiled bigger when Sarlun met her gaze. Dean Parker walked over, passing Suma an Alliance pin. "Will you accept the role?" Dean asked.

She took it, gawking at the piece of Inlorian bar. "Yes. I will lead Shimmal."

"What about the baby?" Elex asked, and the room went silent, all eyes on the couple.

Suma frowned at her husband. "We weren't supposed to tell anyone!"

Elex shuffled his feet. "I'm sorry. It was too…"

Sarlun hugged his daughter tightly. "Is this true?"

"Yes."

"Then we have much more to celebrate tonight!" Sarlun had never been so happy in his entire life, with the exception of Suma's own birth.

Everyone crowded Suma, expressing their blessings, shoving Sarlun aside.

Dean leaned toward Sarlun. "Congratulations on your retirement. And the news."

"The baby is the best thing that could happen. As for retirement, any advice from one washed up has-been to another?" Sarlun asked him.

"Maybe we can take up golf," Dean joked.

Sarlun laughed, shaking his head. "Perhaps I'll do some consulting. I heard the Shandra network has expanded yet again."

"Back to the Gatekeepers? Welcome to the team."

Sarlun shook Dean's hand, feeling the pages of the chapter come to an end. But his book wasn't over yet.

———

Jules entered the double doors, feeling the air change pressure as the elevator descended into Shimmal.

"We can trust her, right?" Dean asked when they settled on the bottom level.

"Zarin? I hope so. If not, we're screwed." Jules put the code into the keypad, and they were granted entrance into the new home of the Black Hole. Suma stood with the young girl, her raccoon eyes unblinking as she stared at the series of screens on the wall.

Jules sat in the empty chair to Zarin's left. "Is it operational?"

"The Black Hole is now ours," Zarin said. "Or yours."

Dean tapped the computer. "How much trouble is Herm giving you?"

"The transition seems to have been smooth," Suma said. "A-0000 and every last personality he stole are now loaded into a separate server. They're clear from the primary network, so Shula or Herm or Darius can't access the system unless given permissions."

"And who can give those?" Jules asked.

"Just me," Suma said. "Perhaps Zarin, if she proves her loyalty."

Zarin rolled her eyes. "I told you guys, I'm here for the long haul. This is epic. I'm in the helm of the Black Hole."

"Speaking of, we have to change the name," Jules told them.

"Right. The Black Hole is synonymous with Shula's program. This will help exchange information across the partners and spread positives, rather than the countless dark negatives the previous iteration supplied." Suma drummed her fingers on the top of Zarin's headrest.

"What about the Stream?" Dean waved a hand in front of his face.

"You know what? I don't hate it," Zarin said.

"Me either," Jules chimed in. "Suma?"

"*Stream*. I think it works."

The console beeped, and Zarin clicked an icon. "Looks like A-Zero is done with his tabulations."

"What did you find?" Jules squinted at the small lettering on the screen.

"*The analysis of the Reflective Worlds is complete. There are ninety-seven Links still connected. That's 74.9% of the previous Links established by Darius. Of the ninety-seven, twelve have unresponsive Gatekeeper guards. Suggest visitation to each of the Links to upgrade or replace the existing robots.*" It spoke in Herm's voice, even though the metallic body was now in a scrap yard.

"How about we start on Earth?" Jules said. "Dean, you ready for an adventure?"

"With you, always." Dean put his arm around her shoulders as they studied the readouts about the newly discovered Links.

Jules had been meaning to spend some time on Earth again, and looked forward to the trip home.

"Zarin, you mentioned the group of people on Earth eager to overthrow us. Can you ping those details to my tablet when you have a chance?" Jules asked.

Zarin tapped the keyboard, and Jules' tablet gave her a notification. "Done."

Jules left the notes where they were and peered at Dean. "Is it too soon to search for our new place?"

"I thought you'd never ask."

ABOUT THE AUTHOR

Nathan Hystad is an author from Sherwood Park, Alberta, Canada.

Keep up to date with his new releases by signing up for his newsletter at www.nathanhystad.com

Made in United States
Orlando, FL
01 November 2024

53387108R00174